MURDER AT THE SCOTTISH BALL

BOOKS BY MILLICENT BINKS

The Opal Laplume Mystery Series

A Most Parisian Murder

Murder in Hollywood

MURDER AT THE SCOTTISH BALL

Millicent Binks

Bookouture

Published by Bookouture in 2025

An imprint of Storyfire Ltd.
Carmelite House
50 Victoria Embankment
London EC4Y 0DZ

www.bookouture.com

The authorised representative in the EEA is Hachette Ireland
8 Castlecourt Centre
Dublin 15 D15 XTP3
Ireland
(email: info@hbgi.ie)

ISBN: 978-1-80550-231-9
eBook ISBN: 978-1-80550-230-2

For Robert Noble, an amazing dancer, DJ, friend and beautiful soul.

If you wish to upset the law that all crows are black, you mustn't seek to show that no crows are; it is enough if you prove one single crow to be white.

William James

ONE

A MOST UNEXPECTED INVITATION

Papua, 1934

The sun filtered through the trees, scattering gold coins on the rainforest floor. A bird-watching outpost stood at the edge of the jungle, a wooden structure festooned with creepers. Ornithologist Lord Edmund Laplume, Lady Phyllis Laplume and their daughter, The Honourable Opal Laplume, were squabbling over how to tie a hammock rope while Opal's poodle, Napoleon, interfered with the end of it.

Effie, their servant, came clattering out of the lodge. She was wearing a straw cartwheel hat that had become floppy in the humidity and needed a good starch. She had a basket of sandwiches and a letter with a wax seal clamped in her hand.

'M'lord, the missionary delivered this,' she said, holding up the important-looking letter. 'It looks like a stag on the seal. Wonder who it could be from?'

Effie went to hand it to Lord Laplume, but Lady Laplume extended her fingers over the hammock and snatched it. 'It's addressed to Lord *and* Lady Laplume,' she said, then fingered it open and held it aloft to read:

Dear Lord and Lady Laplume, and The Honourable Miss Laplume,

Sir Seamus and Lady Blair request the honour of your company at a Christmas Eve Ball, to be held on the 24th of December at Dunvaloch Castle, Isle of Bute, Scotland.

The evening shall include traditional Scottish dancing, carols, a midnight banquet and other seasonal amusements. Highland dress admired, though not compulsory.

We should be most delighted to host you for the festive week, should you wish to remain beyond the ball.

Lord Laplume, I must also entreat your assistance on a matter of some urgency, the details of which I shall divulge upon your arrival. I would value your expertise most highly.

We eagerly anticipate welcoming you to a memorable evening of Highland tradition and Yuletide cheer.

With warm regards,

Sir Seamus Blair, Bt.

Lady Blair

'How very bizarre to hear from an old Edinburgh University professor,' said Lord Laplume. 'I haven't seen or heard from him for at least two decades.'

'Well, we simply must attend,' said Lady Laplume. 'I'm not spending Christmas with grub worms out here.'

'I daresay it'll be splendid,' replied Opal, rather excited. 'But what in the deuce does Sir Seamus need Papa's *urgent assistance* for? Why didn't he just spell it out in the letter?'

'That is what I'm afraid of.' Lord Laplume tipped up his pith helmet and rubbed his brow. 'Assistance in distracting Lady Blair while he hides the mistletoe?... Could be anything!'

TWO

DUNVALOCH CASTLE, SCOTLAND

Christmas Eve, 1934

Opal wiped the condensation off the cab window with a squeaky finger and gasped at what was revealed. It was a staggering gothic castle, perched atop a hill, its spires, towers and battlements standing together as if on an abandoned chessboard. Mist swirled around the base, so thick you couldn't see the portcullis. Beyond was the silver stillness of the sea and mountains spiked with Scots pines.

'It's like something out of a Grimms' fairy tale,' Opal whispered.

Napoleon on her lap, whined as if the castle looked like something more out of a nightmare. His legs twitched as if desiring to run away.

'It's making me want to design pointed steeple hats with flowing veils,' Opal went on. 'Would we ever stock the medieval style in our hattery, Mama?'

'Our London millinery boutique is for formal occasions, not debauched costume parties,' Lady Phyllis Laplume said with a sniff, and gasped as she caught sight of the castle. 'Now *that* is a castle. Not like the cumbersome lumps of granite that *some* people try to flaunt as their ancestral pile.'

The cab was soon consumed by mist and the sound of cawing crows. It was an ominous noise, as if the birds were fending off unwanted guests. But it only gave Opal a stronger desire to get cosy inside the castle. The chauffeur let them out inside the gatehouse, and they walked on gravel up to the main door, which was carved with intricate thistles. In the centre was hung a holly wreath tied with a blue tartan ribbon.

In her woolly mittens, Effie the maid tugged a bell handle, and it produced a resonant *BONG*.

A butler materialised, portly and fat-faced, with a countenance that was very friendly. He was a kind of hybrid between butler and Santa Claus, white beard and all.

'Good afternoon, my Lord. Good afternoon, my lady. Welcome to Dunvaloch Castle.' He bowed, as much as his belly allowed. 'The Honourable Miss Opal Laplume, and...' He looked at the maid to prompt her name.

'Effie,' she said, smiling at him in the knowing way servants did at one another.

'Charmed. My name is McWatt.'

'A very merry Yuletide to you, McWatt,' Lord Edmund Laplume said.

'Sir Seamus and Lady Blair are presently making ready for the ball. Allow me to escort you to your chambers, so that you too may make your preparations.'

'I've always pertained,' said Opal to Napoleon, looking up at him through the dresser mirror, 'that a woman wearing a hat commands authority over men, as they have to take theirs off out of respect. We can keep ours on. But now I'm wearing a tiara... does it have the same power?'

Napoleon flipped out his tongue and wagged his pom-pom tail back and forth in an approving manner to whatever she said.

'I think it does, yes, but in a different way. In a kind of untouchable way, perhaps? But I don't carry it as naturally as Mother does. I try, of course, but with me it's more... theatrical. I fell asleep in it once by accident. It did feel rather decadent though.'

Opal admired her sleeves in the oval full-length mirror. The blue velvet was slit from shoulder to wrist, and a pretty amulet peeked through, studded with seed pearls and opals to match her tiara. Opal rarely got to wear the opal tiara her grandmother had presented to her as a baby. The jewels she'd been named after due to the blue opalescence of her eyes. She'd forgotten how weighty the thing was. Her skirts were rather heavy too, due to the abundance of beaded tassels below the knee.

She performed a tentative little waltz step, watching her reflection, and lifted her hands imagining them resting on a certain man's shoulders... Mr Augusto Sevilla's.

'I wonder if he's already here?' she said to Napoleon, who was watching her with his head to one side. 'Gosh, I'm nervous... I haven't seen him in four months.'

She perched on a pouffe and scratched his curly ear. He came in very handy as a confidant, seeing as Opal was an only child and she had hitherto just talked to herself, Papa always being away on an ornithology adventure and her mother being utterly self-absorbed.

'Fancy having a menagerie of men getting my nerves in a twist. First is Augusto, the man I love... but I have to hide it because he is merely my protection officer while I'm in Scotland and therefore a subordinate in Mother's eyes. Second is the man Augusto is protecting me from... Lord Peregrine, who is suspected to be in Scotland, but not coming to the ball, though I can sense his fiendish presence. Then thirdly, there's Lord Turks-Leyton, the damp squib of a man that Mother is insistent on me spousing. Then, of course, there's the business of Sir Seamus... and that '*assistance*' he needs from Father... What on earth could it be?

She gave the poodle's freshly trimmed pom-pom tail a brush to make it sprout even bigger. 'It seems, Napoleon, you're the only man that doesn't cause me any mental strain or anguish. I'm so glad I rescued you from that coal sack in Piccadilly.'

Opal then took her beloved pup and slipped into her mother's chamber. She proceeded to give Effie moral support while fixing Lady Phyllis Laplume's tiara, which would not stay firm. They managed to stitch it with brown thread into the tiara loops.

'I heard there's a Parisian countess in attendance tonight who is influential on the fashion circuit,' said Lady Laplume. 'We simply must convince her to commission one of our hats. Opal, you have our Laplume Millinery business cards in your pouch, don't you?'

'Of course, Mother.'

Joyful ceilidh music began to swirl in the great hall: the folk drums, flute and fiddle accompanied by the tinkling of crystal glassware and the hum of pleasantries.

'Oh drats. I can't believe it's started and we're late,' moaned Lady Laplume.

Once they were gloved, they tottered out onto the balcony, the beaded tassels on their skirts swishing side to side. Napoleon trotted behind, well aware this was an occasion of the highest order and lengthened his neck to show off his opal collar. Lord Laplume, who was waiting on the half-landing, took and kissed Lady Phyllis's hand, to many onlookers below.

'Keeping up appearances?' Opal quietly teased them. They were always squabbling and would only be affectionate if it was for a performance of marital bliss.

Opal did wish she had someone to kiss her own hand though. That someone would be Augusto, and she wished he was taking her hand to do the same. She scoured the dozens of Brylcreemed heads below to no avail. Where was he? He was supposed to have arrived earlier.

'Lord Laplume!' boomed a voice amongst the crowd. It came from a bald man who must have been around the grand age of eighty and who had even grander nostrils. He sported a doublet, blue formal kilt and exceedingly shiny ghillie brogues.

'Sir Seamus,' Lord Laplume shouted with open arms. 'Come here, you crusted old fossil! I haven't seen you since people thought the war would be over by Christmas!'

'Laplume, you've got a very sunburnt face,' said Sir Seamus, giving Lord Laplume a hearty embrace, then patted his nose. 'Perhaps you can be Rudolph this evening.'

'Good evening, Sir Seamus.' Opal's teeth chattered as she put out her hand. 'Opal Laplume.'

'Ah yes. The Honourable Opal Laplume. In all your twenty-two years, I haven't met you. Shame on me. What a pretty thing you are. Look at those blue eyes. I bet those get you in trouble, don't they?'

'They've been accused, certainly... but never convicted.' Opal giggled and then screwed up her toes when her mother glared at her.

'Bet that thing keeps you on your toes – not the poodle – I mean your mother,' he said, with a cheeky wink.

Lady Laplume gave a forced smile, but it was quite evident she did *not* see the joke. 'Good evening, Sir Seamus. It's been a long time.'

'Only a century or two.' He chuckled.

'Jolly decent of you to have us for the festivities, Blair,' said Lord Laplume. 'Though you *must* tell me what this urgent assistance you require of me is.'

'I'm sorry to have been so cryptic about it in my letter, old boy. But seeing as you're the best ornithologist I know, I thought it could only be you for the job.' Sir Seamus extended his neck forward, and the three Laplumes followed suit. 'You see, it's the puffins.'

'Puffins?' said Lady Laplume very loudly, and a few feather headdresses in the grand hall below flicked up to glance at them.

'Yes, St Kessog's Isle was once teeming with puffins. It's very sad, but they have started to die out... I do fear that if you don't go over in the next few days, they will be doomed.'

Lord Laplume grasped his lapels with the authority of a police constable. 'I will most certainly do my best to find the cause and rectify it,' he said. 'But could it be something to do with the recent evacuation? Why *was* it evacuated?'

'Blasted place became utterly barren for the inhabitants. Since their tweed trade dried up, they had no choice but to abandon ship and come to the mainland. The island is supervised by me now.'

How odd, thought Opal. *I wonder what is harming the puffins? I must help Papa fix this... and with haste.*

'Good evening,' called a woman, coming up to join them on the half-landing. She was dripping in diamonds and wore a sash in the same tartan as Sir Seamus's kilt.

It must be Lady Viola Blair, Opal thought. She was a blonde and handsome woman of fifty-odd, much younger than her husband, with three dark moles dotted around her nose. The Laplumes exchanged pleasantries with the lady of the house. They'd never met before, as it was only Sir Seamus that Opal's parents were acquainted with.

'Sir Seamus,' – she turned to her husband – 'I have to inform you that there are reports of a strange man sitting smoking outside on the battlement.'

'Is he in a yellow plaid scarf?' asked Sir Seamus, knitting his white brows.

'Yes, apparently.'

'Oh, that's the scallywag who was trying to gatecrash earlier,' Sir Seamus said, and his nostrils flared in distaste. 'I told him he'd got the wrong holiday; this is Christmas Eve not Hogmanay first-footing.'

'What's first-footing?' asked Opal.

'It's the tradition when a tall, dark, handsome man is the first to cross your threshold on New Year's Day. To set the tone for the year,' said Lady Blair. 'But by all accounts from the ladies, he does fit that description.'

Tall, dark, handsome, Opal thought. *That could be Augusto!*

'Who did the man say he was?' asked Opal, touching Sir Seamus's doublet sleeve.

'I couldn't understand the blighter's accent. Probably one of Lady Viola's lapdogs. There's a new one every six months,' Sir Seamus said and looked his wife up and down jovially.

Lord Laplume and Sir Seamus cackled like they were in a boys' dormitory, Lord Laplume assuming it was simply a jibe. But when they both saw the look on Lady Viola's face, it became evident that she indeed *did* sometimes have gentleman callers.

'How dare you talk about me like that in front of guests.' She spoke without parting her teeth. 'After all I've done for you. Tell them it isn't true.'

Sir Seamus's nostrils flew out in surprise. 'I don't think they thought it was true until you reacted like that.' He then laughed nervously, strumming his fingers on his top hat that he held at his chest. 'I am sorry, my dear.'

Opal looked down at her pooch. Napoleon looked back up at her with his ears pinned back in embarrassment. *Mama and Papa squabbled,* thought Opal, *but this was a real row.* Lady Laplume hummed an awkward carol and gazed at the vast stained-glass window above the landing. Lord Laplume made a compliment about the fiddle player.

Opal put her hand on Sir Seamus's arm again. 'I don't

suppose that man outside was called Mr Augusto Sevilla? You see, we've been expecting our protection officer to arrive.'

'What?' asked Sir Seamus, bamboozled. 'Yes, yes, Augusto... it did sound something a bit like that.'

Lady Laplume butted in. 'We do apologise, Sir Seamus. We made your housekeeper aware. We are sorry he is a little tardy. We expected him to arrive before the ball commenced.'

'Where did he go?' shouted Opal over her shoulder as she dashed down the stairs.

'He walked away towards the Christmas rose garden! I'm dreadfully sorry,' Sir Seamus called after her. 'We'll see you in the ballroom.'

Opal's heart palpitated in her ears as she weaved in and out of the fur stoles and plaid sashes in the grand hall. With Napoleon in tow, she flew out of the gatehouse and pounded along the hedgerows. She found herself surrounded by what must have been the rose garden. But there was no Augusto. She peeked around hedges and over stone walls. Napoleon scrambled onto the highest part of the battlement he could get to for a militant sweep of the landscape.

Blithering fig. Had he left? Opal wanted to stamp her foot but quashed the childish urge. Napoleon barked once sharply to summon his favourite walkies attendant. But all that could be heard was the whistling of the wind around the towers and the far-off laughter of the ball.

Opal ordered her pooch down from the wall and moped back into the castle with her head hung low. Not the way an honourable, crowned in her ancestral rocks, should carry herself. *What if Augusto thought Sir Seamus awfully rude and decided to leave? He could be terribly headstrong. Would she not have the chance to spend Christmas Day with him? That would have been heavenly.*

Back inside the grand hall, she plucked a mini oatcake with smoked salmon and dill off a swirling tray. She checked nobody was looking and dropped a titbit for her pooch onto the floor. She munched the rest and floated with the current of bubbly guests to the ballroom.

Opal's mouth fell open when she saw the size of the mammoth chandelier glittering above. She remembered she was eating and shut it again with haste. A group of dancers swirled by, revealing the parquet flooring. It was polished like a frozen lake, reflecting the colossal Christmas tree dotted with baubles, tartan ribbons, nutcrackers, and ballerinas in little feather tutus. There were vibrant hues of fuchsia, orange, and chartreuse. Gilded mirrors lined the room, repeating the glorious tree infinitely.

She crept around the edge of the ballroom, eyes dashing back and forth, searching for a particularly annoying gentleman's face and posture. She wanted to hide from Lord Cecil Turks-Leyton, better known as 'Turkey', at *all* costs. She'd danced with him once before, and it was like dancing with a deckchair creaking and folding under pressure and on the verge of collapse.

Her attention was suddenly caught by a rather seasoned dancer, going for it solo in front of the musicians, who were strumming up a Charleston number. As the dancer turned, his dark moustache caught the light like a sabre unsheathed. The easy rhythm of his movement faltered; his limbs stilled, and that unmistakable smile played upon his lips... the one with the dimple in the chin, all too familiar to Opal. It was him. Augusto.

THREE

THE TERRIFYING TEA LEAVES

His lips mouthed 'Opal', and he came towards her in big strides, brushing dancers out of his way.

She smiled at him like an intoxicated fairy. He was about to encircle her in his arms, but she lightly shook her head. Mother would see. Instead, he lifted her hand and kissed the air above it. Napoleon ran in circles around them, his pom-pom tail making its own circles, elated at the reunion.

'My darling Opal. Happy Christmas, my darling!' Augusto said, still holding her hand.

'And to you, Mr Sevilla.' She did a small curtsy. 'How on earth did you get into the ball? They told me you'd been turfed out for having a questionable accent.'

'I might have found a window ajar somewhere,' he replied, eyes twinkling.

Opal glanced at his cuff and noticed he'd snagged a bit of fabric on his way in. She giggled, but not into her hand as he was still holding it. *Oh, please don't ever stop holding it.*

'Opal, my dear, dear thing,' the last voice Opal wanted to hear in this moment interrupted. The creaky-voiced, lopsided aristocrat, Lord Cecil Turks-Leyton, came into view. 'I've been looking for you all evening.'

He completely ignored Augusto and plucked Opal's hand away.

'I've just learned a new Charleston variation, darling. Very continental. May I?'

Before she could protest, he seized her other hand and dragged her to the dance floor, scattering distant cousins and baronesses like frightened grouse.

'Observe!' he cried. 'The sidecar shimmy!'

He jerked sideways like a startled badger, one leg trailing as if it had missed the train. Then he shook his shoulders back and forth in the most mortifying manner. Napoleon growled at him as if whatever he was doing was highly offensive and inappropriate.

'Picked this up in Biarritz!' he cried. 'Follow my lead, Opal, this isn't a solo number.'

'I'm feeling rather unwell, actually. I had a champagne that was a little off,' Opal excused, straightening her tiara.

'How can champagne go off?' he asked, screwing up his facial features as if Opal was daft.

'What's going on in the salon?' she said, pointing at the busy-looking doorway across the floor, desperate to change the subject.

'Oh, there's a witch in there giving tea-leaf readings. Telling fortunes for the new year. Everyone's riveted, but I just want to dance the Charleston before they start the traditional reels.'

'A witch? How curious. I'm going to see.' Opal excused herself with a little curtsy and darted away, grabbing Augusto's hand discreetly as she passed him.

'Who on earth is that?' said Augusto. 'I've never met anyone in my life that dances that way.'

'The man Mother wants me to spend the rest of my life with,' Opal replied with a sigh.

They entered the salon, dim candelabra light flickering around tapestries of hunting scenes. A woman who was unmistakably the '*witch*' sat in the centre of a round table. She had extremely broad shoulders and sat very tall, her flame-orange turban towering above the man at her table. The most noticeable thing about her face was that she only had one front tooth.

Lady Laplume caught sight of Opal and Augusto and beckoned them over. 'Opal,' she whispered. 'This is Seraphina Serle, the witch. But apparently, she prefers to go by the term "*seer*". Just warning you not to call her a *witch* to her face.'

'Oh yes, quite right, Mother. "*Witch*" can have negative connotations, I suppose,' Opal whispered back. 'What's happening now?'

'She's reading the tea leaves of Sir Seamus's lawyer, Mr Martindale,' her mother replied.

Mr Martindale was a nervous-looking chap who wore a monocle and had very small eyes, like a mole. He was drinking gingerly from a teacup, the saucer in his other hand shaking slightly.

'If the tea leaves represent anything about *hard work* or *early mornings* in 1935,' he said, 'I say we toss the cup straight into the fire... bad omens deserve a jolly good roasting!'

Seraphina Serle didn't laugh. She simply looked at Mr Martindale icily as he finished his slurp and gave her the teacup. Seraphina swirled the leaves three times and turned the cup upside down onto the saucer. Then she turned it back up again. Mr Martindale leaned in to look inside. The guests in the room craned their necks.

'Let's see what 1935 has in store for you!' said Seraphina Serle.

'There's crows!' said a red-headed man standing above them. 'They are unmistakably crows.'

'I don't see it!' said Mr Martindale, bringing his monocle to the rim. 'Oh, I think I see now. Yes.'

'Yes, the wings, you see,' said the red-headed gentleman.

'Quiet, Mr Finlay Roberts,' hushed Mr Martindale nervously. 'Let Seraphina speak.'

The red-headed man looked a little peeved at being shut up. His hair, electrifying copper wires that had a gold sheen in the candlelight, seemed to get redder with his temper. A matching copper moustache emblazoned above his lip twitched with annoyance.

'Och, the leaves tell a grim tale!' Seraphina Serle said in such a dramatic way that there was a ripple of gasps. 'Corbies in the cup? That's ne'er a good sign. Death's got his eye on some poor soul, sure as the north wind blows.'

'What are corbies?' whispered Augusto in Opal's ear.

'I believe it's what the Scots call crows,' she replied.

'Near the rim means it'll be happening soon, doesn't it?' Lady Viola Blair said, coming over and trying to peek in the cup.

'Aye,' replied Seraphina, showing her.

'What... what will happen soon? Who's going to die?' said Mr Martindale, his little mole eyes stretched to their limits.

'Nobody will! It's all poppycock. Seraphina, you're supposed to entertain us, not give us fear-induced hair loss!' said Sir Seamus angrily and started to usher everyone out with his arms. 'McWatt! McWatt! Where is our butler? I need him to shepherd everyone out.'

'He said he spilt some soup on his suit and is changing,' replied Lady Blair in a clipped tone.

'Poppycock, did you say?' said Seraphina Serle, whose tongue poked around her front tooth whenever she used the letter 's'. 'My readings have *never* been wrong! Mark my words. *Death* is upon us!'

FOUR

THE TWA CORBIES

Feeling utterly shaken by Seraphina's prophecy, Opal was herded out with the other guests who were grumbling like children who'd had their bedtime ghost story cut short. Seraphina Serle remained at the table, gazing at the tea leaves, muttering things about 'crows' and 'darkness'.

'Out of the way of the tree!' scolded Mr Finlay Roberts to a gaggle of children. 'You will smash the baubles running about like that! Come with me, we shall play...um... I Spy.'

Suddenly, the music style switched. An exultant tangle of fiddles, pipes and the steady heartbeat of the bodhrán came crashing through the ballroom. The traditional Scottish reeling had begun! Opal looked around; she'd lost Augusto in the crowd. So she could learn the dance moves, Opal stood in line and fixed her gaze on the caller. The dancers began whirling in a glorious, tangled latticework of bodies, arms flung wide, feet skidding the polished floor with feverish speed, tartan sashes fluttering like banners in battle, kilts swirling.

Lady Laplume grabbed Opal's arm and dragged her over to partner with Lord Turks-Leyton. There was nothing she could do about it, and before she could take another breath, he had his arm around her waist. Up close, she realised Turkey smelt a little bit off, like dill pickle. Opal took his hand and flashed her teeth politely. She looked over at Augusto, now by the Christmas tree. How she wished his arm was around her instead.

Opal blinked rapidly. Augusto's gaze was fixed on a dark-haired woman on the dance floor. She was quite a beauty, with a full, cherubic mouth and was adorned in more sumptuous jewels than anyone else at the ball. To Opal's horror, the woman looked back at Augusto, but for a beat too long to be a casual glance. Who on earth was she, and why was she giving Augusto such a knowing look? Opal looked up at the clock... it was almost ten. Thank God it was soon to be Sir Seamus's speech, and she'd be free from Turkey's jerking clutches.

'Ladies and gentlemen,' called Sir Seamus, once the band had spiralled to silence. '1934 was a wonderful year, with so much to be grateful for this Christmas Eve!'

'Lord Turks-Leyton,' Opal whispered. 'I'm going to listen to Sir Seamus's speech from the balcony above the tree... if you'll excuse me,'

She then dashed up the split staircase that curled itself around the tree. She didn't want to be next to Turkey for too long and risk his lips veering close. Seraphina Serle was up there too, and Opal leant on the balcony alongside her.

'I am immensely thankful to everyone who has attended this ball and especially our star guest of the evening... Countess Angelina de Brisecloque, all the way from Paris, whose presence makes this ball infinitely more glittering,' Sir Seamus said and lifted his glass in the direction of the woman he was speaking about.

It was none other than the pouty lady Augusto had shared a look with earlier. Opal huffed air out of her nostrils. A Parisian countess? Would Augusto perhaps know her from when he lived in Paris?

'Looking ahead, 1935 shall be a big year for Blair Electrical Enterprises! I'm pleased to announce our latest innovations: the kilt pressing machine and, of course, the Loch Ness Monster detection device...' His nostrils flared as he tittered at his little joke. 'I am also proud to unveil Blair Electrical Enterprises' latest little brainwave – Christmas tree bulbs that positively twinkle!'

With a flourish of his wrist, Sir Seamus grasped the brass Christmas tree switch between thumb and forefinger and snapped it back. A sharp crackling sound came, then a miniature lightning strike burst from the little brass box in his hand. It expunged a puff of smoke, then came a buzzing noise, as if a million bees were trapped inside Sir Seamus Blair's body, making him shake violently. The tree lights flickered as if mimicking his shakes, then became constant. He opened his mouth to yell, but nothing came out, unable to take a breath. Then he buckled to his knees and toppled over sideways. His convulsions stopped, apart from one brogue that was mirror-shined so well that the tree lights danced around in it in freakish greens and deathly reds.

Opal, along with the whole party, took an inhalation of shock, like something had sucked the air out of everyone's lungs at once. Their heads jostled and jumped up, trying to get a view of the collapsed Sir Seamus. From the balcony, Opal could see him perfectly well from above. Suddenly, something else could be heard... a tune began to play. An inharmonious, scratchy melody, a traditional folk-sounding number. Its mood was macabre and mournful. But it was not the band...

Opal peered forward, holding her tiara to her head as if to stop her mind from falling out. Attached to the switch in Lord Seamus Blair's hand were two wires. One for the Christmas tree bulbs, and the other wire snaked around into the back of the tree. She was able to duck down and peek through the bannisters. The wire led to a gramophone, concealed inside the

Christmas tree foliage. A record on it spun wildly, playing out the hellish melody.

'"The Twa Corbies",' screamed Seraphina from the top of the stairs like an irate seabird. 'The tune playing is "The Twa Corbies"! I told you all I saw crows in the tea leaves!' She then flung her hands upwards, emitted a piercing cry, and collapsed in a faint from the exertion of it.

Opal went to help her. She put a hand on Seraphina's large shoulder, but realised she was too big for her to lift. She could then hear the rapid clatter of panicked feet running up the steps to her assistance. Opal let a couple of burly men look after Seraphina and stood back up. She looked over the balcony and saw an oscillating human tide around Sir Seamus's body. The wave surged forward, then retreated in a collective shudder as McWatt, arms spread wide like a shepherd corralling his flock, pushed them back.

'There's a gramophone in the tree!' Opal shouted at McWatt, pointing down to the back of the dense branches.

He looked up at Opal with a face drained of blood and tore through the branches of the tree, several baubles smashing on the parquet flooring. Once inside and with a triumphant yank, he silenced the gramophone's infernal screech. Though not without a final, ghastly wail from the machine that made several ladies clutch their necklaces.

Lady Viola Blair knelt gracefully beside her husband's motionless form. His shoe had stopped twitching. She placed two delicate fingers on his neck and held them there for a long time. Longer than necessary in determining whether someone was dead or not.

'Well?' the butler yelled so loud you'd think he had a megaphone. Lady Blair looked up as if hypnotised, a fog over her eyes, then slowly shook her head.

FIVE

TIME TO RETIRE

The clock on the drawing-room mantle bonged one in the morning. Slumped in the armchairs by the hearth were the only remaining people in the castle, the ones who were staying overnight. The other fifty or so guests had departed soon after the terrible incident.

Left were Lady Viola Blair, Mr Walter Martindale, Mr Finlay Roberts, the Laplumes, Countess Angelina de Brisecloque, Lord Turks-Leyton, Augusto and the servants. Seraphina Serle was recovering in her bed upstairs.

'I'll never be able to use another light switch without thinking of Seamus's death,' Lady Blair wept into her hands. 'He was the love of my life!'

Opal was a little taken aback. To lose someone so suddenly must be a terrible blow. Sir Seamus had been her only companion in this vast, echoing castle. But just earlier, Sir Seamus had humiliated his wife in front of Opal and her parents, and her incandescent reaction led Opal to think their marriage was hanging on by a thread. Could she be acting? Was it true she received her rumoured 'lapdog' gentlemen callers in her own marital home?

'It's a shame we can't get hold of the detective and procurator fiscal until the morning, m'lady,' said the local police constable who had arrived. 'But the scene is secured, the body is covered with a sheet, and nobody is allowed in the ballroom.'

'Please do not refer to my beloved husband as a *body*. Call him Sir Seamus,' wept Lady Blair.

The constable stammered an apology and rocked back and forth on his heels.

'Do we know if it was an accident or if someone tampered with the switch?' asked Mr Martindale, placing a hand on the weeping Lady Blair's shoulder. 'I daresay the fact that the gramophone was hooked up to it to play that dreaded tune would seem like it was deliberate. But then again, perhaps only the gramophone was intended to be hooked up, not Sir Seamus as well!'

'That will be investigated by the detective and procurator fiscal,' said the police constable.

'Surely it's not rocket science to see if a switch had been tampered with in a malicious way?' said Mr Roberts impatiently. 'Whenever did the constabulary become so useless?'

'And who are you?' said the policeman, puffing up his chest.

'Mr Finlay Roberts... the castle falconer. I take care of Sir Seamus's falcons.'

'I know what a falconer is, Mr Roberts. And in answer to your other question, we must not touch *anything* and go by procedure, sir. The switch will need to be dusted for prints. I advise everyone to retire to their rooms. Take a dram of whisky if needs be. Try and get some rest.'

'How are we meant to sleep if there is a murderer in the castle?' Countess Angelina said, her full red lips quivering.

'Now let's not get ahead of ourselves. I doubt anyone would have wanted to kill our beloved Sir Seamus,' said McWatt in a soothing tone, but his expression did not look confident. 'It could have been a most tragic accident.'

'I agree. I don't know who would have wanted to kill him.' Mr Roberts swigged from a tumbler of whisky, then said what Opal was thinking, 'I mean, he was so old, you could almost hear the creaking of the universe whenever he stood up. They wouldn't have had to wait long!'

'We're all doomed without that man!' Lady Viola Blair blubbered into a hanky. 'What am I going to do without him?'

'I'll take your arm, Lady Blair. Let me help you upstairs,' offered the countess.

'Let me take your other arm, m'lady,' said Augusto and supported Lady Blair on the opposite side.

Everyone else followed upstairs like frightened sheep, shiftily looking at one another as if to try and intuit who had blood on their hands. Opal gave Augusto a goodnight nod, and he returned it. The fact that he was leading Lady Viola Blair to her room along with the beautiful countess made her feel a teeny bit green. It was not a feeling she was used to. But she'd been desperately lonely all her life before she met Augusto and was not up for sharing her darling companion.

Opal bid her parents goodnight, hesitating when uttering 'Happy Christmas' as it wasn't quite appropriate and slipped inside her room. She changed and opened the curtains a smidgeon before slipping into bed. She needed a bit of the moonlight to keep surveillance of the room.

It took her a good half hour to doze off. Not because Napoleon kept snoring, beating his pom-pom tail in his excited dreams, but because her senses were on high alert mode. Every tiny rattle of the windowpane and gurgle of the old pipework had Opal flashing her eyes open wide and darting about the room.

She couldn't help but wonder. If Sir Seamus Blair was an electrical engineer and inventor, wouldn't he be the only one who could pull off that intricate set-up with the switch and the gramophone? Rather a dramatic suicide method though. Or could it have been planned for someone else? Or was the person who did it in fact one of the six guests staying in the castle tonight? Opal mentally went over the potential suspects. There was Mr Walter Martindale, Seraphina Serle, Countess Angelina, Mr Finlay Roberts, Lady Viola Blair and the butler, McWatt. As much as he annoyed her, she did not suspect Turkey. Having known him all her life, she knew he had the backbone of a poached pear marinated in cowardice. No, not him. But who?

SIX

THE RED SCRAPBOOK

Opal awoke to the sound of her door creaking open, and a hand emerged through it, holding something dark and long, pointing to the floor. *A gun?*

Opal's lungs created a kind of backwards scream, inhaling instead of expunging a noise. She sat up and scrambled to the back of her bed. Napoleon sprang up on all fours next to her, head low, growling.

'Who?!' is the only thing she managed to shout.

It was still pretty dark, but with the light from the gap in the curtains, Opal could make out McWatt's head poking in.

'Oh, I'm sorry, Miss Laplume,' he said. 'I wasn't meant to wake you.'

Opal exhaled in relief, ruffled Napoleon's head to calm him and switched on the bedside lamp. She'd been the target of a firearm in the past, and her nerves had never fully recovered from it. In the dark, anything of similar size becomes a gun. But she could see now that it was a small Christmas stocking that McWatt had hooked on a peg on the mantle.

'The lady of the house had organised these stockings before

the... err... tragedy of last night. She requested I still dispatch them out to make the day less... gloomy.'

'That is kind,' said Opal and grasped her shoulders. 'It is glacial in here, McWatt. Do you have any matches?'

'I shall light the fire for you, Miss Laplume. The staff are all a little manic this morning. Lady Blair really is not well.'

'I can only imagine.' Opal sighed. 'How are you holding up?'

McWatt struck a match and bent over the hearth. Opal suspected he was tearing up as she heard a sniff. 'I am fine, Miss Laplume, thank you for asking. I shall be chambermaid as well as butler this morning. Would you like me to open the curtains properly?'

'Yes, please, if you will,' said Opal. She was itching to ask him about last night and what he thought happened to Sir Seamus, but knew she must approach it gently.

He swished the heavy tartan drapes aside. 'It's snowed overnight. A "snawy Yule", the locals call it. Though it is hindering the procurator fiscal and the detective from getting here. They're coming from the east, where it's fallen thicker.'

'Oh... that is unfortunate,' said Opal. 'But I have to say that I've never been lucky enough to see a white Christmas.' Then she remembered it was pertinent not to speak in such an excited tone. 'Due to the smog in London and Suffolk, where I lived as a small child, any snow that fell did not stay white for very long.'

Napoleon blinked in the stark light, leapt off the bed up onto the reading stool and plonked his fluffy paws on the glass. Opal had to fling open her eiderdown, wriggle on her slippers and flap up to the window to take a look. She grabbed her dressing gown on the way. She was in the presence of a manservant, after all.

It was so bright she needed to shade her eyes with a hand as you would looking into the sun. Once her eyes had got accustomed, she could make out the snowy mountains, the loch, the sea, the trees dipped in icing sugar, the maze and grounds, the shading resembling a giant snow leopard lying down in front of the castle.

'The stable lads are gettin' the horses ready for church,' said McWatt, and his breath made condensation on the glass. He then pressed a finger lower down on the window.

Opal peered forward. So did Napoleon. He yapped at the sight. There were four hefty, chestnut-brown horses with fluffy white hooves – *Clydesdale horses!* – being led by a couple of chaps in wellies and flat caps around the courtyard roundel. They were making their way to a striking green landau carriage with four giant wheels.

'I say, what beautiful creatures,' said Opal. 'Who are they transporting?'

'Everybody to St Aiden's Kirk for the Christmas Communion Service, Miss Laplume. The snow has mainly fallen on the opposite side of the estate due to the wind, so we should be alright.'

'We're surely not attending Mass after what happened last night?' Opal blinked up at him in confusion.

'The lady of the house says it would be frowned upon not to attend such an important service in the calendar year, and even *expected*, as one needs God in times like these. The constable will man the house,' said McWatt, hands behind his back and chin held high as if relaying a message from the Queen.

'I see,' Opal replied, though she did not exactly. She thought Christmas Day would be decidedly *off*.

She looked into the butler's eyes, they were greyish-blue and held a weight... as if all he wanted to do was cry but could not... or would not... for a very long time.

'How long have you been at Dunvaloch Castle, McWatt?' Opal asked with her head tilted.

'Forty years, Miss Laplume. I had known Sir Seamus for a very long time,' he said, looking out onto the glen.

'What... do you think happened to him last night?' asked Opal in a quiet tone.

McWatt swallowed and walked over to the bookshelf. 'Lady Blair,' he began, whilst running his finger over the books on the shelves, 'was foolish to hire Seraphina Serle to entertain last night. I am yet to fathom how that witch pulled it off, but I know she had strong reasons to want Sir Seamus dead.'

He pulled out a red canvas volume and put it under his arm.

'What's that?' she asked.

'Sir Seamus kept his scrapbooks in this bookshelf. There's some interesting reading about that family of witches, and I want to show the police.'

'A family of witches?' Opal asked, her lashes batting in intrigue.

'Yes. Both of her sisters are witches or "*seers*", as they like to call themselves. One of them is deceased. They were thick as thieves, those three. If I didn't know any better, I'd say it'd been lifted straight from the pages of *Macbeth*. And we all know how that ended...'

'Oh...' said Opal, flapping towards him in her slippers. 'Can I have a look first, please?'

'I'm afraid these are private, Miss Laplume. But please heed my words. Keep an eye on that strange woman. We don't know how long it will be until the law arrives. Enjoy the confectionery.' With that, he turned to leave the room.

'Wait a moment, please, McWatt,' she said, glancing at the bookshelf and getting an idea.

'Why don't you take a sweetie, you really need cheering up. It is Christmas, after all.'

'I couldn't possibly, Miss Laplume,' he said with a hand on his belly, and Opal couldn't tell whether it was his decorum or paunch he was worried about.

'Please, I insist,' she said.

'I guess I could have *one*, for Sir Seamus,' said McWatt,

peeking in the stocking with a finger and plucking a brightly wrapped bonbon out. He put the red scrapbook on the mantle to undo the sweetie, his back turned to Opal.

She very quickly sidled over to the bookshelf, pulled out an identical-looking volume from the shelf and smoothly swapped it, hiding the other behind her back.

'Merry Christmas, McWatt,' she said with a small smile.

'It is Christmas, Miss Laplume, but not a merry one, I'm afraid,' he replied forlornly and bumbled out with the wrong book.

Opal could not resist unhooking the Christmas stocking from the mantle to delve inside and chew on something while she read. Napoleon yapped commandingly for Opal to open it, propping his front paws on the footstool.

'Alright, boy, don't get too excited, there's probably nothing for pups.'

Opal yanked out a treasure trove of treats from the festive sock. A tangerine, some lemon hard candies labelled 'Barley Sugar' wrapped in bright cellophane, a little box of clotted cream fudge, Scottish tablet wrapped in brown paper and spiralised ribbon. And, of course, shortbread... in the shape of a stag.

Napoleon's eyes started to waver like he was giving up hope of anything meaty. He let out a little whine.

'Aha!' Opal said as she pulled out the last item at the bottom. 'Lady Blair, I mean *Santa Claus*, didn't forget you, boy. A pig's ear. You love these, don't you?'

He clamped it in his jaws and dashed away onto the bed, where he could get a panoramic view of any possible scavengers. He then began to snaffle at it with a carnivorous groan from the back of his throat.

Opal popped open the lid of the clotted cream fudge with her red nails. She was able to stab her nail into the square and pop a confection in her mouth. Exquisite. Why did sweets always taste better when you shouldn't be eating them? It was before breakfast, after all. How decadent.

She lay on her stomach on the bed, ankles crossed in the air, and opened the scrapbook on the first page.

It was pasted with newspaper clippings of Sir Seamus's many achievements, from business to philanthropy.

BLAIR ELECTRICAL ENTERPRISES WINS INVENTOR OF THE YEAR

SIR SEAMUS ASSISTS IN THE EVACUATION OF ST KESSOG'S ISLE

Her fingers stopped on a page of a darker theme.
The article was dated a year ago and read:

EUPHEMIA SERLE COMMITS SUICIDE IN PRISON

Serle, Opal thought. *Isn't that Seraphina's surname?*

SEVEN
A SUSPICIOUS SLEEVE

Opal pulled her robe tight, a sudden chill seemingly having crept into the room. Was this Euphemia a relative of Seraphina the witch? The woman in the picture had a very similar face and broad shoulders. Opal read the story:

> Sir Seamus, accompanied by his legal counsel Mr Martindale, saw to the swift imprisonment of Euphemia Serle, notorious among the trio known as the Serle Witches of St Kessog's Isle, after she foretold the tragic downing of a military aircraft off the coast of Dunvaloch. Serle was charged with espionage masked as witchcraft and sentenced to a term of twenty years. Yet the so-called seer did not endure long – she took her own life behind bars.

How dreadfully upsetting, thought Opal, biting her lip, *to be given a sentence like that and feel so hopeless that you had to turn to suicide.* Whether Euphemia was a spy or not, women who dabbled in witchcraft to ease poverty were treated far harsher than others, with awfully severe, medieval attitudes towards them. Not to mention prejudice against women.

'So,' Opal sighed to Napoleon. 'From what we can deduce... Seraphina Serle had a sister who died in prison, and Sir Seamus, with the assistance of Mr Martindale, put her there for "spying". Why on earth would Lady Blair then hire Seraphina to come and entertain at their Christmas Eve ball? And why did Seraphina say yes? She must hate Sir Seamus for what he did. Did she kill him to avenge her sister? That seems to be what McWatt thinks, that Seraphina is trying to hoodwink everyone into thinking it was the ghostly crows that killed Sir Seamus, when she is actually behind it herself.'

Opal got up from the bed, stepped towards the window to take in the snow-covered Munros in the distance and pondered. Seraphina really did seem genuine in her shock at Sir Seamus's death. Opal had been next to her, and she had no doubt the witch had genuinely fainted. Was the poor lady being framed?

Suddenly, there was a distant tinkle of a bell.

'Drats, Napoleon, it's breakfast,' Opal said, opening her closet. 'What should I wear? I didn't pack any black clothes to dress for mourning. I guess they can forgive me for not knowing what would happen.'

Napoleon sat up proudly, puffing out his black furry chest as if to say that he was the one who'd followed the appropriate rules about black attire and mourning.

Opal's festive ensemble consisted of a tartan, trumpet-sleeved dress in imperial purples and yellows. Encircling her shoulders was a plum velvet cape, fur-trimmed and imperious, a matching muff, and pheasant feathers sprigged into her plum fedora. Despite the joy of seeing her look pulled together in the mirror, she sighed.

She'd been looking forward to having an ordinary, joyous Christmas Day with Augusto. Not a day filled with doom, gloom and death. She'd been ever so excited to present him with a gift. A bright green, leather-bound sketchbook and artist-quality charcoal, rather than the flaky sticks he usually drew with. She would have liked to get the book monogrammed, but she'd not had long in Harrods.

'Ahhhhhhhhhhhh!!!!!' came a female yell. Despite the mammoth size of the castle, it carried to Opal's room like it had wings.

Opal sprang up straight, pulled her hat further down over one eye, clicked her fingers at Napoleon and dashed to the stairwell.

Lady Blair, dressed in black mourning attire, had thrown herself on the floor in the doorway to the morning room and was sobbing into her hands. 'Smoked haddock in champagne butter! It was his favourite!'

Despite being utterly shocked at her lack of restraint, Opal dashed to Lady Blair's assistance to help her to her feet. Her husband had just died, but most aristocrats would only release such displays of emotion in private. She did feel sorry for the poor widow... if this outburst was truly genuine. Opal then noticed what had made Lady Blair hysterical.

The breakfast table, that had evidently been planned before the tragedy, was laid with Sir Seamus's favourite Christmas breakfast. The aforementioned smoked haddock glistened in the champagne butter on a silver tray. The table was decorated with a twelve-foot holly centrepiece, studded with dried clementines bursting with the scent of cloves. Opal was rather taken aback by the sumptuous decor but assumed it had perhaps been laid for the ball's midnight feast. Before Sir Seamus's death.

Opal managed to get Lady Blair to sit down and told her it would be good for her to consume something. The other overnight guests of the castle soon joined them. Even Lady Laplume and Countess Angelina, who would, being married ladies, usually take breakfast in their rooms, had come to see what the noise was about. The men, Mr Martindale, Mr

Roberts, Turkey, Lord Laplume and the police constable also took their seats.

'Where is Seraphina Serle?' asked Opal to nobody in particular, draping a napkin on her lap.

'The housekeeper says she's in a state of nervous collapse in her chamber. So she won't be joining us. Besides, she's a pagan so won't be attending Mass,' said Mr Martindale.

'Did you know the Romans chose the Christmas date to co-opt and tame the unbridled pagan holiday of Saturnalia?' said Turkey in his irritating, swotty tone. 'I'll have to ask her if she celebrates that!'

Opal ignored him and tried to get back to the point. 'I am aware there was some history with Sir Seamus and Seraphina's sister Euphemia that did not end too well—'

'You're wondering why I hired her and why she took the job when she must have hated Sir Seamus?' cut in Lady Blair, tears streaming down her cheeks, eyes glazed.

Opal batted her lashes in surprise. 'Well, that's the long and short of the question, yes.'

'She needed the money, and I wanted to annoy Sir Seamus,' said Lady Blair, and started to blubber again into her napkin. 'How I regret tormenting him all the time.'

Nobody had the foggiest idea what to say. They consumed the breakfast in silence, broken only by Lady Blair's sobs and the scrape of knives on plates. Nobody dared to say 'Merry Christmas' or 'Sorry for your loss' to Lady Blair, or 'When can we be excused?' for fear of setting her off further.

Countess Angelina seemed to find the silence unbearable. 'I see you have one of the latest gramophones in here. Why don't we play a Christmas tune... in honour of Sir Seamus? He was always so cheery.'

Lady Blair blubbered a response into her festive napkin. Countess Angelina sashayed in her puff-sleeved red gown over to the 78s collection. She unlocked the cabinet and rifled through the sleeves. Suddenly, she stopped and pulled out a cover. She gasped.

'What is it?' asked McWatt from the sideboard, where he'd been serving.

'Oh... it's nothing,' she said and tried to slot it back, but it got stuck in the tightly packed sleeves.

'Please be careful, Countess,' he said gently but clipped with irritation. 'It is my 78s collection. Allow me to put it back.'

He froze after he took the record off her. His back was to Opal, and she wished she could see what had made him stop moving.

'Do you not think this should be dusted for fingerprints, McWatt?' said Countess Angelina, barely audibly, folding her arms.

McWatt still didn't move a muscle. You could almost hear his brain cogs churning, trying to figure out what to do with whatever record he was holding.

After tapping her foot and looking him up and down disdainfully, Angelina plucked it out of his hands and held the sleeve square on, so everyone could clearly see what recording it was.

Lady Blair screamed like the sound of a needle scratching shellac. The police constable stood up to get a better look.

The brown sleeve, brandished in front of Countess Angelina, had an illustration of two crows in one corner and at the top right was the title: 'The Twa Corbies – Arranged for String Quartet.'

EIGHT

A CHRISTMAS CARRIAGE RIDE

'It's alright, Lady Blair,' said Lady Laplume, rushing over to soothe the screaming widow. 'We will get you some tea, shall we? Darjeeling? What about a nice Christmas blend with orange and cloves?'

'Scotch,' panted Lady Blair when she'd run out of scream.

'It's empty,' said Countess Angelina, as if she'd cracked the entire case. 'Where is the record, McWatt?'

'Still in the ballroom, with the rest of the crime scene, of course!' said McWatt, losing all of his servile niceness. 'And you're right... the detective *will* need to dust it.'

'Please put the evidence down, Countess,' said the constable approaching her.

She obeyed and placed it on the cabinet, then her red-lacquered talons floated onto her hips. 'Don't strain yourself thanking me for finding it! Funny, isn't it, that the record that played in the ballroom last night just happens to be one of McWatt's?' she said, with a stabbing look at the butler as she sauntered out of the morning room. 'I'm going to pet those lovely beasts in the courtyard.'

'Well, I never!' said McWatt when she was out of earshot.

'What is the countess insinuating? That I killed Sir Seamus just because the record that was used was from *my collection*. Anyone could have taken it.'

'Calm down, please, McWatt. Let us depart for Mass. Seeing the vicar will bring me great comfort,' said Lady Blair.

They slung on their winter coats and furs and made their way to the courtyard. Augusto was waiting for Opal by the carriage, looking ever so dashing in his yellow scarf, a dusting of snowflakes on his dark eyelashes.

While helping her into the carriage with a hand, he whispered to Opal, 'I don't go to church. I'm a heathen.'

'Well, you're a devout Church of England goer today,' she whispered back. 'You're my protection officer, you have to come.'

He got in next to her, and the horses trotted, their sixteen hooves gallantly clip-clopping along the cobbles and over a little bridge. The lightest sprinkling of snow falling upon the horses' backs like icing sugar from a sieve.

'Now you may introduce me to our first-footer, Opal,' said Lady Blair, seeming to have perked up a little after a double Scotch and fresh air and now on a delirious emotional roller-coaster. 'I absolutely insist that you be the first person over my front step after midnight at Hogmanay, young man. You look just the part.'

Opal noted how Lady Blair searched Augusto with her eyes, as if she liked the look of him very much. Augusto looked abashed, and the dimple in his chin turned into a bemused curl. He removed his hat but didn't know what to respond.

'It's a tradition here,' said Opal, then continued. 'I do apologise for not introducing him sooner, Lady Blair. We have all been... preoccupied. This is Mr Augusto Sevilla. Augusto, Lady Viola Blair.'

'Very glad to meet you,' said Augusto. 'And my deepest condolences for the loss of your husband.'

'Latin, are you?' asked Lady Blair keenly, leaning toward him, seeming to forget completely about her husband's dramatic death.

'Spanish,' said Augusto.

Opal fidgeted, because she had reservations about Augusto's 'background' that she hadn't quite unearthed yet.

'An Iberian, how exciting. I heard you're the Laplume family's protection officer?' asked Lady Blair.

Augusto nodded, and Lady Blair continued, 'To make sure Lord Peregrine stays away from the Laplumes? I know all about that debacle, but nobody really knows where Peregrine is. Rumours are he's in his hovel in the Highlands. Wearing an eyepatch.'

Opal gulped. She'd inflicted the eye injury on him in self-defence last spring in Paris. No wonder he'd be clamouring around in an eyepatch.

'Augusto will just be around to look out for anything suspicious. Opal could do with a chaperone when I'm not around anyway,' said Lord Laplume. 'You did a very good job in America, I heard,' he said and nodded approvingly at Augusto.

'Lord Laplume, Opal will be safe. Do not worry about that,' Augusto said assuredly.

When they arrived at the church, most worshippers were already inside, and there were even some congregated outside for lack of room. The servants from Dunvaloch Castle had made their own way, and Opal noticed butler McWatt looking like the angry steam from breakfast had not left him, sitting on a chair behind the back pew next to a sad-looking young woman in a wheelchair. She had the same greyish eyes as McWatt, and Opal overheard him introducing her to someone as 'his daughter'.

Oh, I wonder why his daughter is in a wheelchair? I do hope she is alright, thought Opal.

Lady Blair had a front bench reserved for herself and the

guests staying at the castle. All eyes in the church silently watched them walk up the aisle to their seats. It was clear the whole village knew about the disaster at the ball, seeing as some of the congregation had been present when it happened.

Augusto and Opal walked side by side. For a tiny split of a second, Opal allowed herself to imagine a different occasion when she might be walking up the aisle next to him. She looked down at her rhinestone shoes and gown and imagined them white. His brown shoes mirror-shined black. Napoleon squirmed in her arms, jutting her out of her daydream. *Don't be such a nitwit, Opal,* she told herself.

Once in her seat, she couldn't help but notice the number of young men who came up individually to offer their condolences to Lady Blair. One even called her by her first name. The black egret feathers in Lady Blair's hat flicked back and forth as she took the queue of hands in hers, and she failed to suppress the air that she was enjoying the attention.

'Who are all these *fans?*' whispered Countess Angelina in Opal's ear and gave Lady Blair a suspicious pout.

'I... wouldn't like to make assumptions,' Opal whispered back as she eyed a particularly handsome one walking away to the back of the church.

Her eyeline then fell on McWatt. He patted his daughter's knee and whispered something in her ear behind his bulbous hand. The daughter, under a rather neglected, saggy cloche brim, smiled. The kind of smile that would stretch someone's lips if they'd cheated in a parlour game and won. Gleefully amused.

NINE

A FRIGHTFULLY DANGEROUS FLAMBÉ

Once back at the castle, they were met with the disappointing news that the detective and the procurator fiscal still had not arrived. Lady Blair insisted Christmas lunch would still go ahead, on the grounds that the day would be so utterly wretched if they were not to behave like normal. Besides, the Gilded Pheasant en Croûte – hand-latticed puff pastry, painted with twenty-four carat gold – had cost a fortune.

Augusto, being staff and not one of the party, was not invited to the feast and would be lunching with the servants in the kitchens. To Opal, the lack of his physical absence brought home the reality that there was truly a wedge between them in this world, no matter how hard she tried to deny it.

How lovely it would have been to be sitting next to him in this beautiful dining hall. The luncheon candelabras were lit with tall, green candles, and ribbons of tartan fluttered playfully between the polished silver, as though the very spirit of Christmas had come to dance across the banquet. Countess Angelina and Lady Laplume's festive jewels twinkled back at the candlelight. And the gentlemen sat stiffly upright in their wing collar shirts.

Opal was seated opposite Mr Finlay Roberts, the only man not in this attire but wearing a dark lounge suit instead. Opal remembered that he too was staff; he was the estate's falconer. She wondered why he had a seat. He must have been especially close to the Blairs.

'Where are your family spending Christmas, Mr Roberts?' Opal enquired, looking through the candelabra at him. She had to find out more about this man.

'The Blair household *is* my family,' he replied shortly and twizzled his copper moustache.

Opal found his conversational skills rather uncouth. A gentleman, after all, doesn't put a full stop where a lady has placed a delicate question mark. Still, perhaps he wasn't seasoned in the art of civilised supper chat.

'Yes,' added Lady Blair. 'Seamus and Mr Roberts were like father and son. Actually, more like left and right socks in a drawer... always together, weren't you, Mr Roberts?'

'I do not know what I shall do without him,' replied Mr Roberts, looking down at his plate solemnly.

Opal swallowed a generous amount of champagne when she realised she must say something to Turkey, who was sitting next to her. He attempted a wink that looked more like a bee had flown into his eye.

'Champagne isn't *off* this afternoon, I hope?' said Turkey, leaning close. 'It did seem to disagree with you last night.'

'The vintage was excellent...' said Opal, bringing her glass between them as a barrier. 'It was the pairing with a certain company that proved unfortunate.'

'We simply must exchange gifts,' said Lady Blair at the head of the table. 'I need all of the merriment I can to get through the day!'

The servants brought the gifts that had been waiting under the smaller Christmas tree in the drawing room, and everyone got to unwrapping.

Opal had bought her father a new phonograph record with new recordings of bird calls. Though she whispered to him to open it under the table so as not to set Lady Blair off thinking about records.

She next gifted her mother a little handbag with a real zip – how modern!

'I mean, it's a novelty having a zip. But I just can't help feeling as though I'd enlisted in a factory workforce. The sound...' She zipped it closed fast with a screwed-up face. 'Not exactly the dainty purr sound I'd expected.'

'If you work in fashion, you must keep up with the latest technology, Mama.' Opal sighed.

'I jolly well do *not* have to keep up, I just have to keep *tasteful*,' Lady Laplume retorted.

The Blairs had gifted Opal and Lady Laplume an electric hairdryer each. They resembled a chrome snail-shell attached to an arm.

'Oh, wonderful, Mother. Effie will be able to get you ready quicker,' Opal said, then quickly looked around to see if Effie had somehow been lurking. No, she hadn't heard, thank God.

'They are funny inventions. They puff and wheeze like you might take off for Mars at any moment,' Lady Blair said and then smiled nostalgically. 'Like something Sir Seamus would have tried to invent.'

The Laplumes had got Lady Viola Blair an array of Harrods lipsticks. Mr Finlay Roberts got a safety razor and a leather-bound portable radio. Countess Angelina had brought chocolate gifts from Paris. Turkey gave Opal a musical powder compact that played a shrill rendition of 'God Save the King'. *Ghastly,* she thought, through her best smile. Though she contemplated that if Augusto had given it to her, she would have adored it.

Suddenly, a cold draught stroked the back of Opal's neck. The door had opened, and Seraphina's head poked through.

'Ah, Seraphina, my dear,' said Lady Blair, standing up. 'How are you feeling now?'

'A little better, thank you, m'lady,' said Seraphina. 'I thought I'd better eat something.'

'There is a place for you... We are just about to start lunch.'

'Thank you for your kindness, m'lady,' said Seraphina.

It seemed Lady Blair felt a tad guilty for using Seraphina to annoy her husband. From her polite tone, she did not seem to believe Seraphina had anything to do with her husband's death.

After the paper and ribbons were stuffed away in a wastepaper basket, Opal's taste buds were treated to the most exquisite Scottish cuisine. Steaming on mirror-shined platters was Orkney lobster thermidor, drowned in a creamy whisky sauce, haggis wellington and cognac jus with braised red cabbage, wild boar terrine with bramble and port glaze, apples, cloves, roast potatoes and butter-glazed Brussels sprouts with chestnuts.

The guests allowed themselves to enjoy the food thoroughly, but nobody touched the Christmas crackers. Seeing as the man of the house was lying dead in the ballroom, it seemed inappropriate to be as jubilant as to don a paper crown.

Napoleon, who'd sneaked under the table, whined. Opal coughed to cover up the noise and peeked under the tablecloth. 'No, you cannot have the Gilded Pheasant en Croûte. It's dusted with twenty-four carat gold and I'm not sure how your tummy will cope with that.'

Mr Finlay Roberts and Turkey were chattering in low tones across the table. The latter pulled open his fountain pen lid with a zealous pop and scribbled something on a card with a flourish. He then slid it to Mr Roberts with a sideways glance of mischief. Mr Roberts examined it, and his eyes popped forth. Opal thought this rather curious and paused in her munching to watch their exchange.

'What are you two talking about?' Lady Phyllis Laplume

enquired and peered over at the small card as Mr Finlay Roberts was to her right. Her eyes also bulged.

'Oh, just er... billiards,' said Mr Roberts, tucking the card into his inside pocket.

'You're not playing for *that*, are you?' Lady Laplume asked, and a piece of wild boar terrine fell off her fork as if the morsel itself had fainted.

'Oh no, we were discussing house values in London,' rescued Turkey and waved his forked apple in the air.

Lady Laplume rolled her eyes, pulled a clove out of her teeth and waggled her lips around her gums like a camel as if she didn't believe them. Opal didn't either. She wondered whether she'd underestimated Turkey. Could he be up to something shady after all?

Lord Edmund Laplume seemed to bite.

'London property prices are positively shocking,' he said. 'One can hardly tell the difference between a terrace house and a dog kennel these days.'

'Property in London is like the King's Guard. All for show, expensive and useless when you need it to be practical,' said Turkey. 'I can never sleep for the racket outside.'

Glad you won't be visiting me, then, thought Opal.

'For me, it's the *people*. I can't stand how overpopulated it is in the capital. Most of them vagrants and children.' Mr Roberts pulled a grimace when he said that last word... *children*.

'Oh,' said Opal, halving a roast potato and swirling it in gravy. 'I got the impression you were fond of children, Mr Roberts.'

'Good heavens no,' said Mr Roberts. 'Whatever gave you that impression?'

'Last night, you played I Spy with those little'uns. The ones by the tree.'

'Oh... that. I thought they were going to smash the baubles with how wild they were getting,' he replied dismissively.

'I was pleasantly surprised, I must say,' said Lady Blair. 'When I saw you entertaining the kiddies, Mr Roberts. I don't think you mind children as much as you let on.'

McWatt entered the dining hall with the final, extravagant course – a hefty silver platter with the plum pudding sitting on it.

'Aged for three years, steamed for eight hours, served with clotted cream and infused with Highland heather honey,' he announced proudly and carefully laid it down at the end of the table.

'I shall do the honours in Sir Seamus's memory,' McWatt said. 'And I shall use Calvados for the flambé. The flame will be more spectacular.'

He then swiped and dropped a match, and the mountainous treat burst into a blue phoenix.

After a moment or two of clapping and utterances of 'I say!', Seraphina got up and walked hastily down to Sir Seamus's end of the table. 'I don't like the look of that flame, the devil materialises within it!' she exclaimed, and tossed her Chartreuse cocktail over it in a seeming attempt to extinguish the flame.

But instead, the little blue bonfire hissed and writhed into an orange, yellow, white, then even larger purple flame like a testy dragon.

'Youuuuu nitwit!' roared McWatt, hands on his head in panic.

'I didn't know Chartreuse was flammable!' yelled Seraphina.

'It's *alcohol*, you fool! Did you think Chartreuse was fruit juice?' McWatt yelled back, having lost all servile composure.

'Yes, I believe Chartreuse is quite a strong liquor indeed,' commented Lord Laplume, after swallowing a sprout. 'No wonder at all that our pudding lit up like a bonfire!'

'Will you stop discussing chemistry and *help*?' Lady Laplume shouted. She was close to the pudding so pulled her new zipper bag out of the way. Her elbow caught Seraphina, who jutted into McWatt with her hip. The butler yelled and threw his arm forward, catching it on the flame. His sleeve went up.

McWatt flapped up and down like a dragon hatchling. Napoleon stuck his head out of the tablecloth and yapped dramatically as if trying to be a fire engine alarm.

Without a moment's hesitation, McWatt grabbed the turban on Lady Laplume's head, unravelled it, and whipped the fabric on his arm. After a few more hard whips, it dissipated into a puff of smoke.

'Ahhhhh!' screamed Lady Laplume so loudly that she outdid McWatt's noises.

'Oh dear... the scorched turban is a worse tragedy than the scorched arm,' said Lord Laplume. 'It's alright, dear, you've got many more hats.'

Lady Laplume patted her hair frantically into place.

'Is your arm alright, McWatt?' Opal asked.

'Yes, my flannel winter undergarments seem to have protected my arm, though it is stinging,' he said.

'Follow me to the kitchens,' demanded Lady Blair. 'We shall get that iced and bandaged, McWatt.'

Seraphina Serle sank back into her seat and stared into a candle flame, thinking deeply. A footman gingerly served out the dessert with a pudding slice, too shocked to realise the pudding was spoiled. Opal exchanged concerned looks with all the other guests. *Seraphina had pushed McWatt with her hip. Had it been an accident? Or did Seraphina try to burn McWatt on purpose?*

'It's alright, Seraphina,' said Countess Angelina in a low voice. 'We know you didn't do that on purpose. It's those two who have left the room who are the guilty ones.'

Opal almost spat out her champers. All heads jerked in the countess's direction.

She fingered her dangly, ruby earring casually and went on. 'I don't know what they are up to... but from "The Twa Corbies" record in McWatt's collection... to the fact that Lady Blair can never keep her eyes off other men, I think we should all be very wary of them. As soon as I can leave this castle, I will.'

The audacity of the countess to speak out like that, thought Opal, *especially about her hostess.* But she had to concede the French aristocrat had a point. Lady Laplume, who would have put someone of a lower rank in their place for speaking out of turn, pulled her zip-purse onto her lap and stared down at it as if wanting to be zipped inside it.

'Lady Blair and McWatt do not have a hand in the things that have been happening here,' said Seraphina, and her gaze flicked up to the ceiling. 'It is my sister, Euphemia Serle, who is finally getting her revenge! I've felt her stirrin' in the ether, aye, stronger than I've felt her since the night the black crows keened above her cell.'

'Should somebody be taking Miss Serle back upstairs?' Mr Finlay Roberts leant back in his chair and cocked his ginger head at the footman.

The young footman took a few steps forward, then hesitated and froze as Seraphina started to whisper unintelligibly, looking back and forth along the ceiling.

'Revenge?' said Turkey, strumming his bony fingers on the table anxiously. 'Your sister wants revenge for what exactly?'

'For branding her a spy when all she did was see too clearly,' said Seraphina. 'Euphemia wasn't a traitor, she was gifted. She foresaw that military craft's end. But he could not lock up her soul for long. She took her own life, aye, but not in despair... with purpose. So her soul could pass through the veil, where no walls could hold her. She crossed into the spirit world to finish what she could not do in life. Justice was done last night... but only part of it.'

'I say,' said Mr Martindale, springing up. 'Calling Sir Seamus's death justice is not on. Especially when he is still lying dead under this roof. I agree with Mr Roberts, please take this madwoman out of our sight!'

Seraphina shot Mr Martindale a sideways look, which could only be described as black and sinister.

Napoleon's paws crept up onto Opal's knees, his head between them. He was whimpering. Opal stroked his shaking crown. She too could feel the cold, gothic atmosphere settle upon the table. Who else could be next?

TEN

MCWATT'S CASTLE TOUR

McWatt returned to the dining room and made his presence known with a loud cough. It dispelled the eerie atmosphere as abruptly as the bang of a Christmas cracker. Bandages peeked out from the sleeve of his jacket, and he held his arm against his chest like an injured soldier.

'Since we are still waiting for the detective to arrive, I'd like to take the opportunity of giving you all a grand tour of the castle. From an art history perspective,' he said with his normal butler-like pomp.

'That was quick, McWatt,' said Turkey, burnt pudding crumbs tumbling from his mouth. 'Are you sure you're up to it, old fellow?'

'The wool did an excellent job of protecting my arm, so it's only a shallow burn. I've endured more severe singeing while ironing Sir Seamus's trousers.' Then he looked down sadly. 'I... suppose I won't be doing that anymore.'

'Jolly good about the burn,' Lord Laplume said. 'Yes. A tour would be apt. The point being, we really should give Lady Blair some time alone, she shouldn't have to worry about entertaining us on a day like this.'

'Don't let the truth get in the way of a good history talk, eh, McWatt,' Mr Finlay Roberts said and rolled his eyes, as he'd evidently heard McWatt's 'folklore' many times. 'I'll be sitting this one out. I need to check on the falcons anyway. I'll feed them a bite of this delectable lobster as a treat. They shall be wondering where their master is, the poor dears.'

'I *too* must get on with things in Sir Seamus's study,' said Mr Martindale, polishing his monocle. 'There's going to be a frightful amount of probate to wade through. Do enjoy the tour.'

The lawyer and the falconer then left the dining hall. Opal removed her napkin from her lap and stood up with a renewed vim. She was excited by the prospect of a grand tour. The perfect opportunity to poke about and investigate. Knowing the layout of the castle could also prove useful, not to mention soaking up some of the fascinating history.

The timid footman assisted Seraphina, who hadn't stopped muttering to herself, out of the room and up the stairs to lie down in her chamber with a glass of brandy. This left the tour participants to be Lord and Lady Laplume, Turkey, Countess Angelina, Opal and Napoleon. They trundled out after McWatt into the chilly corridor. The butler jerked nervously when Napoleon galloped past him all the way to the end of the gallery and back. Doing a rendition of the 'Hound from Hell' to shake off his nerves from the previous scene.

'Don't worry, McWatt, I'll pop him on the lead,' Opal said. 'Here, boy!'

'That's for the best, as there are a lot of things that can be knocked over. Some extremely ancient!' McWatt's voice echoed in the vaulted ceiling. 'We shall begin the tour in the library.'

On entering, dust pricked the back of Opal's throat, and she had to stifle a cough with her fist. It was a hexagon-shaped, towering room with bookshelves lining each wall. They were neatly slotted with volumes, their titles gold gilt in medieval font. McWatt swooped his good arm above the mantlepiece, presenting a portrait of Lady Catherine Dunvaloch.

'Renowned for her queer sense of humour,' he said in a professor-like manner, 'and for her use of figs as ammunition.'

'Hopefully against Lord Dunvaloch,' Lady Phyllis Laplume sniggered.

'What in the deuce is this?' Turkey said, picking up what looked like a giant pair of brass tweezers from beside an armchair. 'One of Sir Seamus's toys?'

'One of his first inventions,' said McWatt sadly. 'The automatic book selector, he called it.'

It had a mechanical arm and an array of dials labelled with things like 'Mood' and 'Genre'. The tip, like a crab claw, snapped as Turkey squeezed the base. A little bulb illuminated when it touched the edge of a desirable book and clamped it so that Turkey could pull it out.

'It was more of a fantasy concept than anything. Never made it to market, alas.' McWatt sniffed and plonked it back next to the fireplace. He suddenly looked rather upset. 'I owe a lot to Sir Seamus. I'm not sure if Lady Blair will keep me on now Sir Seamus is gone. I have a feeling she won't.'

Lady Laplume coughed awkwardly. Opal knew what she was thinking: That this was a highly audacious statement coming from a servant. She wondered why he was so confident as to confide in them like this. Surely he wouldn't want Lady Blair to catch wind of him wafting this information casually about... to guests of all people?

'Oh?' said Opal. 'That would be a shame.'

'Surely not, McWatt,' said Lord Laplume. 'Without you, the umbrella stand would become a jungle!'

'Yes, we can't have Lady Blair answering the phone, the Germans will get the jam recipe!' sniggered Turkey.

Countess Angelina twittered, but the jokes flatlined with McWatt. Turkey was a berk, and Opal had to concede that her father's 'quips' were sometimes more patronising than humorous.

'I think the whole castle would fall into disarray without you, McWatt,' Opal said sensitively.

'Thank you, my dear. The problem is, Lady Blair doesn't actually know all the tasks I perform. I've been here so long I think she assumes it's magic,' he said sadly. 'Right, next stop the art gallery.'

As the tour party's feet plodded the carpet after the portly old butler, Opal had a muse. She'd previously been trying to concoct a motive for McWatt, but it seemed he could be put out very much by Sir Seamus's demise, on a personal *and* professional level. And he had the disabled daughter she'd seen at church to look after.

The art gallery was lined with amber-glowing torch brackets and populated by a battalion of knights in shining armour. Napoleon trotted up to one with a rather ostentatious feather plumage in his helmet and sat at its feet. He contemplated his reflection in the shining calf armour with his head on the side, then started yapping at the fellow as if giving him orders to rally the troops in the glen.

The arrow slits in the walls bathed the gallery in soft northern light, perfect for displaying the Blairs' collection of Scottish artworks. Landscapes of lochs and stormy skies shared space with charming, somewhat peculiar, pieces like *Highland Sheep in a Tartan Bonnet*.

'Oh, look at the knights with their bagpipes!' said Countess Angelina. 'How gloriously Scottish!'

'I heard that's why you're here, countess,' said Lady Laplume. 'To study Scottish customs.'

'Indeed, I am,' replied the countess, checking her lipstick in the reflection of a knight's helmet.

Opal wanted her to elaborate, but she didn't. *Was she really here to study Scottish customs? For what purpose? And why did*

Opal get the feeling she was more interested in her lipstick than the knight's helmet?

'A masterpiece of pastoral beauty,' McWatt declared of one of the pictures named *Grouse on the Moors, Just Before the Incident*. 'I have a particular soft spot for these twelve paintings, and Sir Seamus kindly said he was leaving them to me in his will. Nobody else likes them, you see. Some people find them vulgar, but I am rather fond.'

'Oh, will they fetch you a pretty penny?' Lord Laplume asked.

'No, no, they don't have any monetary worth, and I wouldn't part with them even if they did,' said McWatt pompously.

Lady Laplume whispered to Opal, 'How frightfully vulgar of a servant to overshare in that manner about Sir Seamus's will. We'll be hearing about what long johns he wears next.'

'I rather like him, Mama. It's refreshing to hear a butler speak so candidly,' Opal replied, then shivered.

The arrow slits in the walls made it chilly, carrying a whiff of salt from the sea beyond, and she was glad once they progressed to a grand bedroom. The vast gothic chamber had a hefty four-poster bed draped in tartan velvet, and it smelt of lavender sachets and fresh linen.

'This room was prepared for King George V's rumoured visit a few years ago,' McWatt explained, 'which never occurred, as His Majesty preferred the salmon on another estate.'

'Dashed poor show,' said Lord Laplume, then crouched down as he noticed something strange under the bed.

'That is the "toasty posterior bedwarmer". Another one of Sir Seamus's contraptions,' said McWatt.

Napoleon prodded it with a paw, as if trying to decipher if it was alive or not. It was a soft cushion-like thing on one side and coils of heating wire encased in padding on the other.

'Did *this* gadget go to market?' Turkey enquired, holding his own posterior, looking as if he'd like to try it out.

'Sadly not,' said McWatt.

'I daresay it would have been a jolly decent house-fire starter,' said Lord Laplume.

'What inventions of his *did* exactly see the light of day?' enquired Countess Angelina.

'Mainly tweed looms...' McWatt waved his arm in the air as if he couldn't really be bothered to go into it.

As the others plugged the heating device into a socket and tried to switch the silly thing on, Opal's eyes were drawn to a beautiful tapestry hanging on the wall. It depicted a battle scene from centuries ago, knights galloping on horseback and clashing beneath dark clouds, their banners flowing behind them. Opal brought her nose close and studied the focal point of the piece: a pompous highland chieftain with his sword raised.

Suddenly, a muffled moaning sound seemed to come from the chieftain. Opal frowned and squinted into his embroidered face. It was as if he was faintly wailing behind his metal visor. *Don't be dense, Opal... the noise must be coming from behind the tapestry. Whoever could be crying back there?*

ELEVEN

BEHIND THE TAPESTRY

'Oh, it is rather hot, isn't it?' said Turkey, lying on the four-poster bed and snuggling up to the heater. 'I must say, I do prefer my novelty frog hot-water bottle.'

Opal took the opportunity to investigate the noise while the others fannied about. It really did sound like the cry had come from behind the tapestry. She brushed her hands down the richly woven wool as she pressed her ear against it. *Oh!* Her hand felt a protrusion behind the fabric.

She swished the edge of the tapestry aside, and *yes*, it was a door handle. An entrance to the connecting boudoir. A lot of these old houses had similar hidden doorways. She put her finger to her lips to make sure Napoleon didn't yap with excitement and gingerly slipped inside. Napoleon brushed her ankles as he followed her in.

It was hard to see inside the boudoir because the shutters were closed and the drapes pulled across. The only light source was a collection of candles burning on the bedside table.

The person propped up in the bed was half in shadow, but Opal could see the one front tooth as the mouth made strange hissing sounds and the occasional wail. The hands covered in fat cabochon rings were hovering over the tops of the candles. It was Seraphina Serle, too deep in whatever spell she was conjuring to notice Opal.

'Seraphina?' asked Opal gently and clasped one of the bedposts... for safety, if for anything.

Seraphina's head snapped in Opal's direction. 'Oh!' she exclaimed. 'What do you want, lassie You gave me a fright.'

'I am sorry, Seraphina. I just heard you from the next room and wondered if you were alright?'

'I am fine, Miss Laplume,' said Seraphina. 'But I have been trying to talk sense into my sister's spirit. I fear her business is not finished and there will be more trouble. She is restless.'

'Oh, Euphemia Serle?' said Opal, trying to sound like she believed her.

'Yes. I want her to be at peace... I'm imploring her to leave Dunvaloch Castle. But she is my elder sister, so never she listened to me, and she is as stubborn as an ox.'

'What is her unfinished business?' asked Opal with a gulp.

'Destroying the second crow. The twa corbies. One was Sir Seamus. I have no idea who the second shall be.'

'Do you really think Euphemia's spirit was able to lift the gramophone into the Christmas tree and set the wires up to electrocute Sir Seamus? Does she have poltergeist powers?' asked Opal. She did not believe a moment of it, but just wanted to hear Seraphina's rationale.

'My sister can do anything,' she said, looking Opal up and down with black orbs for eyes.

'Are you from St Kessog's Isle, Seraphina?' asked Opal, trying to bring the conversation back down to the physical realm.

'Yes. I lived there all my life until the evacuation,' she said.

'I'm going there with Papa soon to help save the dying puffins. Do you know what could be wrong with them?'

'It could be my cat getting them... Morag is her name.'

She smirked. 'No, I'm only teasing, she didn't hunt. I had to leave her with the island caretakers, as I had nowhere decent to bring her home to. Since then, my other sister, Malvina, found a cottage in the hamlet for us to live in, so I've been meaning to go back to fetch her. But I can't afford the boat fare.'

'Perhaps I can bring her back for you?' suggested Opal brightly.

'Would you?' The seer's eyes lit up.

'Of course,' Opal replied. 'Not sure how much Napoleon will like being on a boat with a feline, but we shall make do.'

'You have a kind heart,' said Seraphina, softening her tone.

Great, thought Opal, *I've won her over.* 'Could you tell me a bit about Sir Seamus and his involvement with St Kessog's Isle? Why is he the person supervising it after the evacuation? Does he own it?'

'No. The defence establishment do, as an observation post, but they never use it as such. They appointed Sir Seamus as an honorary warden,' said Seraphina. 'He is the closest landowner to the island. But I think his relationship with the military runs deeper.'

'How so?' asked Opal.

'For many years before the evacuation, Sir Seamus would often visit and disappear for days on end with nobody knowing where he was. St Kessog's is a small island, so it was rather odd. Rumours were he had a secret laboratory for his electrical inventions on the island somewhere.'

'A secret laboratory?' Opal asked, grasping the bedpost harder.

'Yes. Nobody has ever found it. Nor the person that started the rumour,' said Seraphina and looked deeply into the candle flame.

'He also had Euphemia arrested for alleged spying and predicting the crash of the military aircraft, didn't he?' said

Opal, pinching her chin. 'Was he getting involved to prove his vigilance to the War Office, do you think?'

'Yes, indeed,' said Seraphina. 'He got involved with policing everything around these parts; it's so remote, there wasn't really anyone else with the same amount of power as Sir Seamus. Thought he was king.'

'I am surprised that you accepted the offer to entertain at Sir Seamus's ball, seeing as he was responsible for your sister's imprisonment,' said Opal.

'I've less coin than a minister's swear jar,' said Seraphina. 'Utterly destitute. Thank goodness my sister Malvina has found some menial work in the hamlet.'

There was a scratching noise in the darkness behind them.

'What's that?' said Seraphina sharply and almost made Opal's cloche fall off.

It sounded to Opal like Napoleon was picking at something. She crept closer to the shadowy corner of the room. Napoleon, who had been cowering by the radiator from the scary lady, was now picking at something behind it.

Opal knelt down to stop him, but he was determined to dislodge an object that had got stuck behind it. Suddenly, came a tinkling sound and a soft thud.

'What's that? Is Euphemia trying to speak to us through the plumbing?' Seraphina sat up straight and squinted into the darkness.

Opal squatted to look at what had fallen from behind the radiator. It was a little manual, a well-thumbed thing. She couldn't quite read the title, but it had the word *Electrical* in it. And something else. A screwdriver.

'No, no, Seraphina, Napoleon simply got his toys stuck,' Opal said and scooped them into her bag. They seemed a little suspicious somehow, and Opal didn't want the witch to catch on to what she'd done. She quickly changed the subject. 'I think you should get some sleep, Seraphina, you have been overexerting yourself with worry. Rest assured, I will bring your cat Morag for you, and I shall endeavour to find this secret laboratory too.'

With that, she slipped back through the side door and into the grand chamber where the countess was currently sitting on the 'posterior toaster' and demanding that she borrow it that evening.

Together they ventured back to the main staircase. Opal tottered to keep up with her father at the front and whispered behind her hand into his ear. 'Papa, we simply must visit St Kessog's Isle without delay, as I hear Sir Seamus may have had a secret laboratory there.'

'Come again, Bins?' Lord Laplume said, frowning down at her. Opal resolved to tell him all about it later.

Lady Laplume shushed them as McWatt chattered on about the magnificent stained-glass window above it that glittered in verdant greens, like a peacock in the moonlight. The image on it was a shield, boldly emblazoned with a stag surrounded by a wreath of thistles. There was a Latin family motto written on a scroll in the glass panels below.

Opal descended the steps to try and get a better look at the words. *Fortis et Fidelis*.

Turkey put a slithery hand on her shoulder and said, 'It's the family motto. Probably means, if you mess with us, you'll sit on a large thistle.'

Opal twittered artificially and removed his hand from her shoulder as if it was a grubby dishcloth.

'It actually means,' said McWatt, 'Brave and Faithful... Follow me to the drawing room before icicles grow on our extremities. It *is* frightfully chilly.'

The drawing room was beautifully bedecked with wood panelling and clad in portraits of tartan-wearing ancestors, staring down challengingly as if daring you to comment on their oversized noses. McWatt drawled on about the ancient grandfather clock. It ticked, long drawn-out tocks as if resisting the approaching year, 1935. The focal point was the fireplace of mammoth proportions. It currently housed a little blaze that was struggling to warm the cavernous space, but it crackled and glowed in a comforting way. There was a leather armchair swathed in sheepskins and footstools dotted about on top of an exquisite rug.

Lady Viola Blair peeked her head around the armchair to look at them. 'I'm afraid the castle was built at a time when you were expected to huddle next to sheep to keep warm.'

She had reddened eyes from crying, but seemed to have found something to distract herself. She was crafting, knotting cords in the macramé method, making decorative edging for a cushion cover.

'Gosh, did you handcraft the rug as well?' commented Lady Laplume, looking down at the knotted artistry.

'I did, with a few little helpers, yes,' Lady Blair said quietly.

'Well, it is so beautiful it deserves its own title,' said Lady Laplume, clearly trying to cheer the woman up.

'What title? Countess Shagpile? You are a nitwit, Phyllis,' Lord Edmund Laplume sniggered.

'Well, in that case, the rug outranks you!' Lady Laplume retorted.

Lady Blair sniffed, the three moles around her nose bobbing. 'You two should stop squabbling. When one of you exits this life, you regret the bickering!'

'Don't be so hard on yourself, Lady Blair,' said Countess Angelina, fingering the twine Lady Blair was working with. 'When someone departs, the mind has a way of exaggerating past troubles. Best not to place too much stock in it.'

'The countess is right,' said Lady Laplume.

'Thank you, Countess,' said Lady Blair sniffing, then paused her crafting fingers. 'I have to admit I wasn't the one that he fought with most. Mr Martindale and he were at each other's throats at times. The racket I heard coming from the study during their meetings, you'd think there was an amateur opera rehearsal.'

Opal stopped ruffling Napoleon's tummy by the fire. He twitched his nose at her to carry on. Opal tried to think of how to frame her next question in a way that did not sound too meddlesome.

'Mr Martindale seems such a mellow, quiet sort of chap,' said Opal. 'Whatever would rattle them so?'

'Took me a while to find out. Seamus never let me in on business affairs. But they were being sued by a Parisian textile company over a patent for a loom design. Seamus blamed Mr Martindale when it looked like they were going to lose the legal battle. I believe the fight may still be ongoing with the Parisians.'

Opal swallowed. Napoleon huffed for her to continue with his afternoon massage. She was thinking hard. Could Mr Martindale be a suspect? Could he have been double-crossing Sir Seamus and working for the Parisians, for instance?

'Oh, that reminds me, Countess,' continued Lady Blair, wriggling in her armchair to face her. 'You're in with the fashion lot in Paris, aren't you? Were you ever acquainted with the Société des Tissus Parisiens? Forgive my dreadful accent.'

Countess Angelina dropped the piece of twine she was examining and walked to the fire with her hands splayed to warm them. 'No, never heard of them. I'm sorry.'

Easier to lie when your back is turned, thought Opal.

TWELVE

A BUST-UP WITH THE BUTLER

'Who's ready to brave the outdoors?' said McWatt, and on cue, a whistling wind smacked into the side of the castle. 'I simply must show you the Christmas rose garden.'

Before heading out, everyone raided the cloakroom and threw plaid shawls over their coats and yanked woolly deer-stalkers over their ears. Napoleon, though already fluffy, had his bare shaven parts, like a little black lion, and was supplied with his own canine coat to help those parts stay warm. Opal then headed to the powder room and noticed a gold signet ring on the basin. It was imprinted with some sort of animal. Someone must have removed it before washing their hands. Opal brought it out. 'Anyone's?'

'Oh, I know whose that is. I'll return it,' said McWatt and plucked it out of her hand.

The snow-encrusted gravel crunched below Opal's feet as they stepped out onto the grounds. They walked through the gardens and wound their way beneath the bare branches of aged oak trees and yews, their twisted branches casting long shadows on the frosty pathway. The Christmas rose garden was quiet and solemn, and despite it being mid-winter, it was beginning to stir with life. The winter roses nodded gently in the breeze, their pastel petals catching the light of the low Scottish sun. Around them, tufts of grass grew out of the stone walls, the scent of moist ground married the seaweedy air drifting up from the sea beyond.

Napoleon lost his little coat as it got hooked by thistles as he chased a robin around the low hedge maze. In the centre of the maze was a circular flowerbed, blooming with little pink-and-white five-petalled flowers that glistened with frost. More Christmas roses... how delightful.

Mr Finlay Roberts came up some mossy steps. His cheeks were red with cold, and he was wearing his gauntlet, a falcon perched on his forearm. He gestured toward a small turbine house by the loch. 'Sir Seamus's hydroelectric plant,' he said. 'One of the first of its kind in Scotland.'

He then chatted on about the physics of the turbine in some detail. Opal was a little taken aback at hearing a falconer be so versed in the elite sciences.

'Forget the turbine, what a beautiful specimen on your arm,' interrupted Lord Laplume. 'What is the pretty thing's name?'

'Maisie. She was Sir Seamus's best girl,' replied Mr Roberts, giving the bird's head a little stroke.

Suddenly, something exploded out of the maze close to McWatt, sending the butler into a fit of shrieks that Opal at first thought was her mother. A pheasant bolted away and flew over the low wall. Maisie the falcon launched into the sky, evidently startled.

'McWatt! Are you quite alright?' said Opal, dashing awkwardly around the maze to meet him.

'Yes, yes, I'm just terribly skittish,' he panted and patted down his coats. 'You see, my daughter was in an accident when she was charged by a stag and is now in a wheelchair. Ever since, I've been vigilant outdoors.'

'How unimaginable,' said Lord Laplume. 'I am sorry, old chap.'

'Poor girl,' said Countess Angelina, cuddling her muff.

'Oh, how ghastly for her,' Opal said, placing a hand on his forearm. 'I noticed her at Mass. I'm so sorry.'

'It's alright, I'm trying to figure out how to raise funds to get proper treatment for her. I want her to walk again,' he said sadly and looked up into the sky hopefully.

Opal looked over at her mother. Lady Laplume pursed her lips together as if they would fly off in a tangent of disapproval if she didn't. They quivered and then lost the battle, flying apart to say, 'McWatt. I'm very sorry about your daughter, but I do not think this is an appropriate topic to discuss with guests. Perhaps we might steer the conversation toward something a shade less... er... rattling-the-tin-cup in tone? Rest assured, we do our bit for the deserving poor, but—'

'Mother, stop please,' said Opal. 'I don't think McWatt was hinting that at all.'

'No, no, you're mistaken, m'lady. I didn't mean to offend or to hint at charity,' he said, bowing slightly. 'I know that Lord Laplume had to give up his Suffolk estate due to withering funds, and that it was sold to a mustard factory. I wouldn't dream of pressing for money when I know times are hard for you as well.'

Lady Laplume almost dropped her winter muff, while Lord Laplume chuckled behind his glove.

'I'll have you know,' said Lady Laplume, hoisting her muff beneath her bosom, 'the Copperfields estate was sold willingly due to my business being in London and since Lord Laplume has had the lucrative task of setting up a string of bird sanctuaries around the world. We are not, as you put it... in *hard times*.'

'Don't worry, McWatt,' said Lord Laplume, putting an arm around his wife to calm her. 'We were in a pickle after Lady

Laplume put a fortune's worth of millinery cargo on the *Titanic*. You're not all wrong.'

'That is ancient gossip,' said Lady Laplume. 'Many people lost things on the great ship. But if you go about wafting that sort of piffle, I may find myself in urgent need of a very serious word with Lady Blair.'

'My sincerest apologies, m'lady,' said McWatt, looking down at his snowy shoes.

Opal mouthed 'sorry' to him, over her mother's shoulder. Mr Roberts looked highly entertained and was trying to stop the sides of his mouth curling into a laugh, his ginger moustache bobbing up and down.

They all shuffled back inside the castle through the glass conservatory that housed some divine geraniums, mint, lavender, figs and palms.

Lord Laplume had a stern word in his wife's ear. 'Phyllis, my love, let's not make enemies of the staff, eh? You don't know what will end up in your afternoon tea.'

Opal saw a curl of brownish smoke emerge from a fig tree far down the other end of the conservatory. Napoleon saw it too and dashed ahead... he knew where the smoke was coming from. Augusto and his cigarillo.

'How was the staff lunch?' Opal asked when she found him. 'Are they all speculating about what happened last night?'

'Yes, yes, they were. I learned something that may tickle your curiosity.'

'We must confer. But not here, somewhere quiet,' Opal whispered and seized him rather decisively by the elbow and towed him out past the basil and bergamot, away from the conservatory, along the east wing of the castle. Napoleon trotted ahead of them in his own little fantasy that he was leading the way.

They stopped at a suitably remote spot by the wall, concealed by a canopy of ivy. Augusto attempted to steer her gently against the stone wall. She resisted with a hand to his chest.

'No, Augusto, I can't kiss you now,' she said firmly. 'Tell me what the servants were saying.'

Augusto sighed, defeated but not entirely displeased. 'They're all convinced it was Seraphina Serle, and she set it up pretending it was her sister's ghost... but the housekeeper, Mrs Keith, had something interesting to say.'

'What?' Opal said, with a couple of strong blinks.

'That Sir Seamus and Mr Martindale were being sued by a Parisian company over a patent, claiming Sir Seamus's invention was identical to theirs and they'd done it first.'

'I heard the same from Lady Blair. Did Mrs Keith say what the invention actually was?' asked Opal.

'She didn't know any more. She used to hear them talking angrily about it.'

'I see,' said Opal. 'Mr Martindale is getting a head start on the probate in Sir Seamus's study. I wonder where that room is?'

'I believe it's on the ground floor, around this side of the castle,' said Augusto, but he put his arm out to slow her as she stepped forth. 'But, Opal, you're not investigating again, are you?'

Opal gave him a side eye like a cat considering an ajar pantry door. 'Why ever not? It's what I do, isn't it?'

'It is, and you do it very well,' said Augusto. 'Far better than the police detectives we've had to deal with over the past year, but—'

'But what?' Opal said, squaring up to him with her arms folded. Napoleon sat at her heel and huffed with his nose up high as if to ask the same thing.

'You've got into danger many times.'

'That's what you're here for, isn't it?' said Opal.

'Yes... but I can't keep my eye on you permanently.'

'Don't worry, I have a woman's intuition for danger. Also,

I've a feeling it'll be pinned on Seraphina. She is terribly vulnerable and has nobody to look out for her. Would be easy to throw her in the clink, but I've a feeling she's telling the truth about thinking it's Euphemia Serle's ghost.'

'I'm not so sure,' whispered Augusto, suddenly remembering they could be overheard through a window or the carrying wind.

'Well, I heard her earlier, she was talking to her sister's spirit, or thinking she was. She didn't know anyone could hear her. She wouldn't have been putting on an act alone in her chamber, would she?' said Opal, then opened her bag.

'Oh dear, what have you found?' said Augusto, his feet scuffing the ground reluctantly as they walked along the castle wall.

'I haven't had a chance to look properly, but these things were stuffed down the back of her radiator.'

She pulled out the book she'd found in Seraphina's room and gasped when she finally read the full title.

A BEGINNER'S GUIDE TO ELECTRICAL ENGINEERING

It was well thumbed and floppy.

'Doesn't look good for Seraphina if she has this in her room. Anyone could suspect she was the one who set up the wires to kill Sir Seamus and play that gramophone,' said Augusto, shaking his head.

'And there was a screwdriver with it,' said Opal, then frowned, alarmed that perhaps it could have been Seraphina. 'We shouldn't make conjectures without sufficient facts. We must wait for the detective to examine the scene.'

'I wouldn't tell him you've found those. As much as it reflects badly on Seraphina, he equally might think you planted them in there,' said Augusto.

'That is a point. But then again, *anyone* could have planted them there,' Opal said with a deep sigh.

'Could it be dusted for prints?'

'Yes. Thank goodness I have my Christmas banquet gloves on.'

'Well, let's see what this detective is like before you let on how much you know. Detectives aren't always interested in justice. More interested in getting the appropriate culprit.'

Opal went to take his hand. She remembered how awful it was in Hollywood when Augusto was almost shut away forever... or something even more unmentionable.

They continued in silence for a while, gazing into the dusty windows and the walls behind, clad in shady portraits of glowering masters on horseback, until they came to a rectangle of orange light on the path. The light weeping from Sir Seamus's study. Mahogany gleamed in the lamplight, books crammed in every wall, while peculiar mechanical devices lay in half-finished disarray. Opal crept closer and was able to discern a voice. A male one.

'It must be Mr Martindale,' whispered Opal, and shaded her brow close to the glass, but behind the edge of a curtain.

'Don't let him see us,' Augusto warned.

Napoleon dropped low to the ground like a well-groomed tarantula and backed up, getting his nose out of the rectangle of orange light on the path.

'Shhhhh,' said Opal. 'He's on the telephone to someone.'

She could see him hunched forward, the side of his face visible, a glinting monocle pressed into it.

'Yes, indeed, Mummy. It is a ghastly debacle, the whole thing. I don't know why the confounded man couldn't just use plain English. Took me an hour to find the safe and unlock it. Then found the note, which is so cryptic it might as well just be a hanky. This is why I'm calling, Mummy. You're good at crosswords and riddles and things. Well, if you stop talking, I will read it to you...' – Mr Martindale held a small piece of paper to his monocle – 'Mr Martindale, if anything happens to me, follow these instructions: The brave shine, the faithful remain, yet what you seek lies behind pain. But it is spelt...'

Opal screwed up her features, desperate to hear the next

part, but Mr Martindale had spun in his desk chair away and muttered unintelligibly. *Blithering fig*, thought Opal. *I didn't get the rest.* She fumbled to find her sketchbook and pen and scribbled down the riddle.

'Careful,' whispered Augusto, and pulled Opal away from the window. 'He's spun his chair back in our direction.'

'What is he saying now?' whispered Opal and bit the end of her pen anxiously.

They were pressed back against the wall, and Mr Martindale's words weren't clear enough to hear now.

'Come on, let's go back in the castle before he catches us eavesdropping,' said Augusto, his fingers dancing over hers, trying to clasp them.

Opal relented and took his hand. They dashed along the castle's flank, taking care not to slip on the ice and snow. The scullery was below ground level, down a few worn stone steps, and they sneaked in there.

Napoleon made an excited sniffing noise and pawed at stonework in the corner of the architrave. A squeaking little rodent shot out and back inside another crevice.

'Leave him, boy,' said Opal. 'There's no need to show off to us as we know what a master retriever you are.'

She ruffled his head and thought.

'The riddle could be a metaphor for something like a mouse. Mice are terribly *brave* for their size, eyes all *shiny* and vigilant. A pet mouse can be quite *faithful*, as they tend to *remain* in one place while hibernating.'

'And if what you *seek* is his hiding spot, you'll find it *behind the pain* of your finger snapped in a trap,' said Augusto, placing his hands on his hips in exasperation. 'It's useless; you could make any metaphor work.'

'That's not an excuse for not trying,' said Opal, turning to face him with her hands also on her hips.

'I do want to try *something*,' he said, eyes sparking up like a lit match. Then he gently pushed Opal inside the scullery. He pressed her against the brass boiler, his handsome mouth moving close. She had waited so long to be with him... should she? Then a thought came rushing to the front of her mind, and she simply had to blurt it out before it left again.

'One moment,' said Opal, holding him two inches from her mouth with a hand on his neck. 'Sorry. I just had another thought about the riddle. A good one, I think!'

FOURTEEN
HIGHLAND SATIRE ART

'What?' Augusto sighed and took a step back to listen, resting his head on the copper boiler behind with a weary thud.

'It could be about a concept like marriage. Only the *brave* enter, the wedding rings *shine, faithful* spouses *remain*, though I question how many do, and what young fools *seek*... romance, affection and whatnot, ultimately *lies behind pain*... lawyers, and property settlements.' Opal slowly trailed off as she came to a mental dead end.

Augusto's eyes searched her face, and the corner of his mouth twitched into a smile. 'Whatever made you think of marriage?'

Opal felt her cheeks flush... before she could answer, he took her face in his palms. This time she allowed herself to fully enjoy his kiss. His lips were warm on her cold ones, and his hair smelt of cigarillos and the cardamom scent of his cologne. Even her ears, which should have been on heightened alert for any servants' footsteps, seemed to lose their ability to hear anything except his breathing and their lips pressing together in a frenzied longing.

Napoleon evidently got impatient and pawed at Opal's leg.

It made her aware of her discoverable and scandalous position, so she broke apart. They progressed into the castle's labyrinth and ended up in the art gallery that McWatt had shown Opal earlier.

Opal giggled with Augusto at the awful-looking paintings of forlorn sheep. Augusto, a keen recreational artist, was very confused by the artworks indeed.

'The artist couldn't have been in earnest,' he said in mild disgust, his moustache becoming wonky.

'That's what I thought. Or were they intended to make people laugh? McWatt deeply reveres them, and nobody else wanted them, so Sir Seamus left them to him in his will, apparently. We shall have to see if this really is the case after the will is read, I suppose.'

'McWatt either is off his rocker,' mused Augusto, 'has no taste, or very *expensive* taste, and they are worth something.'

'The latter is the only narrative I can get my head around,' said Opal. 'Only through gold-goggles could one see any delight in these eyesores whatsoever.'

'McWatt couldn't possibly be a suspect though, could he?' Augusto screwed his face up as if it was as ridiculous as to think a beagle pup did it.

'Countess Angelina is *convinced* McWatt killed Sir Seamus under the instruction of Lady Blair,' said Opal. 'But if he did do it, he could have had his own motive, it didn't necessarily have anything to do with Lady Blair.'

'McWatt is such a loveable chap, I can't see him doing this,' said Augusto, pacing the carpet.

'He wasn't in the grand hall at the start of the ball because of a "soup spillage". That would have given him the time to set up the gramophone and sort other things out while we were all changing upstairs. But he told me he thinks Seraphina did it to avenge her sister.'

'How could he have made the crows in the tea leaves appear

though? To match the theme of the record tune "The Twa Corbies"?' asked Augusto, straightening a wonky picture. 'That's when the whole crow theme started.'

'That is true. Could it have been a coincidence?' asked Opal doubtfully, peering out of one of the breezy arrow slits. 'He would inherit those ghastly paintings. He said they were worth nothing, but what if he was lying? Maybe they're worth a fortune.'

'Perhaps we can find out?' said Augusto, shrugging.

Opal's eyes fluttered. 'Yes... yes, we could! Let us ascertain the name of the artist?'

Opal zoomed her nose into the bottom right corner of the vulgar painting entitled *Grouse on the Moors, Just Before the Incident* and tried to make out the letters flicked in gold oil paint.

'Strike a match for me, would you, so I can see better,' said Opal.

Augusto struck one and held it in front of the canvas. 'D. Muir pinxit, 1799,' she whispered and then scribbled it in her sketchbook.

'I'd better be careful, as we don't want to incinerate McWatt's payday,' said Augusto, mockingly skimming the bottom of the frame with the match.

'Don't be a berk,' said Opal. 'Now, McWatt would likely get his art knowledge from some of the books in the library. Let's go and inspect.'

Once inside, Opal floated over to a segment of shelves that had 'Art History' written on a plaque. She wriggled out a few volumes. 'If only the subject was fashion and millinery. I know next to nothing about art, but I'm sure we'll find something about them in these.'

'My art knowledge is good, but not in this... esoteric field.'

Napoleon had chosen the most comfortable armchair to take a nap in. So they sat together in a little velvet love seat and thumbed through the dusty volumes. Opal was quite relieved they had the books to distract them; she didn't want Mama to walk in and have an apoplexy.

After a good amount of old book dust had been inhaled, Opal's finger alighted on a chapter in a book called *Highland Satire*, on the artist, Donald Muir.

"'Highland Satire emerged around the late eighteenth century, a blend of humour and rural lifestyle,'" she read. "'This movement was characterised by its light-hearted, sometimes absurd portrayals of the animals, often exaggerating the characteristics of sheep, cows, and even the country folk in a way that invited laughter and reflection.'"

'Augusto, will you get the telephone directory and find the name of an art dealer or gallery close by? Perhaps I can get them on the blower. It is Christmas Day, but I know a lot of art dealers are so on the ball they never stop.'

After sourcing a gallery manager and dialling them on the library telephone, Opal waited nervously, strumming her fingers on the earpiece for the operator to connect her. Once Opal had made the appropriate Christmas-disturbing apologies and made her query, the gallery manager sounded extremely excited... either that or merry from Christmas sherry.

'If they are dated 1799, those are a rare collection that have been missing. Most of Muir's paintings are in Edinburgh, and collectors would be extremely interested indeed.'

'I don't want to keep you from your mince pies and brandy butter for much longer, so I'll get to the point,' said Opal. 'What sort of sum are we talking for the twelve paintings?'

'At least ten thousand pounds. Depending on how the bidding goes, it could go for many multiples of that.'

'Thank you kindly, sir. I wish you a happy Christmas.'

'One moment, madam, don't... don't go yet,' said the art dealer. 'I did have a similar call from a man about a year ago about the same collection. He wouldn't tell me his name or where he had found these paintings, alas. May I ask where you have them?'

'Oh,' said Opal. 'I would not like to disclose that at the moment, I shall be in touch,' she said as politely as she could be and hung up.

Augusto loosened his collar with a finger and made an impressed whistling sound. 'That's got to be at least twenty times McWatt's salary.'

'Certainly enough to get a good doctor for his daughter,' said Opal. 'And it sounds as if he may have made the same call to find out about their worth. He lied to us when he said they weren't worth the canvas they were painted on.'

At that moment, McWatt came into the library with a tray of tea resting on his good arm. There was a dark look on his face. Opal sprang back, making the telephone table wobble. Napoleon barked at the wobbly table as if to reprimand it for not standing still. Augusto coolly turned his head, then folded his arms when seeing the moody manservant.

McWatt's voice was less courteous butler and more brusque butler. 'Detective Inspector Morven Sinclair has arrived with the procurator fiscal. Tea will be served in the drawing room, Miss Laplume... and it seems I took the wrong scrapbook from your bookshelf this morning. I will need to fetch the correct one for the detective if I may be allowed to enter and fetch it.'

'Yes, yes, of course. I'll see you in the drawing room, McWatt, thank you,' Opal stammered.

Opal felt dread trickle down her spine. She knew her face would appear white. Did McWatt hear them speak about the paintings? Did he overhear their discussion, and, if so, just how much of it? He could have been lurking around the corner since the phone call with the gallery manager. God forbid. Were they in danger?

FIFTEEN

THE DETECTIVE COMES FOR TEA

Tea was laid out on a white macramé tablecloth like a little village of silver, surrounded by little hills of baked goods. There were cheese scones, the edges crumpling with crisp orange flakes, Dundee cake and the stag-shaped shortbread biscuits left over from Christmas stockings. With one arm behind his back, McWatt leant forwards and poured an Earl Grey concoction that infused the air with bergamot. It mingled in Opal's nostrils with smokiness from the hearth.

Lady Viola Blair was sitting in her armchair by the fire, dressed in a black shirtdress, a funereal onyx brooch clasped at her throat. A macramé stand that resembled a small clothes rack was standing in front of her with a little wooden pole hanging from it, on which the cords were knotted. Her hands moved fast as if bewitched. Her eyes, gazing down upon her work, were not in focus. Opal wondered, if Lady Viola Blair was truly innocent of her husband's murder, how lonely she must feel in this castle big enough for a hundred people to reside with ample space. But perhaps she was already lonely living just with Sir Seamus, the mismatched duo. It was not really a surprise that she may have taken lovers.

Turkey was sitting next to Lady Laplume, steam from his teacup rising around his gaunt face. He was wearing a baggy suit that looked as if it had been stored in mothballs since the reign of Queen Victoria. His bony knee jutted up inside the fabric, looking almost sharp. *What a drooping, half-portion of a man,* Opal thought.

The guests slurped from their teacups while ensconced in armchairs by the crackling drawing-room fire, and the constable, with his ink book and pad, went around and carefully rolled fingers, blotting the excess, and thanking each person with a quiet nod. Only Countess Angelina gave any kind of protest.

'The Comte de Brisecloque takes a dim view of people manhandling his wife... especially for something as vulgar as fingerprints.'

The room was silent, and the constable froze.

'I would advise against resisting, Countess,' said Mr Martindale, polishing his monocle. 'From a lawyer's point of view, that is my opinion.'

After a moment's reflection, she co-operated with an aggressive tug of her glove and a pout of her mouth. Once this was done, McWatt fetched the new arrival.

Detective Inspector Morven Sinclair looked like the personification of Humpty Dumpty. So short and round, you'd suspect he may roll sideways if it weren't for his cane. A deep trench between his brows gave him the look of a man permanently doubting your alibi, while three visible chins nestled beneath a strained cravat.

'May I present Detective Inspector Morven Sinclair,' said McWatt gravely. 'The procurator fiscal is still dealing with... things in the ballroom.'

'He's not taking Sir Seamus away yet, is he?' said Lady Viola Blair, standing up sharply, the macramé twine on her lap tumbling to the floor.

'Not yet, Lady Blair. Rest assured, the procurator fiscal will be in close contact with you over today's procedures,' Detective Inspector Sinclair said.

'I'm going to speak with him now,' said Lady Blair. 'I want to say goodbye to my husband, if you do not mind.'

Lady Blair whisked out of the room before Detective Inspector Sinclair could say anything else. The line in the middle of his forehead deepened as he addressed the remaining guests.

'Good afternoon, all. And merry Christmas. I'm sorry to say, but 1934 has ended with a murder at Dunvaloch Castle.'

'Do we know for certain Sir Seamus was *deliberately* killed?' said Lady Laplume.

'The tree light switch appears to be tampered with, yes. Then there was the strange arrangement of hooking up the gramophone to play "The Twa Corbies". The conjecture is that the death was *not* an accident.'

'Detective, it was my sister's ghost!' Seraphina said, looking up at the ceiling as if she was hallucinating images on it. 'She came to take revenge on the man who locked her away.'

Detective Inspector Sinclair jumped back a few steps and placed his chubby fingers on top of his belly as he regarded this eccentric lady.

'Will somebody pour her some tea. With *sugar* in it?' insisted Lady Laplume.

McWatt did so, but it only aided in making the seer more excited.

'The tea leaves said it all... The twa corbies!' Her voice quavered like a lamb, and she peered deeply into the cup.

'I think you must go and lie down again, Miss Serle,' said McWatt, aborting his tea mission and jettisoning the madwoman off out of the room under her arms.

Opal looked down into her own teacup and grabbed her chin thoughtfully. *The first we heard last night about the twa corbies, or two crows, was when Seraphina was doing the tea leaf reading. She introduced the 'crow' concept from that moment.*

'I wonder if the Scots named crows "corbies" because they make a caww caww sound? Named after their call, just like the cuckoo, chiffchaff and peewee,' said Lord Laplume, chewing cake thoughtfully.

'I think you'll find it's the same as crow. The sound can be described as crowing,' answered Lady Laplume sarcastically, lacing her hands. 'Pray, can you cease with the ornithology whilst we're in the middle of a murder investigation, Edmund. Do you think you can accomplish that?'

'British people are indeed eccentric,' said Countess Angelina with a nod, slicing down into her cake.

'Uhum.' The detective cleared his throat to silence everyone. 'I will shortly be conducting interviews in the salon, if you would be so kind as to come and see me, one by one, after tea. It is a shame that we couldn't have kept everyone who was at the ball last night in the castle. Logistically, I can understand that would not have been easy. But we have everyone's address, and I will be making calls.'

With that, he turned on his heel and plodded off to the salon. Napoleon, thinking everyone was to follow the detective, happily trotted after him, pom-pom tail whipping side to side. Opal went after him to scoop him back. Out in the grand hall, she lifted him like a little lamb and nestled her nose into the soft bouffant on his head. Noticing Lady Blair chatting to the procurator fiscal, Opal stepped behind a pillar to listen.

'Metal shavings?' The voice of Lady Viola Blair echoed. 'You're telling me... somebody put metal shavings in the Christmas tree light switch to make it short-circuit?'

'Yes, m'lady. There was foul play,' said the procurator fiscal. 'Metal shavings were jammed inside the copper switch.'

'Of course. I just... I guess I wanted it to be an accident so that I didn't have to think about there being some devil who wanted to hurt poor Seamus.'

'We have dusted the record sleeve in the morning room and I've made a comparison with the prints. They look unmistakably like the butler's.'

Lady Blair was silent, then said, 'That is disappointing. It is his record collection, so it makes sense that there should be his prints on it. Besides, he grabbed it off the countess, who was wearing gloves this morning, and the killer could have been wearing gloves or taken it with a hanky.'

'Indeed, m'lady, but we would like to make him one of our prime suspects.'

'No, no. Not McWatt,' said Lady Blair. 'He adored Seamus. No, no… I would keep my eye on Mr Martindale, if I were you. Shady fellow who did not always see eye to eye with Sir Seamus. God knows how he's meddled with the will.'

SIXTEEN

SINCLAIR, SWEETIES & SUSPECTS

It was finally Opal's turn to be questioned by Detective Inspector Morven Sinclair. She rolled her eyes before turning the door handle to enter the salon. Her experience with detectives had *not* been the most pleasant. In the past year, she'd unfortunately had dealings with two. A Parisian one who was so vain he'd put a prized pageant cat to shame and another in Hollywoodland who was so keen to get the case wrapped up and money in his pocket, he aimed his eye on the easiest innocent target. No values between them. She'd outsmarted both of them, of course. This Scottish one already had a bit of a pompous air about him, so Opal didn't have high hopes. Napoleon held his chin high, ready to trot in disapprovingly.

She slid inside, and with an artificial smile, said, 'Good afternoon, Detective Inspector Sinclair.'

'The Honourable Miss Opal Marion Laplume,' he said, his cheeks plumping up in a grin. 'And who is this wee lady?'

Napoleon puffed his nostrils indignantly, jumped up onto the grandest-looking chair in the salon, sat upright and curled his pom-pom tail in beside him.

'*He* is Napoleon,' corrected Opal, perching down next to her poodle and patting the soft padding of his bouffant.

'Ah! Emperor of the Hundred Days!' He chuckled and tapped his pencil on his notepad cheerfully.

'Yes. Waterloo, in his case, is the *bath*.' Opal chuckled. Unexpectedly, she was getting a rather good energy from this man.

'Good job his fur is black then, eh! Good for concealing the muck,' he said, then the crevice deepened in between his brows. 'Now, Miss Laplume, may you start by assisting me with your very fine memory of the proceedings of last night? Start at the beginning of the ball... anything you noticed that was *off* or pivotal to what happened.'

Opal knotted her hands in her lap and talked through her movements. She wasn't quite ready to spill out all of her suspicions and discoveries. She would need to gauge his temperament first. But as she spoke, she was pleasantly surprised by his calm demeanour, eagerness to listen and take seriously what she had to offer. Most unusual for a detective.

When she'd stopped speaking, he dove his sausage-like fingers into a brown paper bag on his lap, pulled out a red and white striped sweetie and popped it into his mouth. 'Berwick cockle?' He offered her the bag.

'Oh, I'll try one,' Opal said, reaching over and plucking the hard sweet out. The minty boiled confection delighted her tongue.

'Now that I've bribed you with a sweetie, please tell me if there was anything *else* you picked up that was amiss, strange... or even normal and mundane. Any detail at all that could or indeed could not have been related to the murder. You never know when a trivial detail unlocks a whole new narrative.'

'Well,' Opal began, feeling a little reluctant to give him her valuable clues, as she liked to be the one to solve the mysteries. She was getting rather good at it, and it gave her otherwise silly life purpose. But she liked Detective Inspector Morven Sinclair, and the killer deserved to be punished. Besides, she could probably use this gentleman's help.

'I daresay,' she said, then lowered her tone, 'it seems most people are trying to blame Seraphina. But I'm not convinced. The others all have motives. I will start with Countess Angelina. I think she needs a good probing if you haven't already interviewed her. She spouts some tripe about being here to immerse herself in Scottish customs as a learning exercise. But there's a whole library here that she hasn't expressed interest in delving into... and what woman of her stature goes about studying? It just seems *off*. Perhaps Angelina de Brise-cloque is a spy sent from Sir Seamus's business rivals, Société des Tissus, in Paris.'

Detective Inspector Sinclair raised his eyebrows and scribbled. 'She is a cryptic creature indeed.'

'I agree.' Opal sighed, then blinked at a framed photograph of the lady of the house that was on the mantle. 'Lady Viola Blair is a strange thing too. Fighting with Sir Seamus over every trifle, but then being devastated when he died. You would have thought before that, that him getting bumped off was her dream come true! She seems to have collected a number of... fans.'

'The feather variety?' said Detective Inspector Sinclair, sucking on a sweet.

'No, no. Young gentlemen. Lapdogs, Sir Seamus called them. At church there was a whole line of them queuing up to kiss her hand and offer condolences,' said Opal, twisting her finger around Napoleon's ear.

'Yes. Perhaps she was a lonely woman. Sir Seamus was always extremely busy, I know,' said Detective Inspector Sinclair, then cracked the sweet with his back teeth.

'Yes. In this enormous castle with only McWatt bumbling about. Though McWatt thinks she will get rid of him soon.'

'Why so?'

'He says she doesn't appreciate or acknowledge everything he does. McWatt is an oddball too. He was late to the ball, supposedly due to spilling soup on his tails. He has a crippled daughter and confesses he'll be acquiring the ugly paintings in the gallery in Sir Seamus's will, as they are worthless and nobody else likes them. But the thing is...' Opal leant forward.

Sinclair leant forward also and stopped sucking the sweet.

'I rang a collector who said the artworks are worth... *a lot!*' Opal's mouth opened wide when expressing the last word, then added, 'The collector also said a man had rung him about the same paintings about a year before, but didn't get a name. Could easily have been McWatt gauging their worth.'

'It could have been Mr Martindale. He is Sir Seamus's lawyer, and in drafting wills, you need to know how much paintings are worth,' the detective mused.

'True,' said Opal. 'But why would Mr Martindale not name himself? Perhaps you can follow up on that, please.'

'It seems, Miss Laplume, that I've been demoted from sleuth to sidekick,' said Sinclair with a sparkle in his eye and a crunch of boiled sweet. 'Do let me know if you'd like the magnifying glass polished.'

'No, thank you. I don't have one, Doctor Watson,' Opal said with a giggle, then resumed a serious tone. 'Though Mr Martindale is an oddball. He was in Sir Seamus's study getting a headstart on probate, and I overheard him on the telephone to his mother – "*Mummy*" – asking her for help to solve a riddle that Sir Seamus had bequeathed him.'

Opal took out her sketchbook and read the riddle aloud.

'"Martindale, if anything happens to me, follow these instructions: The brave shine, the faithful remain, yet what you seek lies behind pain." Then he trailed off talking about the spelling, but I couldn't hear that part.'

'Well, I sincerely hope his "Mummy" won't be able to solve the riddle before we do,' said Sinclair chuckling.

'I'm going to try and crack it tonight,' said Opal determinedly, snapping the sketchbook shut.

'Any other odd behaviours you've noticed among the guests?'

'Well, at luncheon Lord Turks-Leyton offered Mr Finlay Roberts a note with a great sum of money written on it which my mother suspected was a billiards stake, but the men denied this and said it was London property chat... and...'

Opal fidgeted with the clasp on her bag. She was weighing up whether to give Detective Inspector Sinclair the evidence she'd found behind Seraphina's radiator. She didn't want him to jump the gun and arrest the poor woman.

'What have you got in there then?' asked Detective Inspector Sinclair, eyeing the bag, a sweetie bulge in his cheek.

Opal glanced down at her bag. 'Oh, nothing, Detective.'

'It is my job to read body language. When a young lady pinches the clasp of her bag, then let's go and then pinches it again... she wants to show me something.'

Blithering fig. She was caught out. She clicked open the clasp and removed the electrical manual and Phillips screwdriver, placed them on the chair beside her and pulled her hand away as if they were scalding.

'I found these behind the radiator in Seraphina's chamber. But I believe there's a strong chance someone planted them there to frame her. I can understand how it must look. That she used the manual and screwdriver to orchestrate Sir Seamus's electrocution. But I've watched her reactions very closely. After it happened last night, she fainted, and it was a genuine faint... very hard to fake, smacking the floor. I also overheard her talking to her sister's spirit, imploring her ghost to leave the castle. She truly believes it is her sister, Euphemia Serle, getting revenge on Sir Seamus. Do you know the background, Detective?'

'Indeed, I do. Sir Seamus had her sister imprisoned for espionage, and she took her own life. Tragic.'

'Indeed. I feel dreadfully sorry for her. There's another thing Seraphina let on to me.' Opal stood up and pinched another Berwick cockle out of the detective's brown paper bag. She popped it in her mouth and said, 'There's a rumour Sir Seamus has a secret laboratory on St Kessog's Isle.'

'Is that so?' said Sinclair. 'A laboratory to work on his electrical toys?'

'Yes. It may hold a key to *why* he was killed,' said Opal. 'What's more, now that he's dead, we can't leave it to rot with nobody ever discovering it.'

'Your father has been trying to convince me to let him go to St Kessog's first thing in the morning. Lord Laplume says the puffins are dying, and it may be too late if left any longer.'

'Yes, we simply must go,' said Opal. 'Please permit us, Detective.'

'Well, I had insisted everyone stay in the castle, and I had told your father I'd think about it. But seeing as you're so keen to find this secret laboratory... you've twisted my arm.'

'Thank you, Detective,' said Opal. 'Will you be coming with us?'

'No. I have plenty to be getting on with in the castle. I shall give you twenty-four hours to be back, and make sure you have something interesting to tell me.'

'I will find the lab if it's the last thing I do,' said Opal.

The portly gentleman rounded up his pencil recordings with a definite stab of a full stop, then said, 'You, my dear, are very astute indeed. Shrewd. Logical. Aware. You notice things.'

'Well,' said Opal, tinting pink, 'I must say, Papa calls me "Bins" because I'm like a pair of binoculars for him when he's birdwatching.'

'Might I employ you, unofficially, as a little helper of mine?'

'Napoleon too?'

'Goes without saying indeed.'

'Of course,' said Opal, then smirked at him with her head tilted. 'Will I be recompensed?'

'Yes,' he said. 'With Berwick cockles.'

'Well, sir, I suppose that's what I would have spent the money on anyway.' Opal laughed.

'Ah! But only I know where to get them from.' He winked, then leaned forward. 'I'll tell you why I think it's important we work together. It's because people will confess things to you that they won't to me. You're already slightly ahead of the game, and I fear if I can't beat you, I'd better join you.'

Napoleon beat his pom-pom tail on the cushion once.

'Yes, I meant the two of you,' the detective corrected himself. 'I wish you luck... and if we do not speak again, it was an honour to meet you.'

'What?'

'The sea looks a little choppy.'

'Stop it, Detective.' Opal laughed when she realised he was teasing.

'But if I were you, I'd work on that riddle before you depart... it may hold the key.'

SEVENTEEN

FINLAY THE FALCONER

Opal went to relay the news to her father that they were permitted to go to St Kessog's Isle and could depart first thing. She found him with Mr Finlay Roberts in the southern tower of the castle where the falcons lived.

It was draughty and sawdusty with stone walls and slit windows that let in just enough light to stop you from mistaking a falcon for a gargoyle. The birds were a collection of regal-looking goshawks, who clasped their blocks and groomed between their glossy feathers. Leather jesses and hoods hung from hooks. Every now and then, a falcon would let out an indignant call, clearly wondering why their master, Sir Seamus, had not come. Opal desperately wanted to stroke one but knew it may sacrifice her finger.

Mr Finlay Roberts had a docile-looking bird with half-open eyelids held abreast on his leather glove. He was feeding it a tiny cutlet of raw beef. 'They're sleepy from their afternoon flight,' he said.

'I wonder if they're grieving for Sir Seamus,' said Lord Laplume. 'Frightfully intelligent creatures, they possess the emotional depth akin to a small child.'

'They may be missing their usual routines, which can be stressful,' said Mr Roberts. 'But they are hardy little blighters.'

'I really need to get to St Kessog's Isle before the puffin population declines further. Whatever the cause, it'll need weeding out without haste.'

'That is the thing, Papa,' Opal said, clinging onto his elbow. 'I've just come from my interview with Detective Inspector Sinclair, and he has given us his blessing to go... for the puffins, but we must be back within twenty-four hours.'

She glanced sideways at Mr Roberts. She didn't want to mention the secret laboratory in front of someone she didn't completely know or trust yet.

'That is splendid, Bins! Jolly good show. Thank you for talking him round,' said Lord Laplume, rubbing his hands together. 'I shall hotfoot it down to the jetty and speak to the skipper about the mail boat. I'm sure we can get a lift with the crew.' He looked at Mr Roberts. 'I'm afraid you'll still be held hostage on the estate, won't you?'

'Oh, it won't be long before the detective realises it's that batty Seraphina Serle behind it all,' said Mr Roberts, drawing a gentle finger down the bird's neck. 'It's plain for everyone to see.'

'You really think it was she?' asked Lord Laplume, as innocent as a baby deer.

'Conjuring up that nonsense of crows in the teacups, then the gramophone playing the creepy crow song,' said Mr Roberts. 'She could have wired it all herself if she had learned the instructions. She is not a stupid woman. Well, she *is* if she thinks we will all believe in that ghost she's fabricated.'

'And you think she did it in revenge because Sir Seamus incarcerated her sister Euphemia?' asked Opal.

'Of course. Those three witch sisters were as thick as thieves. They've played tricks on the public for years. Arrogantly believing we will fall for their guff.'

'Seraphina said that Euphemia's ghost is now after someone else. That the "second crow" is yet to be slaughtered.'

'We will be keeping a close eye on her. I'd lock her in the west wing if I had my way,' said Mr Roberts. 'I may suggest it to her ladyship.'

'I'm sure Detective Inspector Sinclair and the procurator fiscal will keep things under wraps,' said Lord Laplume and gulped.

It was time to retire for the night. Augusto had, on her request, now been assigned a bedroom in the main quarters of the castle so he could come to the rescue should there be any 'night terrors'. His presence down the hall, combined with the sharp ears of her canine sidekick, gave Opal comfort. But something was niggling her brain. The riddle. She feared Detective Inspector Sinclair was right, and it may have to be solved before she left for St Kessog's Island in the morning, as it may be the clue that would help her find Sir Seamus's secret laboratory.

If anything happens to me, follow these instructions: The brave shine, the faithful remain, yet what you seek lies behind pain.

Shining and remaining. What shines and remains? A lamp that's bolted down? A star that is constant? An engagement ring? Lady Blair's ring? But Lady Blair seemed anything but faithful. Opal started to go a bit batty with a kaleidoscope of thoughts that got more and more absurd. She came to the conclusion that the riddle could quite literally mean anything.

Napoleon was not helpful. Whenever a bluster of snow swept across the window, he'd paw at it making an awful ruckus with his nails on the glass.

'Napoleon, I adore every single curlicue of your being, but you really can be a pain in the backside. Those panes of glass are centuries old, you are going to damage...'

She paused. Then batted her lids in quick succession. The words she'd used had jigged her brain... pain... and pane. The last thing Mr Martindale said to his mother was, '*lies behind pain. But it is spelt...*'

What if it was *pane*, not *pain*? As in a *pane* of glass, not a *pain* in the backside. She yanked her bedside lamp chain and scrambled for her sketchbook. Her fingers flicked through the hat sketches to find the riddle.

She remembered McWatt's reference to the family motto. Brave and Faithful. *Fortis et Fidelis*. Might this be emblazoned somewhere on an object in the castle? A necklace, an ornament, a seal inside a book?

Clink, clink, clink, snaffle. Napoleon's pom-pom paws danced on the glass, trying to catch the butterflies of snow.

Of course, Opal, you nitwit! The stained-glass window in the grand hall. Fortis et Fidelis is written on the scroll. What you seek lies behind pane. Could '*what you seek*' be outside on the ledge behind the stained-glass window?

Opal looked out at the abysmal night sky. No matter how compelling the mystery was, she couldn't quite brave the arctic temperatures outside. Perhaps she could stay inside and take a candle to illuminate the glass to see what might be on the other side?

She got out of bed, slid on her silk nightie and plucked a candle out of a wall sconce. She lit it with matches she retrieved above the hearth.

'Right, boy, you can come with me, but do not bark or I might end up on the other side of a bullet. There are guns in this house, after all. Everyone's up in arms tonight, and I don't want them to think we're killers snooping about the castle.'

They slipped out of the chamber and, through the cloisters, she could see the window... the beautiful emerald hues shimmering in their faceted glory. She coordinated her footsteps with the low tocks of the grandfather clock in the hall, trying to disguise the sound as much as she could.

The moon shone through the stag's eye, looking down upon her with fear, as if it was mid-prance, dodging a bullet. Now directly below it, she lifted her candle to illuminate the multi-coloured panes. The scroll stood out on white, opalescent glass with the words *Fortis et Fidelis* in black.

Opal went on tiptoes to shine her candle through the glass, straining her eyes to see if there was something outside on the ledge. No luck, it was too opaque.

BONG. BONG. Opal spun and flattened herself against the wall. Then sighed with relief as she realised it was the clock chiming two in the morning. *Blast it.* Napoleon groaned low in the back of his throat as if daring the clock to have another outburst.

She returned to searching the glass again. She smoothed her hand over the panes and noticed something peculiar. The black rectangle directly below the motto had an extra-thick iron ridge. It looked as if it could come away. She dug her fingernail behind the gap and... yes! The pane popped down like a lid.

Inside was a slim box, that must have been affixed from the outside. Opal brought her candle to illuminate the contents.

It was a little round brass thing. She pressed the side button, and it snapped open like a clam. It was a compass, though just a bog-standard one. She brought the candle flame closer. How queer. Someone had scratched the outline of a seabird... a puffin?

She closed it in her palm and carried it back to her room, ascending the stairs with quiet purpose.

Suddenly, a murmur from the mezzanine caught her ear. She stopped dead. *Who on earth?* In the moonlight, a fluffy slipper protruded from one of the cloisters. The voices weren't speaking English. Spanish, perhaps? A man and a woman.

Augusto? He was the only Spanish speaker in the castle – or so she thought.

She continued upward, stomach performing slow revolutions as the truth was confirmed... she could make out the profile of Augusto's handsome nose. Then a giggle. It was undoubtedly Countess Angelina; none of the other women in the castle would emit such a ridiculous falsetto sound. Then Countess Angelina's fluttering fingers emerged as she giggled about something in the lowest tone she could. They were loud, enough for Opal to catch a crisp *'buenas noches'*. Spanish for *'goodnight'*... and with that, they vanished into their respective rooms along the corridor.

Opal tingled with jealousy; she could feel it in her fingers and toes. She cupped her bob, trying to shake it off, but the emotion only morphed into irritation instead. What was Augusto gabbing away to her about? And why hadn't he told her the countess spoke Spanish? It was utterly heart-wrenching that they could converse in his native tongue, and she could not. Her feelings then shifted to sadness.

Opal bowed her head and made for her chamber, utterly stricken. How *could* he? There was most certainly something going on between those two.

She stroked Napoleon's comforting furry midriff on her pillow. Then tucked the eiderdown up to her chin, still clutching the compass, and drifted off at last, worn out by the sheer effort of thinking.

Opal awakened to the crows cawing at first light. Effie came to light her fire, and soon after, Lord Edmund Laplume knocked. Opal called him in, sat up in bed and began to brush the soft curls on Napoleon's ears.

'I assume Augusto will be coming with us to the isle?' said Opal. She imagined a rosy-toned scene of Countess Angelina and Augusto frolicking around the conservatory together, and she did not like the picture.

'Of course, we're not paying him as a protection officer to loaf around scoffing shortbread while you're on an unpoliced, remote isle, are we?' Lord Laplume replied and stabbed at the fire with the poker. 'There's just one thing... and I implore you not to complain about this,' said Lord Laplume, pulling his shoulders back to assert himself. 'Your mother is coming with us.'

Opal groaned and flung the dog brush onto the eiderdown. She loved her dear mama, but not on mucky field trips; she was always positively ghastly on them. 'Won't she need to look after Lady Blair?'

'Apparently that's what Countess Angelina is going to do,' said Lord Laplume. 'Your mother has been finding it hard to sleep here, and I can't say I blame her.'

'Won't it be worse to get to sleep in a cramped croft on a remote Scottish isle teaming with squawking seabirds?' said Opal.

'That is almost exactly what I said. But she's got her hot-water bottle, brandy, and she's lugging along Effie.'

The stable boy led the horse that carried luggage and provisions for the Laplumes to the castle jetty. They walked along the granite blocks, moss-edged and weathered from generations of storms. Rusty-iron mooring rings lined the edge. Gulls circled overhead, crying into the brisk sea wind. The sun was out, and the snow had melted, leaving the sand sparkling. Their sea chariot was waiting for them. It was a tiny, patched-up mail boat, rocking gently.

'Oh, it's terribly utilitarian,' said Lady Laplume, looking at the sacks of letters and crates of potatoes. 'How many hours will we be cooped up on this sardine can with a motor?'

'Three hours, Phyllis, dear,' Lord Laplume replied with a sigh.

'You know, since the *Titanic* disaster, all boats give me anxiety neurosis.'

'Phyllis, that was more than two decades ago, and you weren't even *aboard* the *Titanic*.'

'My beloved hats were! My spirit was in those glorious confections. The finest artworks I ever created. Now the glass beads I had lovingly stitched onto them are decaying on the ocean floor. They are probably the only remaining materials.'

'I don't think beads have feelings, my dear.'

Augusto held out an arm and helped Lady Laplume onto the mail boat. The crew consisted of a young boy of around fifteen years of age with a goofy grin who introduced himself as Clyde and his father, clearly the captain, a quiet man who was just referred to as 'Skipper'.

The boat swung out, and Clyde had to take Lord Laplume's hand to steady him aboard. The boy ogled Lord Laplume's signet ring with round eyes.

'That is a fine ring, my lord,' Clyde said. 'I'm going to have one of those one day. I saw one recently that was engraved with a cow on it. I'd never seen one like it before.'

I say, a cow design, that rings a bell, thought Opal. Had she seen a signet like that recently? She had a vague memory that she indeed had.

With her sleuthing brain switched on, she thought she'd ask if the skipper or his son knew about the secret laboratory.

'Nay,' the skipper replied, but smirked. 'I guess he could have dug a hole and stuck a rock on top of it. Though there are thousands of rocks and boulders on St Kessog's. I wish you luck.'

Opal sighed. She had to concede he was right. It could be anywhere. She alighted the boat, avoiding Augusto's hand and taking instead the skipper's. She had not forgotten about his antics last night.

After a rather freezing journey, during which they cocooned themselves in thick woollen blankets, they arrived at St Kessog's Isle. From a distance, it looked like a hunk of chocolate cake that had been nibbled at by mice in the pantry. The cliff side was jagged and porous, and the top was green and speckled white. As they sailed closer, Opal realised the little white speckles had orange feet and beaks and grey wings and were swooping and diving into the sea. Puffins!

'There aren't as many fishing as there should be. They do seem ill, poor little blighters,' said Lord Laplume.

Opal wondered what on earth could be hurting the puffins. Did Sir Seamus's secret lab perhaps have something to do with it? Regardless, she'd have very little time to figure it all out.

EIGHTEEN

MR & MRS MOFFAT'S CROFT

Soon, the Laplumes and Augusto were eating Scotch broth inside a little stone croft in the home of Mr and Mrs Moffat, the only inhabitants on the little island, who had remained as caretakers and watchmen for Sir Seamus. The croft house squatted sturdy against the blustering winds of the North Atlantic, standing out as a little clump of stones against the heather-clad hills beyond. It had a thatched roof that sagged a tad under the weight of decades.

Inside was impressively warm despite the holey stone walls. The thick beams overhead seemed to hover like a mother bird's wings protecting its nest. A central hearth crackled cheerfully, doing its best to keep the chill at bay. The air carried a trace of salt and smoke, as if the room itself had been perfumed with the island's elements.

Mrs Moffat placed a carousel of home-made condiments on the table. Among the jars was a pot of Copperfields' mustard. Lord Laplume saw it and tried to spin the carousel to hide it from Lady Laplume, but his wife had already spotted it.

'Why on an island at the edge of the very earth would we

have to find this confounded mustard brand?' Lady Laplume said. 'Get it away from me!'

'What?' asked Mrs Moffat, stroking back her cloud of white hair in alarm.

'Copperfields was our estate up until 1916 when it was taken over by this very mustard factory,' explained Lord Laplume. 'It is a sour subject for Lady Laplume.'

'We *sold* the estate *willingly* to the mustard factory as my business was up in London,' insisted Lady Laplume.

'It looks like Copperfields' mustard is doing very well. We really should have insisted on being shareholders, Mama,' teased Opal.

'Well, you seem to have the largest croft on the island,' Lady Laplume redirected the chat.

'We didn't use to. We got to move in when Sir Seamus took the island over,' Mr Moffat responded. A leathery old chap with his long beard plaited into a thin sprig sprouting from his chin.

'Now... we come bearing some bad news, I'm afraid, of our good friend Sir Seamus,' Lord Laplume said, placing his spoon down and sitting up straight.

Mr and Mrs Moffat were shocked to hear of Sir Seamus's passing. They would only receive newspapers, letters and provisions a mere once a week, so nothing had reached them just yet. Ironically, Opal soon learned, this isolation from the outside world was one of the reasons that so many St Kessog's Isle residents got fed up and decided to evacuate, especially since the tweed trade was drying up. Mr and Mrs Moffat loved the island and did not mind the isolation.

The news of Sir Seamus's death was a blow to the Moffats, who very much liked the old fellow. Then they started positively reeling when they were told how he died and how many people were accusing Seraphina Serle.

'Seraphina Serle! She wouldn't hurt a fly. She's too superstitious and would believe it would come back to her,' said Mrs Moffat.

'I very much agree,' Opal said. 'However, I found some damning evidence in her room, behind the radiator. It's possible it was planted. There was a how-to electrical manual that she could have used to orchestrate the booby-trapped light switch, plus a screwdriver.'

'An electrical manual?' asked Mr Moffat. 'That couldn't have been hers!'

'Why?' asked Opal.

'Seraphina Serle cannot read.'

'What?' said Opal.

'She couldn't possibly have read that instruction manual; she never went to school. She wove tweed since she was twelve. She never learned to read, and this is why she took up the seer trade with her sisters. It was one of the very few options available to her.'

Opal gasped. This certainly meant that someone planted the book in Seraphina's room. But who? And why would they want to frame the poor witch?

NINETEEN

THE PUFFIN CIRCUS

'I sincerely hope Seraphina conveys this information to the constabulary, and they let her go,' said Opal.

'I'm not sure it'll be as easy as that,' said Lord Laplume. 'They may say it's simply another cover-up. You can't really *prove* that you can't read, can you?'

Opal couldn't wait any longer to probe Mr Moffat. 'There is something else that may help Seraphina. Do you have any knowledge of a secret laboratory Sir Seamus had on the island?'

Mr Moffat's face froze in a blank expression for a few moments, and then he laughed heartily. 'That old rumour? Absolute poppycock. Sir Seamus would stay in the room your father will be sleeping in when here, or he'd go fishing. I have lived here all my life and know the island like I know my own freckles on my face. I can assure you, there's no secret lab.'

Opal scraped the remnants of her bowl, feeling rather defeated. There was a possibility that Mr Moffat was sworn to secrecy and could be trying to keep her away from it. So she didn't bother showing him the silly compass. But she had to admit that the idea of discovering Sir Seamus's secret lab had excited her. The fact it actually didn't exist muddled her theory of why he had been killed. But perhaps Mr Moffat was mistaken. If the lab was indeed secret, Sir Seamus would not have shared its location with anyone. She vowed to keep an eye out this afternoon for anything suspicious.

After lunch, the puffin expedition got ready to head out and included Opal, Augusto, Lord Laplume and Mr Moffat. They set off on foot with maps towards the part of the island where the puffins nested in the cliffs. Lady Laplume, Effie and Mrs Moffat had stayed at the croft mending fishing nets and discussing tweed.

Opal trudged behind the others, kicking stones, agitated. Augusto brushed his hand against her back in acknowledgement of her mood. Her mind raced; she could not stop thinking about poor Seraphina and who on earth would want to set her up. She wanted desperately to send a telegram to Detective Inspector Sinclair, but the mail boat would not be returning until the morning. She'd have to wait. If she was arrested, Seraphina would still need to stand trial, so it wouldn't be too late. As long as she wasn't planning on emulating her sister's demise in prison... Opal needed to focus on finding this clandestine lab.

'It is truly riveting living here alone,' said Mr Moffat into the wind. 'I feel as if I'm King of the Isle.'

'That you are, Mr Moffat,' said Lord Laplume.

'The puffins are the true sovereigns,' said Mr Moffat rather sadly. 'I feel like renaming the isle for the puffins. Puffin Point? A benediction that would help them survive?'

'Yes, or as you share it with them, what about Mount Muffin?' suggested Opal. 'Moffat and puffin combined.'

'It would be dreadfully disappointing if some famished, sweet-toothed pirates saw it on the map and found it wasn't made of muffin,' said Lord Laplume.

'Look!' called Augusto, pointing to a rock. 'A nest of puffins!'

'Indeed,' said Lord Laplume, 'but the young look malnourished and pretty wretched. So does the mother. Doesn't look to be due to predators to me. More of a disease.'

They edged as close as they could without scaring the birds.

'What do you need us to do, Papa?' asked Opal.

'I will access the habitat and survey the population. Puffins nest in burrows on steep cliffs or areas with grassy, soft soil. I need to find out whether they have enough fish and sand eels to eat. I could also check for any predation that may be taking advantage of the fact that the birds are sick. There may be introduced species such as rats and foxes. I need to ensure that the island is predator free.'

'Golly, where do we start?' said Opal, holding her hat on in the wind.

'We shall start by counting the puffins. Both alive and any deceased. Noting the sex individually and then the young. It's going to be hard to decipher the sexes as they are almost identical, but the males are slightly larger.'

Opal looked around her at the colony of puffins. They had a jolly huge task ahead of them.

'Let us split up,' said Lord Laplume. 'If I count the birds that are on the east side of the island, Mr Moffat can cover the north. Opal and Augusto go down south, where the beach is, and see what you can come up with. We shall do the west later.'

Opal made a mental note to scout out any sign of Sir Seamus's lab while they were at it.

'What if we count the same bird twice?' asked Mr Moffat.

'That is bound to happen, but we will do several rounds of counting to get a good estimate. I'm not going to tag the poor little blighters.'

The group broke up, and Opal trudged alongside Augusto until they were out of earshot. The terrain was exceedingly rocky, and Opal's walking boots slipped on some moss. Augusto slid his arm around her waist to catch her and held it there as they persevered towards the shore.

'Keep your eyes peeled for any nook, cranny or a loose rock leading to a cave or hole,' said Opal. 'Though I know it could literally be anywhere. I just need a starting point.'

Opal enjoyed the feeling of his strong arm around her waist. But it felt duplicitous that his other arm could easily be wrapped around Countess Angelina's if she, too, had slipped.

'Well,' Opal said. 'You and the countess seemed jolly chummy up in the mezzanine. What was the big joke?'

Augusto blinked at her innocently. 'Ah, *mi corazón*,' he began, which was already an outrageous liberty considering how little Spanish Opal spoke.

'Don't *mi corazón* me,' Opal snapped. 'What were you two giggling about? Plotting a coup? Comparing notes on your jawline? And why so late at night?'

He looked mildly pained and loosened his grip on her waist.

'Countess Angelina could not sleep and went for a walk. I heard her footsteps and thought it best I check who it was. I am a protection officer, after all. We got talking and she mentioned that she'd seen this fellow and Lady Blair on Christmas Eve in the library.' Augusto smirked. 'They were tipsily dancing together in a Latin fashion – or attempting at least. The countess did a great impression of his ostentatious moves and had heard him say that he didn't like the music in the ballroom because it... muddled the energy of his hips.'

Opal wanted to remain stoic and did not want to laugh, but she burst out in a snorting kind of explosion; she couldn't help it. '*Muddled the energy of his hips?* Quite a line. I think I would like this gentleman. I wonder who he is.'

'A very good friend of Lady Blair's, I'd wager,' said Augusto, raising his brows.

He tried to swing Opal round in a mock imitation of Lady

Blair and her dancing partner. But Opal clamped her arms by her sides.

'Stop. Buffoon. I haven't forgiven you yet, you know,' she said, and she hadn't quite.

'I am telling the truth, Opal,' he said.

'I know,' said Opal. She did believe him, but she still wasn't overjoyed by it.

There was another long silence as they clamoured over a set of steep rock formations covered in limpets and barnacles. Opal wanted to change the subject to something less bitter than the countess, but she couldn't help it. It was the main thing that had been irking her.

'I didn't know the countess could speak Spanish,' Opal said, trying to sound intrigued rather than perturbed.

'She is very good at it,' Augusto said, completely missing Opal's concern.

Opal was focused on the rocks and couldn't see his face, but she could almost hear him smirk and his chin dimple curve to the right.

'Yes, I imagine it's easier when one only needs to know the words for flirt, giggle, and "where is my cigarette?"'

Augusto stepped closer, all dark eyes and dangerous dimple. 'You are jealous, Opalita.'

'I am not,' Opal scoffed. 'And don't call me Opalita. Just because you've found another Spanish speaker at the castle doesn't mean you can *slather it on* when talking to me.'

He smiled. 'Yes, Miss Laplume.'

Drat the man, Opal thought.

'Goodness,' gasped Augusto.

A moment later, Opal beheld what Augusto had seen. The coastline was utterly magnificent. The sea breeze carried the scent of kelp, ruffling the wildflowers that clung to the grassy tops of the cliffs. A violet sea frothed onto the sand and dragged glittering pebbles back away with it. And then, the feathered royalty of the island: the puffins. Dozens of them, though looking thin and sluggish, were like little tuxedoed mariners, dotting the seascape. They waddled, bobbed and peeked up from burrows, their bright beaks in flame colours, highlighting their every move. Opal watched with joy as from a high perch on the cliff, a more healthy-looking puffin dove, like a swift flick of charcoal against the blue surf. Below it, waves crashed and threw up spray like smashed crystals.

'I must sketch you here,' Augusto said, scrabbling a hand inside his jacket to retrieve his sketchbook. 'Sitting just here in front of the cliffs.'

'I daresay it would be a damn shame not to capture this vision. We can't be too long, mind, we have a circus of puffins to count, not to mention a secret lab to find.'

She sat where he directed her, her scarf billowing out behind her as she watched the happy seabirds. Napoleon nestled in beside her and let his tongue billow like the scarf. She looked back at Augusto when he looked down at his work. Opal adored seeing Augusto sketching. His hand movements, so considered and gentle, as if each mark had great consequence. Then, at other points, he would scrub and dash the page like he could do no wrong. She always thought it a great waste that he hadn't the privilege of going to a classical art school. But his skills were certainly sophisticated, as if he had done so.

'That's far prettier than I truly am,' said Opal, when she saw the drawing.

'On the contrary. It's not nearly as pretty. That is why it is always a challenge to draw you.'

Opal's cheeks warmed. She smiled up at him, though she didn't believe a word he said, he was such a charmer. She looked back down at the drawing with her head tilted. He'd focused mainly on the profile of her face, looking out to sea, her small, pointed nose and sharp peepers. The lashes were dark flicks, that seemed as if they trapped all kinds of details and perceptions in their brush. He would usually focus on fashion, but it seemed now that every time he drew her, he would focus on her... closer and closer in on her face.

'You forgot to capture the North Atlantic and avian wildlife,' said Opal quietly.

'Oh yes,' said Augusto, not seeming to notice before. 'I did, didn't I. But that really isn't my focal point. Or my main interest.'

His face was very close to hers now. They locked eyes above the sketchbook. He placed it down on the rocks and took her face. His eyes were so dark and beautiful she feared that if she looked at him any longer she'd never be able to... resist his kiss.

She let him kiss her for a moment and then gave in and kissed him back. She'd never really kissed like this before. In Hollywood, it was simply a soft press of the lips, a melting sensation. But this was indeed something more. Opal was thoroughly enjoying herself, but something was nagging at the back of her brain. Countess Angelina's flirtatious giggles echoing in her head like a haunted doll in the doll's house of Opal's mind. Taunting her. *Stop, Opal, you can't fall even more deeply for him, you are clearly not his main interest.*

Napoleon got nervous at Opal and Augusto's unusual behaviour. First in the scullery, and now out here. What on earth could be up with them? Exchanging scents without sniffing first? How rude! Or is it a polite bite-off? Or snout wrestling game? And he was being left out of it! He circled the pair in one direction and then the other. He then leapt on a rock and started barking at the puffins, as he knew that was naughty and would break the pair apart. Opal was half irked but half grateful at the obligation to pull away.

'Napoleon, remember what I told you about endangered

birds,' she said. 'We wouldn't want miniature poodles to become extinct, would we? We must respect and protect the puffins.'

To try and avoid Augusto's grasp, she picked up the sketchbook and charcoal off the rock and started to draw the patterns the birds made in the sky and the swooping splashes into the water, daubing a bit of her lipstick to colour the beaks. She wanted to sketch one closer up, so she ventured forward onto the sand.

Augusto followed close behind, and after a long sigh, said, 'I must say, being on this island feels incredibly isolating and lonely.'

'I know what you mean. But it has to be good for perspective, hasn't it,' said Opal.

'What do you mean?'

'It's rather like a metaphor, isn't it? For life. You're born alone, you leave alone, and in between, only a handful of people ever truly know you. I'm lonely rather a lot of the time, you know. But what I've realised is... it's worse if you fight it. You have to learn to accept it.'

'You're not alone, Opal,' Augusto said, taking her free hand. 'I'm here with you.'

'But not all the time. We're not inside each other's minds. What I mean is... I think life might be about learning to accept that we are, on a certain level, alone. I've always found that deeply unsettling, but on an island like this... I guess you have no choice.'

Augusto squeezed her hand in response.

She took in a sharp breath when she noticed a shape in the sand that should not be on a deserted island. A footprint. Many footprints, walking away. She crouched to look at the indentations. They were so clear she could tell they were hobnail trench boots.

'Papa doesn't wear these,' Opal said when she heard Augusto approach. 'And Mr Moffat was in wellies. The mail boat men were in wellies too. I wonder who it could be? They are headed west... Could the secret lab be there?'

Opal suddenly had an unpleasant, familiar twisting feeling in her stomach. She'd seen such boots before. But where?

TWENTY

A CATATONIC PUFFIN!

They followed the footprints, Opal feeling more and more nauseous until they were introduced to a fishing hut. A beaten-up-looking thing made of wooden planks.

'Whoever it is, he's not lurking in there, is he?' whispered Opal.

'I don't think so,' said Augusto, pointing to the ground. 'The footsteps veer off into the grass where they can't be traced... but I will make sure.'

He stalked across the muddy path, boots squelching as quietly as he could, and flung open the warped door of the hut, his other hand inside his lapel.

Empty.

'Look,' said Augusto, pointing above the triangular roof of the hut. 'That puffin looks exceedingly ill. Poor thing. It's in a catatonic state and has a queer look on its face.'

Napoleon made a perplexed squeak and cocked his head sideways. Opal shaded her eyes and looked up at it in concern. Then blew a raspberry of laughter into her hands.

'You nitwit,' she said, jabbing a finger at it. 'That is not a catatonic puffin. That is a *weathervane* shaped like a puffin.'

'Oh, I knew that,' said Augusto, brushing down his coat, a little abashed. 'I was, how you say... pulling your leg?'

'I daresay that's poppycock,' teased Opal.

The hut was cobwebby inside and had the lingering scent of crab. There was a little shelf covered in old fishing paraphernalia, and an ancient compass lay rusting on a bench. Not exactly a clandestine laboratory.

'So... this laboratory. What was that riddle that was supposed to help us?' asked Augusto, looking around the hut hopelessly.

'Oh, I cracked it,' said Opal.

'You did?'

'It led to a secret compartment inside Sir Seamus's stained-glass window, and it had this silly compass inside.' Opal sighed and pulled the thing out of her pocket.

'Golly... well done,' said Augusto, eyebrows raised. 'But how is it meant to help us?'

'If only I knew,' muttered Opal.

She popped the lid open in an absent-minded manner and paced around the hut, studying the faint engraving of the puffin inside the lid.

She noticed something exceedingly odd. While pacing near the shelf, the dial began to spin... wildly. But when walking away, it stopped abruptly.

'Well,' she murmured, looking up at the ceiling. 'The puffin weathervane is directly above; either the puffin has developed a magnetic personality, or something's still alive in the wiring... making the compass spin.'

She stepped back. The needle settled down. Forward again... and it spun like mad.

'There really is a magnetic disturbance,' she said excitedly. 'Something mechanical. Maybe electrical.'

She looked up at the ceiling again. There were tiny blackened streaks on the ceiling, swirling in circular shapes.

'The puffin weathervane,' she said breathlessly. 'It is directly above. Would you be so kind, Augusto, as to give me a leg-up?'

'Yes, anything for Opalita,' he said, and kicked his leg in the air like a cabaret dancer.

'No, silly. Lace your hands and hoist me up onto the roof to see our catatonic puffin friend.'

They exited the hut, and after a few attempts and many utterances of 'whoops', 'I say', and 'sorry', she was straddling the narrow, tarred roof of the hut like an indignant squirrel, eyeing the puffin-shaped weathervane.

It was made of painted steel, had a proud beak, pert tail, wings tucked back as if preparing to declare war on a mackerel. It also seemed rather too elaborate for a mere weather-predicting ornament.

On closer inspection, the beak could be twisted, she discovered, as could the tail. *How bizarre*, she thought. She pulled out the compass from her skirt pocket and studied again the puffin that was etched. The beak pointed south, and the tail was pointing east in comparison with the compass face below it.

What if she adjusted the weathervane beak and tail the same way?

With a breath, she twisted the puffin's beak due south. It clicked. Opal's eyes flicked back and forth. *That sounded interesting.*

Then she bent the tail to point east... toward the lighthouse, whose beacon stood stoic against the horizon.

'Done,' she whispered.

But nothing happened.

Not a whir, not a shake, not even a puff of smoke. The hut remained profoundly hut-like. She felt a little silly thinking it may perhaps lower on a hydraulic lift down into a 'Blair lair'.

Just then, a muffled yell floated up from the distance. Napoleon stood up on his hind legs on a rock and barked eastward. The poodle was right... the yell was coming from that direction. The direction of the lighthouse.

'I'd better go and investigate,' said Augusto, his face going white. 'Let me help you down first. But wait here.'

Of course, Opal did not wait... she followed him, a dozen or so yards behind.

'AAAAGH! Blasted granite steps!'

That sounded like Papa.

'Lord Laplume?' called Augusto, running.

'Father?' Opal called, clambering after him.

A moment later, her father emerged from the fog near the base of the lighthouse, rubbing his shin and cursing.

But Opal was not looking at her father. She was looking at the stone slab beside the lighthouse's base. It was rising... silently, steadily, on metal hinges.

'I say, what is happening?' said Lord Laplume. 'I tripped on that!'

She hobbled across the pebbles and reached it just as it revealed a steel trapdoor embedded beneath.

'Drats... how do we get in?' said Opal, smoothing her hands over the metal.

The thing had an odd-shaped handle and a figure of eight indentation. It seemed to Opal like something could fit in the indentation, like a key in the same sort of puzzle piece.

Augusto reached it seconds later. 'Ah,' he panted. 'This looks promising.'

'If we can get it open, that is,' said Lord Laplume.

Napoleon came to see what the fuss was about and find out when someone was going to fulfil their ball-throwing duties. They were at the seaside, were they not? He nuzzled Opal's hand to hint that whatever brass thing she was holding, it would be good enough for him to play with.

'Napoleon.' Opal sighed. 'If you played fetch with this, you'd crack your teeth.'

Then she gasped. 'That's it!' The compass was a physical key. She popped it open and laid it flat in the eight-shaped indent. It fit perfectly.

'Here goes!' Opal said excitedly and with a jittery finger, pressed it down.

The lock mechanism shifted and the hatch squeaked open.

TWENTY-ONE

THE BLAIR LAIR

Inside was a narrow spiral staircase descending into cool, humming darkness.

'Shall we?' Opal asked, eyes round and electrified.

Augusto flicked his cigarillo away and insisted he go first, hand inside his lapel.

Opal very nearly emitted a squeak of excitement. She had been right after all. Yes! Sir Seamus *did* have a secret laboratory, and it might just hold the key to why he was murdered.

The laboratory was far larger than Opal had imagined, lit with weak yellow bulbs that buzzed like sleepy bees. Military-looking filing cabinets lined the walls. Maps hung from pegs. A long metal table was covered in half-finished gadgets with tangles of copper wires spilling out. Sir Seamus's handwriting was everywhere... notes, formulae, calculations, newspaper clippings pinned like butterflies to the walls.

In the far corner was a metal desk. On top of it was what must have been the pièce de résistance of everything Sir Seamus had been working on. It looked rather like an angry brass octopus... wires akimbo, valves and dials dotted all over it and a small Bakelite switch labelled 'ON'.

Opal's fingers twitched.

'Don't touch that button, young lady,' said Lord Laplume, marching to her side. 'At least not until we find out what it does.'

'True,' said Augusto. 'Could even be explosive.'

Opal picked up a little notepad on which Sir Seamus had scribbled a memorandum to himself. She read the title aloud, '"The Aerial Interference Discombobulator"' I'm assuming this is the name for this... thingamajig.' She eyed up the brass octopus, bemused, and then kept reading. '"Designed to scramble enemy radio signals in flight using 'broad-spectrum oscillatory jiggery-pokery', though it also has a knack for interrupting the BBC's Shipping Forecast. It is to be mounted behind the pilot's seat." It then has a load of technical detail I can't make head nor tail of.'

'So... Sir Seamus was secretly working on gadgets for the air force,' Lord Laplume said.

Opal put down the notebook and yanked open the top drawer of the desk. There were some folders labelled 'Subject to the Official Secrets Act, 1911' and 'War Office Directive IX'.

'I daresay you are correct, Papa,' Opal said, shuffling through them. 'It certainly does look like Sir Seamus was inventing electronic apparatus for the military. I haven't the foggiest what any of them mean though, do you?' She handed them over to him.

He sifted through with a furrowed brow. 'No, I'm sorry, my dear, this sort of thing isn't my forte. But at least now we know there may be some military element to the mystery.'

'Possibly,' said Opal. 'And he had Seraphina's sister imprisoned for alleged spying on a special forces aircraft. So there is indeed a connection to Seraphina. Though I'd like to think she was innocent. I'll take these back for Detective Inspector Sinclair.'

'Well?' said Augusto. 'Are we going to press the ON button?' He waggled his finger teasingly around it.

'I think we'd like our limbs accounted for and eyebrows unscorched, if you don't mind,' said Opal in a schoolmarmish manner.

Just then, Napoleon jumped up to bite Augusto's waggling finger, thinking it was a game, and his nose knocked the button on with an echoing 'flick' sound.

'No!' shouted Opal. And everyone crouched low, arms shielding their heads.

Nothing happened.

'Err, I daresay it's not plugged in,' said Lord Laplume after a few moments.

Opal sighed with exasperation, straightened up and proceeded to snoop in all the nooks and crannies of the lair.

They were about to depart when Opal spotted a drawer they hadn't opened yet. It had a label in which Sir Seamus had scrawled, 'Silk-sniffing Charlatans!' Opening it revealed a set of ledgers with writing in French.

Opal's heart gave a little jump.

'*Société des Tissus Parisiens*,' she whispered. 'It's the company Sir Seamus was fighting with! I'm sure Countess Angelina *lied* when she said she didn't know who they were!'

She pulled open a folder and pressed it flat on the desk.

Inside was correspondence. Dozens of letters on heavy cream paper, signed in the looping hand of the director of the Parisian company. Diagrams of machinery that looked like tweed looms, patents, legal arguments, veiled threats.

'This is it,' Opal said. 'The Parisian textile company Sir Seamus was fighting with. They accused him of wilful patent infringement of one of their tweed looms.'

'And that's why someone killed him?' Augusto said quietly.

'Angelina is Parisian. She *lied* about knowing about this

company. They could have sent her as an assassin,' Opal said, hands on her hips, satisfactorily.

'I highly doubt that,' said Augusto. 'And she may have lied so as not to get involved.'

Opal winced with annoyance. 'What makes you so sure? Mr Martindale thinks so, and why on earth is she even at the castle? "Cultural studies" my foot!'

'Okay, Opal,' said Augusto calmly and put his hands on her shoulders. 'There are many motives flying around. We must not be hasty.'

'Well, she is *now* my prime suspect,' Opal said defiantly.

Napoleon sat up at her feet and made a puff sound through his nose as if to say 'mine too'. As the countess had very rudely never bothered to stroke him.

'We must not forget the puffins, my dear girl. I will continue east. Let's meet back at the croft around six for supper.'

Opal watched her papa march off determinedly, the Atlantic roaring in the distance. Opal allowed herself the smallest of smiles. After all, it wasn't every day one found a secret laboratory beneath a lighthouse, triggered by a magnetic puffin with a mechanical beak. But who else might know about this lab and its contents? And what might happen to her if they knew she had discovered it?

TWENTY-TWO
WHISKERS AND WITCHERY

Augusto, Opal and Effie lent Mrs Moffat a hand with supper preparations while they waited patiently for Lord Laplume and Mr Moffat to return from their puffin patrol. Lady Laplume didn't want to seem too idle and resolved to regard the task as a holiday activity, so tried her best at cutting kelp. Her nostrils flared in bemusement as she applied herself with dainty, diplomatic chops.

'This... dare I call it seaweed? Is it just garnish or is it actually edible?'

'Garnish?' Mrs Moffat laughed. 'No, m'lady. We eat everything, including the cod's eyeballs.'

Suddenly, the most beautiful black cat slunk into the kitchen, shoulders undulating like a tiny, mystical panther. She walked straight up to Napoleon on the mat, curled up and used his pom-pom tail as a chin rest. Napoleon froze. Utterly astonished. *Whatever should he make of it? If he moved his tail away... would she bite?*

'How utterly darling,' said Opal, inhaling with delight. 'This must be the Serle sisters' famous cat... Morag?'

'Aye.' Mrs Moffat nodded, drying a copper pan. 'She's made a bonnie wee friend, I see.'

'The fact they are almost the same size and both with the same onyx fur probably bonds them as if they were from the same sort of little club,' Opal said, gazing down at the breathing bundles of hair.

Napoleon looked up at his mistress with droopy eyes as if to say *'you've got to be joking; she is a cat, my sworn enemy.'*

The door knocker clanged, and Mr Moffat and Lord Laplume's heavy boots scuffled into the kitchen, their cheeks flushed pink with sea brine.

'The puzzle of the perishing puffins is solved,' Lord Laplume said, rubbing his hands together contentedly.

'Really?' said Opal. 'That was quick, Papa. I say, well done!'

'What was the matter with them?' asked Lady Laplume, then jolted upright when one of the seaweed bulbs sprayed juice when she cut it.

'Toxic algae blooms!' said Lord Laplume, arms out wide.

'Come again?' said Opal, pausing with a potato peeler.

'Came across an unpleasant green scum in the bay... algae blooms that are toxic to fish. Many dead and floating kippers and sand eels. The poor puffins were being poisoned by them. We found a crate of copper sulphate in the old storehouse and used it to clear the water.'

'Oh... so will the puffins be alright now?' asked Augusto.

'Yes, within a few days the fish will return, and the puffins can feast unharmed. I've instructed Mr Moffat what to do if the beastly algae blooms re-emerge.'

'You're a saint, Lord Laplume,' said Mrs Moffat.

'Oh, I wouldn't go that far,' said Lord Laplume, playing with his scarf, abashed, but enjoying every moment.

Morag got up and rubbed her head on Lord Laplume's calf, purring as if to thank him too.

'Goodness gracious, I thought Napoleon had been shaved and given green glass eyes!' said Lord Laplume. 'Who is this?'

'It's Morag, Euphemia Serle's previous companion,' said Mrs Moffat.

'What happened to Euphemia, Mrs Moffat?' asked Opal, wanting to know the Moffats' opinion on the witch. 'She wasn't really a spy, was she?'

'Euphemia Serle? No. She had an eerie abundance of second sight. Ever since she was a wee bairn, Euphemia had an unnerving habit of knowing things she ought not to know,' said Mrs Moffat, poking the cod on the stove.

'Aye. She predicted, for instance, that old Stanley McManis's cow would go mad and attempt to throw itself into the sea, which it promptly did on a Tuesday morning in 1897,' said Mr Moffat.

'By the time she reached adulthood, Euphemia's reputation had outgrown St Kessog's limited audience, and with the tweed trade hanging by a thread, she drifted to the mainland, where she began holding séances for society folk who delighted in a bit of well-bred terror,' said Mrs Moffat.

'It was at one such gathering a few years ago, in the candlelit drawing room of a rather too-interested widow, that Euphemia fell into one of her most horrifying trances. Her eyes rolled back and, jaw spasming, she gasped out a prophecy so chilling that it sent an eighty-year-old baronet into a faint. She described, with alarming accuracy, the sinking of a military aircraft, down to the date, 4th June 1931, the time, seven a.m., and the location,' said Mr Moffat.

'The company were all suitably riveted and entertained and then thought nothing of it... until a fortnight later, the morning of June 5th, they looked at their morning papers. The very plane she described was sent to the bottom of the sea; in precisely the manner she had foretold.'

'By Jove!' said Lady Laplume.

'Well strike me purple and call me Percival,' said Lord Laplume, slamming his glass down on the table.

'This is positively lulu!' exclaimed Opal.

'Unfortunately, Sir Seamus, who'd had to deal with this disaster as it was just off the coast of Dunvaloch, thought it was less lulu and more malicious. He suspected a violation of the Treaty of Versailles and thought she must have been working somehow with the Germans.'

'So, she went to prison?' said Opal.

'Yes,' said Mrs Moffat sadly. 'She was never going to be able to survive in a place like that... a child of the mist. She needed to be free.'

Opal glanced at her father and then at Augusto. They both flashed their eyes as if thinking what she was thinking... perhaps that invention they had found in the laboratory had been on board the plane, and that was why Sir Seamus was so angry at Euphemia.

'What an ordeal,' said Opal and changed the subject. 'And poor Morag, never to see Euphemia again.'

'Her sister Seraphina Serle wanted to take her when everyone was evacuated, but didn't have a solid place to live at the time,' Mrs Moffat said.

'Actually, I promised to bring her back for Seraphina now that her sister has found a cottage in the hamlet.'

'I would resist,' Mr Moffat said with a sigh, 'as we are fond of little Morag, but she does belong to the Serle family and it's only right you take her back. Thank you, Opal.'

'I sometimes feel like that cat *is* Euphemia,' said Mrs Moffat. 'She used to follow her around like a little shadow, and when she meows, she even sounds like her.'

Everyone looked at the cat, who was stretching in a wheelbarrow position with bright green eyes reflecting flickers of orange from the fire. Then suddenly came the sound of a distant shotgun.

BANG.

TWENTY-THREE

THE VENDETTA THAT WILL NOT VANQUISH

The gun blast made the cat's eyes dilate in a split second, and its ears shoot back. Then it sprang up onto the bookshelf when everyone yelled and jumped up.

'What in the name?' shouted Augusto.

'I… I have no idea what that could be. We're supposed to be the only ones on the island! Unless it's the mail boat crew, but they left this morning!'

'The skipper and Clyde don't bring firearms, not that I know of anyway,' said Mrs Moffat.

'Where did it come from?' yelled Lady Laplume, clutching her husband's arm.

'West,' said Mr Moffat. 'The echo from the shot must have resounded off the cliffs that side of the isle.'

'What do we do?' said Opal.

'Swim for it,' said Lady Laplume. 'I'm not sure I can stay on this island.'

'Do you have any guns of your own?' said Augusto. 'I'm carrying.'

'Of course we do. Think I'd risk my island being

conquered?' Mr Moffat took a shotgun out of a cupboard and slung it over his shoulder. 'You and I, let's go and investigate.'

'Don't take BOTH the guns!' said Lady Laplume. 'Let Edmund keep one so he can protect us!'

'Of course, m'lady, sorry, I wasn't thinking,' said Augusto and handed his piece over to the trembling hands of Lord Laplume.

And with that, Augusto and Mr Moffat escaped into the night.

Nobody dared speak in the croft, their eyes were on stalks trying to listen for a shot. The time went by ever so slowly. They played a game of cards and sipped whisky in the manner of men trapped in a submarine waiting to be rescued.

The door handle turned. Opal held her breath. Lord Edmund Laplume very quietly cocked the gun and slowly pointed it at the door with both hands.

Opal ducked down to protect Napoleon and stop him from barking.

The door squeaked open.

Opal could see indigo night sky and a hand holding something white... a letter.

Augusto emerged.

'It seems a friend of yours delivered a letter for you in a very dramatic fashion,' said Augusto, handing Lord Laplume the envelope. 'We found it tied to the dock. The purpose of the gunshot was meant as a warning and to draw attention to the letter, it seems.'

'But who is it from?' said Lady Laplume, peering over Lord Laplume's shoulder.

'Lord Sterling Peregrine,' said Augusto.

Opal's mouth fell open.

'He was sailing off in the distance and even gave us a sardonic wave,' Augusto continued. 'He had a black eyepatch on. That surely was him?'

'Yes,' said Opal. She suddenly realised why the boot prints had looked so familiar. She'd never forgotten the clunky footwear Lord Peregrine had worn when he had accosted her in Paris. 'His must have been the boot prints I saw earlier, not Sir Seamus. He's been spying on us for sure.'

'For God's sake, read it aloud, Edmund,' said Lady Laplume anxiously.

Lord Edmund Laplume,

You have taken much from me, dear chum. Your birds of paradise sanctuary in Papua has throttled my poaching business, and I find myself in need of restitution. Allow my men free passage to hunt in the region once more, and this little matter need not escalate further.

Should you refrain, I will see both your precious little bird sanctuaries in ruins. Your puffins of St Kessog's will scatter, your name will be blackened in high society, and the Papuan forests you hold dear will be stripped bare... by me, or by those less inclined to negotiate.

Do the sensible thing, Laplume. You know where to find me.

Lord Sterling Peregrine

Lord Edmund Laplume spoke the name with aggressive emphasis on the consonants, and like each word had a big full stop after each.

'That tyrannical maniac,' Opal hissed. 'Why won't he just stop terrorising our family? You've been proven innocent of his son's death, Papa. He must have reconciled with that.'

'He lost a lot of money when we got the diamond back. Now I've gained that hefty finder's fee and destroyed his poaching expedition, I think it's a double bitter pill to swallow.'

'He didn't *lose* the money, Papa, he *stole* the diamond from you in the first place!' shouted Opal, fizzing with rage. 'And he has evil bones, so bad things are bound to happen to him.'

'We must keep the guns with us tonight. Thank the lord we are leaving tomorrow,' said Lord Laplume.

'Don't be alarmed, Mrs Moffat. It is us he is after, he won't be bothering you once we've gone,' said Lady Laplume, noticing Mrs Moffat wringing her dishcloth in anxiety.

Opal grabbed her father's notepad out of his coat pocket.

'We need a countermove to immobilise him before he does something drastic,' she said. 'Keep him guessing. I'm going to write a letter back to him.'

She began to scribble, her knuckles white with how hard she gripped the pen.

Peregrine,

You mistake me for a man who bargains with larcenists. I do not.

But since you insist on playing this game, let me remind you of a few matters you may have overlooked.

I hold records – oh yes, quite detailed ones – of your past dealings in Papua. Shipments of rare birds and pelts, bribes to corrupt officials, and a rather interesting letter from a certain Dutch officer who, I believe, would love to discuss your activities with the authorities.

Should anything unfortunate happen to either of my bird sanctuaries, I will not hesitate to release these documents. I imagine the Board of Trade, the Zoological Society, and the authorities in Papua and London would be most interested. And let us not forget your friends in high society – how quickly they turn when scandal strikes.

However, I am a reasonable man.

You will cease all operations in Papua immediately. In

exchange, I will ensure your name remains unsullied, and you will be free to pursue your more legitimate interests.

Consider your next move carefully. The hunter can so easily become the hunted.

Laplume

'But, Opal,' said Lord Laplume, 'these are lies. I don't hold such evidence.'

'It doesn't matter if it's lies or not. It gives us the leverage we need, even if it's false. We can certainly gain, or even forge, some fake evidence. Play him at his own game!'

'But, darling Bins... I am not a liar.'

'If you don't mind me speaking out of turn, my lord,' said Augusto. 'But your astute daughter is right. He has to be neutralised, or your bird conservation projects could be burnt to ashes.'

'He's capable of anything, that one,' agreed Lady Laplume.

'There... you're outvoted, I'm afraid, Papa. We shall be posting this to his dwellings as soon as we are back on the mainland.'

Opal sat cuddling a basket on the mail boat back to Dunvaloch. It was covered in a tweed blanket, and inside was huddled Morag. Napoleon touched his nose with hers through the weave; they'd become a sweet little duo. Yin and Yang, calm and spritely, the cat was poetry and the poodle was prose.

'What's the cat on here for?' asked the skipper, lifting his cap and peering into the basket.

'Oh, the least thing I could do was bring the Serles' cat back for Seraphina. She has a home with her sister in Dunvaloch hamlet where it can live. And I'm sure she'll be out of custody soon, once we prove she can't read.'

'Seraphina Serle?' said young Clyde, the skipper's son, thoughtfully, winding rope around his wrist. 'I know that name.'

'I assume there are rumours about her being responsible for Sir Seamus's death. So, I guess you would have heard her name because of that,' said Opal.

'No,' said Clyde. 'I spoke to her... last night. She came to me on the dock all cloaked in black. She asked a favour of me.'

Opal's eyes opened wide and she inhaled sharply.

'What? What did she ask you to do?'

'I'm sworn to secrecy,' he said and looked out to sea with a jaw clamped firmly shut. It was evident he wouldn't offer the information.

Oh dear, thought Opal, *yet another secret to pry out of someone's mouth.*

TWENTY-FOUR

NOTES FROM THE NETHERWORLD

The island party shuffled in, damp and disgruntled, and collapsed before the fire. Lady Blair, Mr Roberts, Turkey, Countess Angelina, McWatt, and Seraphina had been marooned in boredom for some time. Mr Martindale wrestled with probate in the study, while Detective Inspector Sinclair busied himself with castle sleuthery.

'Hot toddies all round,' said Mr Roberts, his hair glowing a rose-gold by the fire. 'McWatt. McWatt, old chap. I'll help you fetch them.'

The two departed to fetch the very much needed reviving beverages.

'You all must be perished,' said Lady Blair, wrapped cosily in a sheepskin.

'You poor thing,' said Countess Angelina, tucking a lock of hair behind Augusto's ear. 'It's been such tempestuous weather. I tried to get a little fresh air earlier and noticed the flag in the tower was wrapped right around the turret, the wind is so strong.'

Opal no longer needed warming up, the hot infuriation at

how sickly Countess Angelina was being with Augusto radiated through her veins.

'Oh, it wasn't too bad,' said Augusto, brushing her hand away gently and glancing at Opal.

Opal gave him a cutting stare.

Turkey tried to slather on the concern in a similar fashion, untying Opal's scarf. 'A very ambitious escapade for such a delicate young thing. That barren crag of an island doesn't even boast a doctor. Terribly unsafe.'

'I had a wonderfully enriching, splendid time, thank you, Turkey,' said Opal, wrapping her scarf up again.

'That was a barmy pursuit, if you ask me. I hope it wasn't in vain?' said Lady Blair.

'It was unspeakably dreadful,' said Lady Laplume, nursing her seasick stomach.

'It wasn't in vain, no, Lady Blair,' said Lord Laplume, propping his feet onto a footstool in satisfaction. 'Toxic algae was the culprit. Easily remedied with a sprinkling of copper sulphate. The puffins will be fine.'

'Thank you, Lord Laplume. Sir Seamus would be overjoyed,' said Lady Blair.

'And... we brought Morag back for you, Seraphina,' said Opal, opening the lid of her basket and lifting out the sleek creature.

She dashed straight for Seraphina, as if following only her scent and leapt onto her lap. Napoleon followed her and sat at the foot of the armchair, keen to be close to his new comrade of the fur kingdom.

'Oh,' said Seraphina. 'Me wee mixy. Oh, thank you, Miss Laplume. How I've missed our girl. The stars will reward you handsomely, I know that.'

The seer's remaining front tooth hopped happily onto her lip, and she whispered something that sounded serpent-like into the cat's ear. The cat purred loudly and rubbed its head on hers.

Opal couldn't help but sense it was as if Seraphina was speaking to Euphemia through the cat.

After hot toddies, oat cakes and Roquefort for a dinner substitute, everyone retired to their chambers for the night. The schedule for tomorrow would be a nine o'clock meeting with Detective Inspector Sinclair in the morning room.

PPPPHHHHHHAAAAAAAAARRRRRRRRR, NAAAARRRRR, PHAAAAARRRR!!!!

The most ghastly, strangulated wail bleated out, ricocheting around the cloisters in a horrible soup of noise. Opal's body snapped up into a perfect right angle. *What an infernal racket! Was it... bagpipes? In the middle of the night?*

Napoleon began to bark into the darkness, running round in circles clockwise, then anticlockwise, utterly in a tizzy! Among the ruckus, Opal could hear doors slamming down the corridor.

Someone had switched the lights on outside, and it lit up Opal's door frame. She scrambled out of bed and threw on her dressing gown and slippers.

Stumbling out, she was confronted by her parents. 'By Jove,' Lord Laplume shouted, his hands on his ears. 'It sounds like a battalion of geese engaging in a heated debate with a lawnmower!'

Everybody, including the servants from the bowels of the castle, came in their nightcaps and overcoats thrown over to see what the devil was going on. Augusto strode ahead of Mrs Keith, the housekeeper, and the cook. Countess Angelina, Mr Roberts and Turkey followed. Opal noted a few people missing – Mr Martindale, Lady Blair, McWatt, Seraphina and Detective Inspector Sinclair.

Mr Roberts led the way towards the ruckus with the countess bumbling close behind.

The sound was definitely coming from the gallery in the

east wing of the castle. The knights in shining armour looked very creepy indeed. The two guarding the tower had both carried bagpipes before, but now only one of them did.

'What scallywag is piping up the east tower?' shouted Mr Roberts. 'This is no night for pranks!'

'Has anyone noticed what tune they're playing?' said Countess Angelina, grasping Augusto's shoulders.

Opal blinked in recognition. Golly. It was the same harrowing arrangement of notes that was played out on the gramophone after Sir Seamus's death.

'Yes!' replied Opal. '"The Twa Corbies!"'

'Shhhhh,' said Mr Roberts. 'I'm going up.'

Mr Roberts switched on the tower lights and began his ascent at a brisk shuffle. Turkey was next, hesitant and slow due to his spinelessness, causing a minor pile-up. All the women, apart from Opal, remained below. She gave the wriggling Napoleon to Effie, the maid, to hold. She grabbed the icy handrail and set off after her father.

It was chilly and damp, the arrow slits providing mild relief from claustrophobia, revealing grey clouds speckled with stars. The bagpipes got louder, and Opal had to cover her ears.

Just as Mr Roberts almost reached the top, the bagpipes stopped short, as if they were just cut off. It was like someone had plucked a bumblebee out of each of Opal's ears. Peace... apart from a faint ringing.

Mr Roberts yanked open the tower door with the 'clank' noise of the ironwork on wood.

He stepped out, and a whistling wind blew down the tower, and Opal's hair billowed. She craned her neck around her father's body, but the curving wall blocked her view.

'Good God!' Mr Roberts shouted. 'There's nobody here!'

Everyone quickly emerged onto the top of the tower. Indeed, it was empty. Apart from a set of bagpipes lying on the stone floor. The pipes splayed out as if dropped in a hurry.

'How can there be nobody here?' said Turkey with chattering teeth.

Opal's teeth also chattered in the bitter cold, but mainly due to the ghostly creepiness of the situation. 'There is no way off the tower, is there?' she said, as everyone peered over the edges.

Augusto came close to Opal and put his arm around her to shield her from the wind. She shrugged him off in case Papa saw.

'No. It is a dead drop, the entire way around,' said Lord Laplume. 'No way off, unless you're a bat or a bird.'

'No trap door either,' said Augusto, crouching and touching the grey stones.

'Are... are we certain the pipes were played from up here?' said Opal, pinching her chin and blinking fast in thought.

'The torches are still lit around the battlements so we can see the ground around the castle, and there's nobody down there, and you'd be sure to see them hot footing it,' said Lord Laplume, his bedcap flailing violently in the wind.

'And why would there be pipes up here if they weren't played up here?' said Augusto, staring intently at the instrument.

'Somebody playing a sick and nefarious joke,' said Mr Roberts. 'That confounded tune as well. "The Twa Corbies". Must be the same tyrant who was responsible for hooking the gramophone up to the tree switch.'

'Or perhaps... a ghost,' said Turkey, inspecting the sky, eyes bulging in terror.

'Foolishness,' said Lord Laplume. 'Let us go back down. This is worse than a ship in a tempest.'

Opal had one last thing to point out. 'When playing bagpipes, would there not be saliva or condensation left on the mouthpiece?' She knelt down and lifted the Bakelite tube with thumb and forefinger. She brought it close to one eye. 'I daresay there is some condensation. Could it be from human breath or from the conditions outside?'

'It certainly looks like breath to me,' said Mr Roberts, crouching to her level.

'Opal, you will catch a cold,' Augusto said. 'Let's go back in before you freeze to death.'

Opal, knowing she'd be no good at sleuthing with the flu, obeyed and let Augusto lead her to the tower door.

But on the way down, Opal noticed a piece of frayed, cream-coloured thread on the bracket that nailed the handrail to the wall. It was directly under the last window. She untied it from where it was caught and stuffed it up her sleeve.

Everyone returned to their beds, white faced and jittery. Opal was still very much rattled, phantom bagpipes echoing inside her skull. On the pillow, Napoleon curled up on top of her head like an enormous warm wig. Whenever he'd tried this in the past, Opal had gently removed him. But tonight, it proved a great comfort to have him there and she managed to drift off.

But Opal was awoken once again. Her eyelids shot back but immediately squinted at the morning light blasting through her window. Napoleon leapt off the pillow like a cannonball. It was a high-pitched sound but came from a set of female lungs. Opal once again pulled on her robe and almost fell over trying to shuffle her slippers on in haste.

Effie was at a doorway on the opposite side of the cloisters. Opal could see the back of her maid's cap quivering in terror. Opal was the first to get to her, though she could hear others pacing behind her. Opal gasped and pinned her eyelids back when she saw what had caused the maid to scream. Lying on the carpet of his room, as still as a toppled mannequin, was Mr Martindale.

TWENTY-FIVE

X MARKS THE SOLICITOR

Mr Martindale was on his back, lying quite straight with his arms placed unnaturally across his chest as if he was going up for a blessing at Mass. He was in striped pyjamas and his feet were bare and blue. The whites of his eyes were pink, and his pupils were extremely dilated, staring up at the ceiling. But the most morose thing was the two black feathers in an X-shape on top of his chest.

'Two crow feathers. The Twa Corbies,' Opal said to nobody in particular, shuddering.

Effie dashed down the stairs, stifling sobs with her hand. Lord and Lady Laplume, Mr Roberts and Lady Blair approached the doorway.

'What the devil?' said Lord Laplume as he took in the dreadful scene with the others. Mr Roberts dashed to check Mr Martindale's pulse, though the man's skin was so blue he must have been deceased for a good few hours.

'Come on, Lady Blair, let's go down and call for help... again.' Lady Laplume took the shoulders of a stunned Lady Blair and walked her away.

Opal swallowed hard and then took in the state of the room

around Mr Martindale. It must have been a noisy attack with bangs and crashes. The desk and nightstand were upturned. There were books from the bookshelf strewn across the floor. The way Mr Martindale lay there, unnaturally, like a mummy, was decidedly arranged by whoever killed him.

'When could this have possibly happened?' said Opal. 'I mean, it would have caused a racket, all the bashing of the furniture. Did anyone hear it?'

'I didn't, we will have to consult the others though,' Lord Laplume said, scratching his head wearily. 'Did you pick up on any noises coming from this room last night, Mr Roberts?'

'No... no, I didn't,' he said quietly.

'Could this have happened while the bagpipes were playing?' said Opal, pacing on the rug. 'On purpose, to... to distract everyone?'

Mr Roberts and Lord Laplume looked at each other and then back at Opal. They were all mentally recalling who had not been present at the tower during the bagpipe ordeal. It was four people. Lady Blair, McWatt, Seraphina Serle and Detective Inspector Sinclair. Could one of them, minus the detective, be the killer? None of them uttered these words, but Opal could tell what calculations were going on in their minds.

'This would imply two culprits.' Opal pinched her chin and fluttered her eyes at the ceiling. 'For it would take one person to be playing the pipes and the other to be carrying out this brutal attack whilst we were distracted by the racket. Who out of Lady Blair, Seraphina Serle and McWatt can play the pipes?'

'I don't know about Seraphina, but Lady Blair and McWatt certainly can't,' said Mr Roberts.

'Whoever was responsible wouldn't be foolish enough to admit they could play,' said Lord Laplume. 'Let's leave the poor man for the coroner or whatever they call it up here.'

'The procurator fiscal,' corrected Mr Roberts.

'Wait, what's that?' Opal said as she zoned in on Mr Martindale's fist.

'Don't touch him, Opal. His body will need to be dusted for prints,' Lord Laplume said touching her shoulder.

'I know that, Papa. I'm not dense,' she said and crouched down low like a frog. She could see a greyish-blonde tuft of ratty hair, sort of screwed up in a ball, and a little broken string with onyx beads on it. It looked as if Mr Martindale had pulled at someone's hair and necklace.

'A bit of a daft killer to leave this sort of evidence in his grasp,' said Opal. 'Though you never know how dark it was or how fast the killer had to get out of here.'

'What was the cause of death, I wonder?' asked Mr Roberts, his shiny brogues stepping beside her.

'Being bashed about, I suppose. From what we can deduce from the state of the room,' answered Lord Laplume.

'Look,' said Opal, craning forward to see. 'The back of his head, there's some blood. He was either bashed on the head or fell and hit it.'

She also noticed on his cheek was a little indentation of a thistle shape, like the press mark you'd get on your bare leg if it was squashed on textured fabric on a chair. There were various thistle emblems decorated in the theme of the room. Thistle wallpaper and embroidery on the bedding, and a vase full of the dried flora. Why would a thistle mark also be on his cheek? And those ominous feathers! What kind of a message was the killer trying to leave?

The police constable and procurator fiscal arrived in the doorway, faces sullen. A breathless Detective Inspector Sinclair arrived behind them in a red silk smoking jacket, making him appear like a tomato. He commanded everyone to dress and go down for breakfast... if they could stomach it. He would give instructions from there.

Opal was reluctant to leave the scene but obeyed, glancing

down at the clump of hair in Mr Martindale's clutch once more before she left the room. She noticed this time it was matted slightly as if pulled out of a hairbrush, rather than directly pulled from someone's head. She couldn't help but try to remember what colour hair Seraphina Serle had, but the seer always had her head swathed in a turban. Would she be sitting at the breakfast table without one? If not, however could she get a peek at Seraphina's hair?

TWENTY-SIX

HAIRS, HYPOTHESES, AND HYSTERIA

Opal pulled on her clothes with fumbling fingers, full of adrenaline... *There was a killer in the castle... and they would be attending the breakfast.* Once she managed to button her warm tweed suit, she topped it off with her fedora and exited her room, Napoleon in tow. The double fright of the night had caused him to remain on high alert, ears pricked.

'Opal,' a voice hissed. She felt as if a spirit had poked a finger in her ear.

Whipping her head aside, she was relieved to see the face of Detective Inspector Morven Sinclair poking around the edge of a door. He ushered her into the stuffy reading room with a hooked finger.

'Detective Inspector Sinclair,' Opal began.

'Keep your voice down,' he whispered hurriedly and twisted his pipe in his fingers. 'We need to keep this brief as I am needed in Mr Martindale's room to help the procurator. But I expect you have information to relay to me from your island trip?'

Opal nodded and continued in a wispy voice. 'Indeed, sir, and it is most intriguing. Firstly, Seraphina Serle could not have used that electrical manual I found in her room because she's illiterate. Cannot read a sausage. She couldn't have orchestrated it.'

'Intriguing indeed,' Detective Inspector Sinclair said, putting his pipe in his teeth and burying his hands in his red silk pockets. 'Can be hard to prove that someone is genuinely illiterate. If you can try to get more evidence, that would help. Next clue?'

'Well... long story short. I found Sir Seamus's laboratory, and he had been inventing classified apparatus for secret military operations.'

'I'm not at *all* surprised that he was up to that,' said Detective Inspector Sinclair stoically.

'Some sort of radio interference device for planes. This sheds more light on Euphemia Serle and why he had her imprisoned. But then the plot became skewed when I found some documents in a drawer. He'd been fighting with a Parisian textile company over a patent for a tweed loom,' Opal said and pulled out the roll of documents she'd pilfered from the drawer from her bag. 'I have a strong suspicion Angelina is an ally of this Parisian company. An assassin they sent, perhaps?'

Opal's eyes flashed with satisfaction at dobbing in her amorous competition. But then tried to remove the vitriol from her stance by taking her hands from her hips.

'There's more to her story, you are right,' said Sinclair, taking the crumpled papers out of her hand and stuffing them in his pocket. 'This gives me a lot to go on. Thank you, my dear. Now go and join the others. I will be down to instruct everyone in due course.'

Opal's Mary Janes clacked on the tiles on the way to the morning room very slowly. She wasn't sure what state the inhabitants of the castle would be in. On entering, she noted that she was last to join breakfast. Everyone was there, apart from the police constable, Detective Inspector Sinclair and the procurator fiscal. Nobody said a word, their mouths opening and shutting as if thinking what to say and then deciding against it. The only sound was McWatt dribbling coffee from a pitcher into Countess Angelina's cup and Lady Blair, who was a symphony of sniffs, hiccups, and the odd warble sound like an opera singer being tickled.

The food was a sober buffet of eggs, rashers of bacon and oatmeal porridge cakes. A fork emerged into the centre of the table and pronged a hard-boiled egg. It was the fork of Seraphina, who sat at the far end of the oval table, a queer smug look on her face. As if she had proved herself correct, the second 'crow' had been murdered. The twa corbies were defeated. To Opal's frustration, the seer had worn a head wrap again that morning, not a strand of hair poking out. Her eyebrows were grey, so it was a good chance her hair could be the mix of blonde and grey that was in Mr Martindale's fist, but Opal couldn't be sure.

Opal cast her eyes over everyone else's hair. She did not see any blonde mingled with grey. But aha! Lady Blair was at least half a century old, so could indeed have some grey in her blonde locks somewhere, but it was hard to tell unless Opal got close.

She floated towards the vacant seat close to the blubbering lady of the house and sat down opposite her. Opal's eyes fanned open wide... *Indeed, Lady Blair did have greys mixed in with her mousy hair. Could it be a match?*

'Has anyone informed Mr Martindale's wife? Family?' Lord Laplume broke the vocal silence, scraping butter onto a slice of oatmeal cake.

'It is up to me. But I simply cannot do anything!' spluttered Lady Blair.

'It is surely standard procedure that the constable will

inform Mrs Martindale,' said Lady Laplume soothingly. 'Don't you worry about anything.'

Rhythmic plods of feet approached the entrance. As if the devil spoke, the constable entered, followed by the procurator fiscal. The constable had a pair of handcuffs swinging from a finger.

'Miss Seraphina Serle, I am arresting you on suspicion of the murder of Sir Seamus Blair and Mr Walter Martindale.'

TWENTY-SEVEN

DOUBLE TROUBLE AND THE WITCH'S WRATH

'Naaawwwww!' Seraphina howled, her face becoming like a screwed-up prune, her snaggletooth quivering. 'It was my sister Euphemia's spirit… she got her revenge on those two men, the twa corbies!'

'Enough of that guff, Miss Serle.'

'Noooooooo!' she cried louder as he took her shoulders.

Opal could feel Napoleon cower between her legs under the table.

'No, Constable, please. There must be a mistake. I do not believe Seraphina committed these murders.'

The constable ignored her and grappled with the woman. The men stood up, not sure if it was appropriate to help.

'You can't lock me up like my sister! I won't be taken!' she yelled, yanked her shoulders free and hurtled towards the servants' quarters.

Napoleon darted after her, followed by everyone else. Augusto was just coming up the stairs and put his arms out to grab her.

'Let go!' she bellowed. 'Or I'll blind your name to the wind!'

'What's going on?' Augusto shouted at the constable.

'She's been caught red-handed,' said the procurator fiscal, close behind them.

The constable grabbed her and, together with Augusto, they took her flailing body and locked her in the study. Napoleon started yapping at the door she was hammering on as if to give her a good telling-off.

Opal stood by a jardinière, blinking in helplessness. Detective Inspector Sinclair came down the stairs, now dressed in his pinstripe suit, showing many chins in confusion.

'Would you be so kind as to inform me of what's going on?' Detective Inspector Sinclair asked of his enforcement colleagues. 'I was just getting dressed, and you've decided to arrest Miss Serle while I've been absent?'

By this time, the entire inhabitants of the castle, including the servants, had gathered in the hall, clutching each other in fear of the '*monster*' wailing and bashing around in the study.

'I'd been searching the bedrooms,' said the constable. 'Behind Seraphina's wardrobe, I found these.' He shook a cloth evidence bag in the air and then poured the contents out onto the telephone table.

It was a hairbrush clumped with blonde and grey hairs, a broken string of beads reminiscent of the ones found in Mr Martindale's hand and a mints' tin.

'Look at this,' said the constable, opening the tin. It had little metal shards in it that winked in the lamplight.

'The metal shards that had been stuffed in the lamp switch and the hair and beads in Mr Martindale's hand, though we still need to work out how she did it all. We've got our murderer,' he said and snapped closed the lid of the mints' tin with thumb and forefinger satisfactorily as if it was the wrapping of the entire case.

'And we can deduce the motive was revenge against the imprisonment of her sister Euphemia Serle, who committed suicide,' said the procurator fiscal in a deep, deadpan tone.

'But what about the bagpipes?' said Opal. 'How would she manage to pull that off?'

'She was not present when the rest of you investigated the tower, so it was likely her doing,' said the constable.

'She has been trying to push the ghost narrative on us all, relating it to that creepy song, "The Twa Corbies". Saying crows appeared in the tea leaves, the melody on the gramophone and bagpipes, the crow's feathers found on Mr Martindale's chest,' said Lady Blair, now becoming angry rather than sad. 'It is most suspicious.'

'What if she's telling the truth?' said Opal.

All eyes edged sideways at Opal as if she was batty.

'Not about the ghost. I don't believe in ghosts!' she scoffed. 'I mean, perhaps that's what she truly thinks has happened. The *real* murderer has orchestrated it to look like Seraphina staged ghostly phenomena to cover up her crimes.'

Napoleon barked in agreement with his mistress, sitting erect, puffing up his breast.

'But who else would have a motive to kill both Sir Seamus and Mr Martindale?' said the constable, puffing up his chest to match Napoleon and rocking back on his heels.

'We don't know yet. There's not been enough time to cover all bases,' said Opal.

'With all due respect, sirs,' said Detective Inspector Sinclair, addressing both the constable and the procurator. 'The Honourable Opal Laplume is right. Someone could be framing the poor, vulnerable woman. I do not appreciate this rush to accuse when you have not allowed me to finish my investigation.'

'Detective Inspector Sinclair,' said the procurator fiscal. 'We have more than enough evidence to bring her into custody.'

'Are you not a little over-confident?' said Sinclair.

'What do you suggest, Detective? If we do not keep her

under wraps, she may flee, and we can't burden Lady Blair any longer by locking her up here.'

'Indeed, I want shot of the woman,' said Lady Blair, purposefully loud so that Seraphina could hear through the door. 'It's becoming all very plain to me that she is to blame!'

'You're telling me,' said Opal, 'that Seraphina Serle, from the Isle of St Kessog's, who is completely illiterate, was able to engineer a light switch to hook up to a gramophone and add the metal shavings inside the copper switch. Knowing it would have enough voltage to kill a person!'

'You have to get her out of my home at the very least, gentlemen. She's positively raving,' pleaded Lady Blair, clasping her hands in a praying position.

'She will be taken into custody,' replied the procurator fiscal and side-eyed the door handle, which Seraphina was rattling on the other side. 'Once Detective Inspector Morven Sinclair has got *up to speed*, we can pursue.'

'Don't worry, Seraphina,' said Opal, her feet castanets of passion as she marched to the door and pressed her nose and hands against it. 'I will take Morag to your sister. We won't give up on you. Please write the address on a piece of paper and pass it under the door!'

'I cannae write!' said Seraphina. 'But thank you, Opal. It is number seven, Ambrose Cottages, Dunvaloch hamlet.'

'Opal, please stop this impertinence this instant.' Opal's mother grabbed her elbow and hissed in her ear. 'You are upsetting Lady Blair.'

'I think it best everyone vamoose,' said McWatt. 'Go back to breakfast.'

'Indeed,' said Detective Inspector Sinclair. 'Everyone disperse. We don't want a scene when Seraphina's transport arrives.'

Everyone skulked away, shoulders slumped, seeming half

relieved that the killer had been caught, but eyes still protruding and darting at one another, as if not entirely certain.

Opal and Augusto went with Detective Inspector Sinclair into the salon, where their ears got some respite from Seraphina's wails.

'I will be conducting more interviews here and then will head to Edinburgh soon after. I will need to make a visit to Mr Martindale's office.'

Opal folded her arms and said, 'Augusto, will you escort me to the hamlet to drop off the cat to Malvina Serle?' in the same tone she sometimes spoke to Napoleon.

Napoleon looked up at her in confusion. *Did his mistress have another new dog as well as a new cat?*

'Of course. The killer is still among us, and I won't be letting you out of my sight,' said Augusto.

'Then we shall catch up with you in Edinburgh, Detective Inspector Sinclair, as we will be attending Sir Seamus's funeral there.'

Opal, Augusto and Napoleon left Detective Inspector Sinclair to scribble furious notes in his pocketbook and went up to fetch the feline.

As they scaled the stairs, Opal whispered to Augusto, 'On the way to Dunvaloch hamlet, let us check the bottom of the east tower.'

TWENTY-EIGHT
MALVINA'S COTTAGE

The snowstorm had withered into a shower of glittering snowflakes, and the snow underfoot was beginning to turn to slush. Augusto carried Morag's basket in his woolly mittens. Opal felt his free mittened hand lightly stroke hers as they passed under a trellis arch, dead vines curling along its rusty frame. She took it and felt safe and held.

As they walked along the battlement wall, Augusto was quiet, probably using his artistic vision to analyse the view. The land below had turned a lush green, though stubborn patches of snow clung to the hollows like cow print marks splashed across the terrain.

They turned right and approached the base of the east tower. The site of the phantom bagpipe mystery. Opal looked up at its great, looming presence.

'It's far too high for anyone to jump off and survive. There is no foothold or any way for someone to get down,' said Opal. 'I honestly do not think anyone in the tower was playing the pipes. It must have been a subterfuge set of pipes left on the floor and the sound was coming from somewhere else!'

'It certainly sounded like it was coming from the tower,' said Augusto.

Opal watched the flag ripple and lick the sky. It was the Union Flag, a reminder of Sir Seamus's bond of martial duty and allegiance.

'The flag...' Opal said, shading her view with a hand. 'Didn't Angelina say it was so windy last night that it was wrapped right around the tower?'

'I can't remember anything anyone says when you're near,' Augusto replied.

He put his hand under her chin. She glanced down at the mittens and started laughing. 'I'm so sorry, I just can't take the mittens serio—'

He cut her off by kissing her. It was more delectable than the clotted cream fudge in her Christmas stocking and lasted far longer. She was anxious someone might spot their clandestine affections and pulled away, turning her head to the right. She opened her eyes and looked down inside the holly bush.

'Look!' she said. 'There's some cord! A jolly long reel of it.'

It was cream-coloured and was dangling on the branches of the holly bush as if it had been tossed there. Opal plucked the end of it and brought it to her nose. She recognised it as the macramé cord that Lady Viola Blair used in her craft.

'I saw a piece of this fraying cord tied around the handrail inside the tower stairwell,' said Opal, popping open the clasps of her handbag. 'If I compare it... yes, yes, it is the same cord!'

Opal salvaged it from the spiky leaves and stuffed it into her bag. Napoleon was the opposite of helpful and snapped at it as if it was spaghetti in a meaty jus.

'You're saying it was tied to the handrail and then afterwards tossed down into the bushes below,' said Augusto, showing the underside of his dimpled chin as he gazed upwards.

'The evidence seems to be saying so, yes,' said Opal, pinching her chin in thought. 'I do wonder if it had something to do with the fact that Angelina saw the flag wrapped around the tower earlier that evening. It may not have been the wind. It may have been tied around the tower, as a kind of sound funnel.'

'A sound funnel? To make it sound like the bagpipes were playing in the tower when they were actually coming from somewhere else?'

'Yes, indeed!' said Opal. 'Perhaps tied to the corner eyelet of the flag, wrapped and brought down into the stairwell under the door? Then once the bagpipes stopped playing, someone yanked the cord from the handrail and let the flag fly free. The cord then fell down into the bushes.'

They began to wind along the serpentine path and tried to unknot the significance of the cord and why Lady Viola Blair's macramé cord was used. As they approached the loch, there came a cacophony of yells in the distance. Napoleon stopped and barked in distress.

It was evidently Seraphina being bundled into the police vehicle. The door slamming. Morag made a high-pitched moan from the basket.

'It's alright, Morag,' said Opal. 'We will sort it out. We will prove that arrogant procurator fiscal wrong!'

Dunvaloch hamlet was a very small rural settlement indeed. Perhaps only a few dozen stone cottages dating back to the 1500s, low and thatched. Some were nestled into the hillside, others stood alone amid green fields. Wild hedgerows, bracken, and ancient trees fringed the winding road.

The smallest of the cottages was the Serles' address. It was covered in moss and had snowdrops scattered like crowds of fairies in the front garden. Augusto held the cat basket while Opal knocked on the front door. The knocker was a Green Man's face, one of those old pagan symbols. It stared at Opal as if looking right through her soul. She shivered and stepped back.

A woman creaked open the door. Her white hair was swirled in a bun above her head and she had exceedingly bad teeth. Perhaps the poor dears didn't have a dentist on St Kessog's Isle because Seraphina's teeth had nearly all fallen out. She had the weathered but wicked-looking face of someone who had seen things no one ought to see and had enjoyed them tremendously. She eyed Opal up and down.

'Och no, I cannae read your palms today. The moon's in a strop with Jupiter, and Venus is no' speaking to anyone,' she said and went to close the door again.

'Good morning, I'm not actually here to have my palm read. I'm Seraphina's friend,' Opal said, clearing her throat nervously. 'I'm sorry to tell you that she has been arrested.'

The wrinkles in the woman's face drooped sadly. 'Just like they did Euphemia.'

'Yes, we know. I'm so sorry about that too. We want to help. We have brought the Serle family cat, Morag, back from St Kessog's Isle for you,' Opal said, stepping aside to reveal the basket in Augusto's arms.

'Morag!' said the woman, and her eyes flashed excitedly. Her tone completely changed after that. 'I'm Malvina Serle, Seraphina's sister. Thank you so much for bringing the cat back. That's what Seraphina wanted once we'd found a home here. We couldn't bring Morag with us when we were originally evacuated, as we had nowhere to settle. And now we've got our humble abode, Seraphina's been carted off.'

'It's alright... we've got a plan of how to get her out. Well, half a plan,' said Opal. 'May we come inside a moment, please?'

The woman let them in and offered to brew them some nettle tea, which they gladly accepted. Augusto placed the basket on the kitchen table, and the woman scooped up Morag like a newborn baby.

The cottage was a museum of pagan treasures: bunches of dried herbs hanging down from the low ceiling. Collections of rocks on a long shelf with the odd animal bone. Wax dolls peered from a shelf, seeming to read Opal's thoughts with their glass eyes. The scent of lavender and incense wafted past Opal's nose with the draught brought in from a rattling window.

'Ma wee bairn. We've all missed you, you velvet little goblin,' cooed Malvina, nestling her face into the cat's fur. Morag purred heartily.

While the kettle boiled on a hook over the fire, Opal explained that Seraphina had been accused of reading an *Electrician's Guide* in aiding her murder of Sir Seamus.

'How can we prove to the police that Seraphina can't read? They think she is lying when she uses this as her defence.'

'That is a tough one,' said Malvina. 'I can testify to it if they'll listen. I can't read either. She won't appear in any of the St Kessog's school records, if they even exist. Notice the lack of a bookshelf in this abode. We never needed to read. We worked the tweed looms and learned stories from memory, listening to our mothers and aunts. St Kessog's was our life, we never thought we'd need to read or write. My father could just about, but he didn't think us lassies would need to.'

'Testimonies could help. Was there anywhere she went where an official had to help her with reading and filling out a form or anything?' asked Opal.

'We haven't been in Dunvaloch hamlet long, but the bank clerk used to help her with her passbook and withdrawals. Oh, and the chemist would read her medicine instructions for her and draw symbols on the bottle.'

'Oh, do you have a bottle somewhere that I can show the constable?'

'Aye, she must have kept some half-used thing in here.' She

rattled around in the cupboard. 'Here we are... a tincture of laudanum.'

Opal took the brown bottle and brought it close to her nose. The pharmacist had very sweetly drawn in pencil on the blank part of the label. Two spoons and a sun for morning, then two spoons and a moon for night. Then seven little suns underneath to indicate seven days. Dunvaloch Dispensary was written on the top of the label.

'Thank you kindly. I should take a visit to Dunvaloch Dispensary and also to the bank to collect the evidence.'

'Say, after all that, they still think she is lying,' said her concerned sister, opening a can of sardines for Morag. 'They could say Seraphina orchestrated this illiteracy cover-up years ago.'

'Yes, especially if they're determined to pin it on her. We may need a backup plan. There must be a direct or spontaneous way we can prove she can't read a sausage,' said Opal, strumming her fingers and looking up at the ceiling, blackened from candles.

'This is terribly cruel,' said Augusto, 'but what if we asked the prison guards to put a note under her cell door saying someone close to her has died and see how she reacts? If you could read and were lying about it, you'd still look and not be able to hide your emotions?'

'I think that would be the very last resort,' said Opal.

'But I like the note under the door thing,' said Malvina, scratching her chin with a long nail.

'What about,' said Augusto, sticking a finger in the air in jest, 'sticking up signs around the prison saying gobbledegook and some saying "Exit". Then shout that there's a fire and let her out and see which way she runs? She'd probably follow the gobbledegook signs as she can't read, and that would prove it.'

'Thank heavens you didn't become a behavioural psychologist, Augusto,' Opal said and nudged him a little. She didn't want Malvina to think they weren't taking it seriously.

'True, but if I did... at least I'd understand *your condition*. Someone really ought to,' he said, determined to flirt at this inappropriate moment.

'*My* condition?' Opal frowned.

'Yes, your *heart's* condition,' he said and jabbed a thumb at his chest, looking earnestly at her as if they were alone.

'Oh, I see. *That* condition,' Opal said and looked shyly down at the table and then back up at him coyly. 'If you ever did figure it out... I suspect society would ask you to kindly forget it.'

Opal had played this little joke as a tester to see if Augusto would bristle at the mention of their class difference. She had never voiced her worry over societal expectations and their romance before. But he smiled and did not seem offended at her little comment about their differing situations. Just a soft smile as if he'd been wise to her internal fretting from the start. And what's more... he didn't hold it against her in the slightest. Not a jot. Quite the opposite... he looked as if he rather expected it, and found it all rather charming.

'That is a risk we may need to take, isn't it?' he said, his eyes steady on hers.

There was a silence, and all you could hear was Morag's purr in the corner of the room. Opal's cheeks filled with pink as she desperately thought of what she could reply. Malvina leant forward as if engrossed in a romance novel playing out on the stage of her kitchen table. Mercifully, Augusto broke the silence.

'Malvina, help me read this woman,' he said, taking his teacup and leaning back in his chair to survey Opal.

'May I?' said Malvina, splaying her fingers out on the table, whipping her green eyes between her subjects. 'I'll perform a couples' scrying? It's a form of divination using a bowl of water... the images that appear in it will reflect the future of your relationship.'

'Oh, no,' Opal said, with an exceedingly nervous giggle. 'There is no coupling here. Augusto is my protection officer. I'm terribly sorry if we gave the wrong impression. But no, thank you.'

Augusto folded his arms, and a smirk made the cleft in his chin curve sideways.

'But you must,' insisted the seer, pointing a long nail at the teacup. 'Look at the way the nettle tea is quivering. The magnetism between you both is simply unheard of.'

Opal was now so pink you'd think she'd swallowed a whole bottle of red food dye. She most definitely could *not* look at Augusto. The old woman took what she called the 'scrying bowl' – a wide, shallow black stone dish – and filled it with water from the squeaky tap. She then placed it in the centre of the table and lit a candle beside it, its flame dancing on the surface of the water in the bowl.

'Now, ye handsome lad,' Malvina said, her voice a rolling Highland burr. 'Ye must look deep into the water. Let the mind drift. Let the heart speak to ye.'

She circled the bowl thrice with a crow feather, murmuring in Gaelic, her voice rising and falling like the breeze in the glen. She plucked a pinch of salt with thumb and forefinger from a small pouch and sprinkled it into the water, and the candle flickered violently. Morag hopped onto the table and emitted a noise that could best be described as a kettle just before boiling point. Napoleon whined under the table and backed up against Opal's leg for comfort. His pom-pom tail was tucked right under his body. For once, he was completely out of his depth.

'Euphemia is speaking to us through Morag,' whispered Malvina. 'She likes the look of you two together.'

Opal and Augusto blinked at each other. Augusto fidgeted with his hands nervously as if he almost believed her. Opal leant forward and looked into the bowl. 'What do you see, Augusto?' she whispered.

He tentatively leant forward as if to look over a terrifying cliff edge. He then paused, his nose above the water, knitting his brows together as if straining to see anything at all. 'Eeeeh... Our faces?' said Augusto.

'No, no, no,' Malvina chastised and glared at him like a blockhead. 'You're only looking upon the two-dimensional surface.' She then tilted the bowl towards her. 'A strong bond, you have, a partnership guided by *duty*, strengthened by *trust*.'

Opal, without meaning to, exhaled, relieved that the forces of destiny could go in the right direction for them. Augusto caught her eye. She quickly looked back into the depths of the bowl.

'But...' Malvina's brow furrowed. The cat's hellish yowl ceased. A chill slithered into the room and curled around Opal's ankles. Opal and Augusto exchanged glances again.

'But?' Opal prompted, lowering her chin and gazing at the seer.

'There is... a thing. A thing that comes between ye.' Her eyes danced over the water's surface, widening slightly. 'A shadow... nay, a presence... something beginning with the letter "C", then the next word beginning with "A".'

Augusto's chair leg squeaked as he fidgeted. Opal gritted her teeth. *Blithering fig! It's Countess Angelina, isn't it,* she thought.

'A and C?' Opal asked, blinking innocently and playing dense.

'Aye, an "A" and a "C" is what the water is saying... without a doubt.' Malvina nodded, her voice now a whisper, as if she feared the letter itself might overhear.

There was a pause. Then, as one, Opal and Malvina turned to look at Augusto to get his input.

He swallowed under pressure. 'I don't suppose there's a chance it's... eeeeh... canine armpits?'

'Canine armpits?' Opal had to splutter a giggle. 'Dogs don't have arms! It would be leg-pits.' She mistakenly blew the candle with her breath as she laughed. It sputtered and went out. The water in the bowl darkened. Morag hissed and shot behind a sack of potatoes.

'I don't know... when you pick Napoleon up under his leg-pits he gets all the attention, and there's none for me,' Augusto said in mock seriousness. Napoleon huffed under the table, still curled in his frightened ball.

Malvina shook her head solemnly, still committed to the scry. 'No, laddie. Not canine armpits or leg-pits. But... whatever it is... it will change *everything*.'

'Curried artichokes? A cuddly... Alaskan?' said Augusto, pinching his chin in silliness. Opal guffawed silently into her palm.

Malvina was visibly ruffled by his facetious suggestions and snapped out of her trance. Her pupils seemed to constrict back to normal size as she pushed the water bowl aside. Opal knew in her bones, if there was any credibility at all to the water scry, the C & A must be Countess Angelina, but there was no way she was going to say it out loud and let Augusto know how much the woman played on her mind. She'd had enough hocus pocus for one morning anyway.

'Let us go and collect references now, Augusto,' she said with a sigh and picked up Napoleon's lead. 'Thank you kindly for the water scrying, Malvina. It was truly fascinating and an experience I shall never forget.'

'Will you do your best to help Seraphina, lassie?' the seer asked, seeming suddenly sad.

'Of course I will. I am set on it.' Opal smiled kindly. 'Good-bye, Malvina. Goodbye, little Morag.'

TWENTY-NINE
OCH AYE THE HOOF

Napoleon was exceedingly happy to be out of the crone's hollow and was back on trotting form. Soaking up the oohs and aahs Augusto received from the locals around the chilly but charming hamlet of Dunvaloch, they made their calls. The pharmacist and banker knew exactly who Opal was talking about when she described the lady with only one front tooth who couldn't read and always talked about the star formations and gave them tips on the weather that always turned out to be correct.

On the corner of the village was a little barber's shop, poky with only two sinks and chairs. Inside was the skipper who drove the mail boat to St Kessog's. He was having his face shaved, and Clyde, his son, was waiting outside, scuffing his feet with his hands in his pockets, staring at something in the window.

It was a racing newspaper propped up against the glass, open at the page for the odds for the next upcoming race on Rothesay Common.

'Good morning, Clyde,' said Opal and joined him in gazing at the horse racing paper. 'I say! What a gas some of the names are! Och Aye the Hoof, Wee Scunner, Neeps 'n' Tatties.'

'Lang Legged Lassie is the one apparently,' he said, looking at the notebook in the barber's back pocket that had various names and odds scribbled on it. He pressed his nose on the glass; it was pretty evident he wanted to bet on that horse.

Opal shot Augusto a side-eye, and he raised his eyebrows. Opal sighed as she knew it was beneath her, but it was the only leverage she had.

'Aside from being highly illegal,' said Opal. 'What's stopping you from making a bet?'

'I'm too young,' he said. 'Father is very religious and won't stake me either.'

'Well,' said Opal, leaning on the glass and folding her arms. 'I too heard that Long Legged Lassie is the *one*. At the ball the other night, they were *all* talking about it. Very good odds to boot. But, of course, being the daughter of a baron, I wouldn't dare get involved in such low pursuits.'

Clyde looked at Opal as if she was cruelly wafting cash about his nose.

Opal looked up at Augusto. 'But my protection officer here could stake you,' she said and winked up at him. Augusto rolled his brown eyes.

'First...' Opal said, blocking the barber's entrance with a swooping arm, 'you're going to tell me *exactly* what favour Seraphina Serle asked of you.'

Clyde looked utterly torn. He breathed out a dragon of condensation and shifted from foot to foot.

'She came to the dock and handed me a great deal of money. She wanted me to play "The Twa Corbies" tune on the pipes from a cliff. There's a spot in front of the giant rock to amplify the sound so it comes into the castle. It was behind a tree so that I was concealed.'

Opal's mouth fell open.

Clyde continued and looked at his feet. 'She said to start at three thirty a.m. on the dot and to stop once I'd seen a person pass the last window before the top of the tower. Then to run home. She said she'd have more jobs for me in future, but not to tell a soul.'

Opal's head felt like it had been clanged with an iron. *Seraphina was involved after all? And there truly was nobody in the tower! It was simply the sound of bagpipes being directed from the cliffs in the wind. The flag had been prepared and wrapped around the tower to create a sound funnel to send the sound down the stairwell. The set of pipes placed on the floor was a subterfuge.*

But Opal still had a niggling feeling Seraphina couldn't have planned all this. She didn't know how to read, so what were the odds that she understood enough physics to redirect sound this way? Opal knew what to ask.

'Did the person who spoke to you only have one front tooth?' asked Opal, taking his shoulders and looking at him firmly in the eyes.

'I don't know, she was in a cloak. The hood was covering the face,' said Clyde, shaking his head with his shoulders up at his ears.

'Tall?'

'Yes, tall and broad.'

'Voice and accent?'

'Old lady like, sort of... squeaky. Strong Highland accent.'

Suddenly, footsteps clip-clopped up the pavement and interrupted them. It was Mr Finlay Roberts, walking with purpose but somewhat glumly.

'Morning all,' he said. 'Not in the queue to get the chop, are you, Augusto?'

'No, no,' Augusto said, stepping aside.

'Ah, the skipper got there first,' he said, glancing through the window. 'Can't quite believe I'm at the barber's for Sir Seamus's funeral. Like a father to me that man was.' He sadly ran his hand through his hair, and his gold signet ring glinted in the winter sun.

Augusto and Clyde uttered a few nervous words of consolation to Mr Roberts while Opal's mind unscrambled what Clyde had told her a few minutes earlier. She just could not understand the flip in the narrative.

This simply cannot be! Was it Seraphina after all? She nudged Augusto and tugged on Napoleon's lead; she simply must inform Detective Inspector Sinclair of everything she'd learned.

THIRTY

FUNEREAL FOLIAGE

Shaking the snowflakes off her hat at Dunvaloch Castle, Opal was disappointed to hear McWatt tell her that Detective Inspector Sinclair had already departed for Edinburgh. Opal was then told to join everyone after lunch in the drawing room, for Lady Blair had a request. Opal couldn't help but notice the air inside the castle felt more tranquil now that the '*witch*' had been removed, and the inhabitants seemed to breathe a little slower now they assumed the killer had been caught.

Lady Viola Blair and Mr Finlay Roberts declared that everyone would, as a group, fetch foliage from Sir Seamus's favourite tree. It was in preparation for his funeral, so that it could be laid on his coffin and decorate the pews and hang from the pulpit. Lady Blair was terribly emotional about it and was insistent on it. She tossed out all suggestions Lady Phyllis Laplume made about getting a florist in Edinburgh to source the same flora there. No, no, it must be Sir Seamus's special pine. It was imperative they bring a piece of Dunvaloch Estate with them to forge a proper farewell.

Lady Blair explained that the late Sir Seamus's favourite falcon, Maisie – who would also be brought to Edinburgh for the funeral – loved this particular Scots pine which she always sat atop. Sir Seamus used to come and sit on his bench and gaze at the little 'crannog', the small island he had built for wildlife in the centre of the loch. He'd watch Maisie soar around it and dive for prey. He would sometimes sail up to his pine and sit under it to fish. His 'Serene Tree', he named it.

There was, however, one obstacle to getting to said tree: the ice. It was thick and almost permanent-looking, bright white and perfect. It was just asking for ice skates to glide upon it, as smooth as a knife icing a cake.

Under the shelf of wellies in the boot room was a trunk that housed all manner of skates, and Opal selected a simply ripping red pair in her size. She'd skated many times growing up at Copperfields Hall so was a fair hand on the ice. Joining her was Lord Laplume, Mr Roberts, Turkey and Clyde. The latter had been roped in to help at the last minute.

Lady Phyllis Laplume and Lady Viola Blair insisted they would watch from the bank and direct which cuttings to take. Augusto made the excuse that he was better equipped to help if there were any accidents, if he was on the bank. But Opal could tell it was a cover-up for him not being confident on skates. Augusto waited behind with the ladies, who included, to Opal's annoyance, Countess Angelina. They were chatting away about some guff, but Opal did her best to ignore them and placed one foot on the ice, muff held abreast as she pushed out.

'I say, the ice is excellent. It's like flying,' Opal said, feeling a childish rush. 'While vertical, if you know what I mean.'

'The lake is so perfect for curling, it's such a shame we didn't get to play,' said Cecil Turks-Leyton as he smoothly slid onto the white sheet next to her.

'I daresay it would have been a little inappropriate to engage in such blithe pursuits after a double murder,' said Opal and skated right past his hand that was trying to hold hers.

'Slow down, Miss Laplume,' said Cecil. 'If you fall, I won't be able to catch you.'

'That's jolly decent of you to care, Turkey, but I'm a competent skater and I have a protection officer for anything of that nature,' called Opal, her voice echoing among the mountains.

'Not as good as your papa though, eh?' said Lord Laplume, whizzing past her with Mr Roberts close behind him.

They made it to the little crannog and Sir Seamus's 'Serene Tree'. The twelve-foot pine was indeed very calm. A soft rustling sound brushing through its green mane and you could almost feel Sir Seamus's presence. Maisie, who had been let out earlier, came and landed on it as if perching on her master's shoulder.

'Oh, there's Maisie, our little cherub,' called out Lady Blair when she saw the bird, and then made a faint weeping noise.

Opal noticed Clyde had only just stepped out on the ice. His skates were making a scraping sound a bit like chalk down a blackboard, and he was wobbling terribly to try and keep his balance.

'These ice skates are terrible,' he groaned, as one of his feet seemed to get stuck in a groove he'd made. He tried to pull his foot out by pulling his knee with both hands.

His face went red with both embarrassment and exertion as he was determined not to ask for help. Opal put the branches she'd picked down and prepared to skate over to help him.

He started to lean his weight onto his front toe and wriggle. But there came then an almighty sound.

Craaacccckkkk.

The mountains and all creatures seemed to hold their breath and watch Clyde.

Craaaaaack. Craaaaack. Craaaaaaccccckkkkkkkk.

Four great forked splits in the ice spread out from his heel.

Clyde's eyes wavered with terror.

'Slowly bend and lie out flat on the ice!' yelled Lord Laplume. 'You need to spread out your weight!'

Clyde began to crouch but the ice could not hold. There came a sound like a lightning bolt cutting through the sky and Clyde went down into the loch. Water splashed upwards and Clyde yelled like a small child. His arms flailed in the air and scrambled at the ice for something to grab onto. A triangular chunk broke off in his hand and his head submerged into the dark water. All Opal could see now was a black jagged shape like a deformed star and Clyde's flat cap and nose bobbing up every so often to catch a sip of air.

The ladies on the bank screamed and held onto each other and Countess Angelina ran back towards the thicket. Was she intending to help? Augusto hesitated, feet planted wide apart, about to follow her but then decided to run off in a completely different direction.

'Saints preserve us!' stammered Turkey, pathetically clutching a tree branch in terror.

Mr Roberts pulled up his sleeves and skated towards Clyde as fast as he could. Opal clenched her toes hard, in fear that he, too, would go under. Mr Roberts dived onto his tummy when he was about five feet away from the hole. Then he began to crawl slowly as flat to the ice as he could to create as much surface area as possible.

He might not be able to pull Clyde out alone! thought Opal in a panic. *Every moment we waste, Clyde could lose consciousness or be swept away under the ice by the current.* Driven by sheer panic, Opal went to put her foot on the ice to skate to the rescue.

'No!' said Opal's father sternly and placed a hand on her shoulder. 'If you go under too, I'll never forgive myself.'

'We can't just stand here while Clyde is drowning!' yelled Opal, shaking all over, listening to the frantic splashes and gasps coming from the hole.

'Mr Roberts is his best hope. Augusto, I assume, has gone to fetch help too. But we can at least try to break off the biggest branch we can find to assist them,' Lord Laplume said.

They got to work, Lord Laplume using his skate as an axe to chop at the wood, and Opal leant over it with all her weight on her tummy to help make it snap. She looked over her shoulder at how Mr Roberts was getting on.

He had almost reached Clyde. On the bank, Angelina had returned with a large branch she'd found, but it was quite thin at the end and sprouting with little twigs. She lay at the edge of the loch and slapped the long branch down over Clyde's jagged hole. He had just spluttered up for a breath and Angelina's branch had smacked him on the head and pushed him under.

Surely that was an accident! Opal thought. *Why would Countess Angelina want to hurt Clyde?*

'Oh, no, no, I am so sorry!' the countess screamed.

Clyde's hands shot up into the air in an effort to grab onto the branch, but with a devastating crack, it snapped off.

'The branch isn't good enough, I'm sorry!' Angelina called out, flailing the broken branch back and forth, but it was now too short to reach his hands.

Mr Roberts had now reached the boy and grabbed one of his hands. He reached into the water with his other hand, presumably to try and grab onto the boy's jacket and yank him out, but it was taking longer than expected.

'He's gone under!' Mr Roberts bellowed.

'Don't let go of his hand!' Lady Laplume screamed.

Mr Roberts held on, but his arm was sucked forward into the water, now up to his shoulder. Opal and her father tried their best to snap off the large branch. With one last whack of the skate, Lord Laplume managed to chop it off. He then lobbed the thing as far as he could along the ice to get it in the grasp of Mr Roberts.

'If I reach for the branch, I'll have to let go of his hand!' shouted Mr Roberts.

'Go on, Papa. You'll have to skate to them as the branch isn't close enough!' Opal urged.

'My weight, along with Mr Robert's, the ice might not stand it. We might *all* go under,' Lord Laplume whispered to Opal in frustration and fear. Opal had never seen him so frightened.

'I can't hold him much longer. He's getting sucked away,' shouted Mr Roberts.

Opal's heart thudded as the falconer let go of the boy and pulled his dripping arm out of the black chasm. Opal pressed her hands to her chest, imagining poor Clyde being dragged into the freezing blackness with no oxygen, trapped under a ceiling of icy death.

Mr Roberts scrambled for the branch that the Laplumes had hurled to him. He then shoved it down the hole to see if Clyde would take hold.

'The housekeeper is calling for the fire brigade and doctor!' shouted Augusto, pounding towards them like a horse, wielding a great pickaxe. He was followed by a couple of servants with blankets and hot flasks.

'He's gone under! Augusto, help us!' shouted Lady Laplume.

'Which way is the current travelling?' Augusto yelled.

'He was sucked in that direction!' shouted Countess Angelina, pointing anticlockwise around the edge of the loch with a shaking finger.

Augusto had thought far ahead in bringing the pickaxe and ropes looped around his shoulder. He started to swing and bring the great thing down upon the solid white floor as if cracking marble. Of course, there was a risk he would impale Clyde, but it was either that or the boy would drown anyway. He heaved the pickaxe back and brought up great triangular slabs of ice with it. He carried on two yards up and two yards up again.

'Stand at the holes!' he instructed the women, tossing them ropes. 'If he slides past, we can throw him the rope.'

'He won't be breathing by now,' Lady Laplume cried. 'The poor boy is surely unconscious if not...' She clearly couldn't bring herself to say 'dead'.

Yet Augusto kept smashing rescue holes around the edge. The loch was big enough for the cracks not to destroy the Laplumes' way back off the crannog. They skated back to the opposite side of the loch, took off their skates and dashed around to the others. Mr Roberts, by now, had also crawled to safety and sat blowing into his hands that were purple with cold. A servant threw a blanket over his shoulders.

'Look!' shouted Lady Laplume, pointing across the loch. 'Clyde's hand!'

A deathly-white hand popped up limply inside one of the holes. The current slowly pulled Clyde through, first his arm, then his white face, staring blankly and bloodshot up at the sky, bobbing up and down through the surface. From that far distance, Opal could not tell if he was conscious or breathing.

Opal let out a scream. She couldn't help it. Augusto and Lord Laplume dragged Clyde out of the water under his arms and laid him up on the bank.

'The Schafer method!' said Lord Laplume. 'We need to expel the water from his lungs.'

He bundled a blanket up and dropped it on the grass. He then rolled Clyde's body face down with his chest over the blanket for padding. His face was turned to the side. Lord Laplume then knelt either side of the boy and pressed his hands down on the base of the young man's back in an effort to force the water out of him.

Angelina and Lady Blair knelt and rubbed the boy's hands to try to bring some colour back.

Suddenly, a slight cough and gargling sound came. *Thank God,* Opal thought.

But then there came a splutter and pink froth emerged from Clyde's mouth.

'I think... I think he's breathing again... very faintly,' said Lord Laplume, his ear to the boy's mouth. 'Get him inside to the warmth of a fire!'

They rolled him in the blanket, and Augusto heaved him over his shoulder in a fireman's lift and ambled as fast as he could into the castle. The closest fireside was in the kitchens, which was where they took him.

Opal helped undress Clyde at the fireside with Angelina and Lady Laplume, while everyone dashed about fetching things that could possibly be of assistance.

'Clyde, Clyde, can you hear us?' Opal said to him.

He just stared blankly at the ceiling like a caught fish, his breath so shallow it probably wouldn't be enough to keep a baby alive.

The bell out in the gatehouse rang, and Lord Laplume raced out to see if it was the doctor.

Come on, come on, Clyde, breathe properly, Opal inwardly begged. She then noticed something queer when she was untying Clyde's ice skates. She was holding the blade with one hand to keep it steady while the other hand undid the laces. She felt a sharp pricking sensation and had to take her hand away. There was the thinnest of cuts on her palm. The skate's metal blades were extremely sharp! Someone had sharpened them! Was this the reason the ice cracked?

THIRTY-ONE
THE BOOT ROOM

Opal silently held her cut palm and looked around at everyone busily trying to revive poor Clyde. Opal didn't know whether to speak out or not. She didn't know who she could trust in this room. She would tell her parents, Augusto and the detective later.

'I'm going to put the skates back into the boot room,' said Opal and stood up, cradling them in her arms.

Angelina rubbed and patted the boy's blue feet.

'This castle is cursed,' said Lady Blair, staring down at him blankly. 'A dark shadow has swallowed us. Perhaps Seraphina was right, and this is Euphemia's revenge.'

'Why would Euphemia want revenge on poor Clyde?' asked Opal.

'Perhaps she's just cursed the entire estate?' said Lady Blair, swaying slightly. She looked up at the ceiling and through it as if trying to peer into another world. Her shoulders shot up violently when Lord Laplume burst back into the room.

'It was the confounded fire brigade,' said Lord Laplume puffing. 'I sent them away. We need the doctor immediately.'

'I'll ring again,' said the cook, 'but he should be on his way.'

Opal snuck out with the skates while the commotion was going on. She made her way to the boot room where she could have a good inspection of the blades. She sat on the trunk and brought them close to her eyes.

It was undoubtedly meddled with. The metal was clearly filed down. Opal wondered who had given this pair for Clyde to put on. Perhaps it had been Lady Blair? It had been her idea to fetch the foliage. Hopefully, poor Clyde would survive and be able to tell her.

She placed them down inside the trunk and tilted her head.

Would she need the skating blades as evidence? There was a little skate-upkeep kit in a leather case in the corner of the trunk. It included a screwdriver. Opal got to work unscrewing one of the blades from one of the boots. Her fingers stopped twisting when she noticed one of the screws was odd. They were all silver with the Phillips insert, but one of them was brass coloured with a tiny number three stamped on the corner. Must be the size of the screw? But why was it different to the others? She checked the other skate. No, only one odd screw.

She wrapped the blade and screws she'd dismantled into her hanky and stuffed it deep inside her coat pocket.

On the way back to the kitchens to help Clyde, Opal heard the doorbell clang. *Oh, praise the heavens, it must be the doctor.* She made a beeline for the front door and hurried the doctor along with his bag to where Clyde was lying.

The doctor whipped out his stethoscope and thermometer and went to work with swift and purposeful gestures. The servants, along with Mr Roberts, Turkey, Lady Blair, Countess Angelina, Augusto and the Laplumes stepped back and held their breath. He then pulled the stethoscope out of his ears.

'He's not dead,' he said in a low voice. 'But not exactly revived yet either. His breathing is so terribly weak. His temperature is too low. All you can do is keep him warm and watch for if his eyes make a flicker of sense. If his brain's been starved of oxygen for too long, he may never wake properly. Or if he does, he may not be the same boy you knew.'

'Oh, please God help him,' said Opal, clasping her hands together. Napoleon whimpered and nudged his nose against the boy's arm. Clyde continued to have the look of a glassy-eyed doll.

'What a wretched day!' wept Lady Blair into her hands.

'You must go and bury your husband, Lady Blair,' said the housekeeper, Mrs Keith. 'You have a lot to arrange. I will look after Clyde, and his parents will be here soon.'

'It's just so God awful,' said Mr Roberts, knocking back the hot toddy he'd been given and flexing the fingers of his frozen arm.

Opal couldn't bear to be in that room any longer. She felt like her nerves might snap and she would become a crumpled mess on the floor. She picked up Napoleon, slumped him over her shoulder and dashed out, pressing her face into his fur.

If someone has done this to Clyde, she must find out who it was. It is unforgivable to take the life away from someone so young.

But then again, he had played the bagpipes, which got him mixed up in all of this. He may have known who the real killer of Sir Seamus and Mr Martindale was. Was this the reason he had to go?

She dashed past the pantry and out into the inner court-yard, adrenaline pulsing through her veins. She placed Napoleon down and aggressively parted the tablecloths that were hanging from washing lines so she could get through to the other side. She had no idea where she was going, but she just had to get away. Throwing her back up against an outbuilding and breathing heavily, she dug her hands into her hair to try to stimulate some brain function.

Napoleon looked up at her in concern and brushed at her leg with a paw. Opal simply looked at him through a gap in her fingers and was unresponsive. He seemed to take it upon himself to do some detection work for her, since she was out of action, and began to explore the yard. His pom-pom tail was erect, in detection mode. It quivered uneasily when it heard the neigh of a horse. Perhaps he was edging close to the stables? He lifted a paw considering whether he was brave enough to venture where beasts did not speak his language and wore metal kicking armour on their feet. Their size did not seem to bother him, as Napoleon was unaware of how small he really was.

Opal watched him take tentative steps on the damp cobbles and decided to follow him... perhaps seeing if the calm beauties would enable her to think better. She followed the scent of straw and found it strangely comforting. A reminder of her childhood surroundings in Suffolk. Something made her scuff to a halt in the dust.

There was a blacksmith's forge to her left: a low, soot-blackened structure with an open front, where a certain warmth was emanating from. Opal entered with light steps, a hand held outwards. Just along the forge wall was a grinding wheel... worn from use, mounted to a wooden frame, and spun by a treadle.

Opal remembered the groundskeeper on her childhood estate, Copperfields, sharpening shears on it with a miserable scowl on his face and a broken cigar in his mouth. This thing was most certainly for sharpening metal.

Finding out if it was used to sharpen Clyde's skate could prove difficult though. If there was a blacksmith about, perhaps he was asked to do it or knew who'd used his grinding wheel...

THIRTY-TWO
THE BRASS SCREW CLUE

Napoleon dashed in after Opal, making her jump. He began to sniff up at a workbench as if it might, on the off chance, be presenting a chicken wing. But he clearly smelt nothing but greasy tools and hopped back down to the ground with a huff. Opal's eyes pulsed wide... she'd seen a jar of brass screws amongst the items.

Examining the jar, she noted they did indeed match the one she found in the skate, and what's more... twinkling at her like a silver fish darting amongst a school of goldfish... was a single silver screw. She sprinkled them out onto the workbench.

A shadow darkened the entrance and blocked the light on the workbench. Napoleon barked. It was Mrs Keith, smoking and looking stern.

'What brings you in here? I thought you were helping us with the poor laddie.'

'Oh, do forgive me, Mrs Keith. My nerves were dangling by a thread and I thought it best I not cause any hysteria. It can be contagious, you know. I was just taking a look at the forge. Reminds me of home.'

'I needed a moment too, so I came out for a smoke,' she said, numb with shock. 'What's that on the bench?'

Opal swallowed. Should she let on that she knew someone had sharpened Clyde's skate blade? She couldn't tell from her shaded face whether Mrs Keith looked angry or was curious. Perhaps she should keep it to herself and just ask what she really wanted to know.

'Who uses the grinding wheel?' Opal asked, tossing her chin in the direction of the thing.

Mrs Keith exhaled smoke as if to scoff, and said in an irritated tone, 'The only one who uses it nowadays is the stable boy for the horseshoes, it's rather obsolete other than that. Why?'

'When did he last use it?' Opal asked.

'I don't know, Miss Laplume,' said Mrs Keith, holding a hand to her head as if nursing a headache. 'It was making a racket early this morning. I assume he was using it then.'

'Where is he now?' asked Opal.

'Not here. He left late morning to go back home. Lady Blair won't need him while she's in Edinburgh for the funeral. The groundsman will tend to the horses for a few days.' Mrs Keith, stamping on her cigarette. 'I better get back to poor wee Clyde. You'll need to get ready to leave for Edinburgh soon. I'd avoid coming through the kitchens as it is a desperately sad scene.'

'Oh, is... is Clyde still alive?' Opal said in sudden panic.

'Yes... just... at the moment anyway.' Mrs Keith's voice broke in distress, and she vanished behind a billowing washing line.

Opal breathed a sigh of relief and went into the stables. The sight of the four calm chestnut Clydesdale horses was the only thing that stopped her from crying. There were four in a row, stocky as anything, munching hay and making puffing noises. Their names were on plaques for their particular stalls – Torin, Lachlan, Rory and Struan. They were all facing away from Opal, munching in their troughs.

Perhaps if I could see the underside of their hooves, I could tell if the stable boy had changed any of their horseshoes this morning, Opal thought. If they were bright, clean metal with sharp nail ends, then we'd know it was the stable boy who'd used the grinder.

Opal leant over the wooden beam. *How on earth am I going to see their feet? Put on a ragtime record and watch them do a jig?* Opal thought bitterly.

She looked down at Napoleon and considered braving the castle again. Napoleon looked at the horses' hooves and back up at Opal. Then, with his tongue flopping out in smug ingenuity, he trotted inside under the gate and into their pen.

'Napoleon,' Opal hissed. 'Come out! You could scare them and they could kick you from here back to the Laplume millinery shop!'

Napoleon ignored her. It seemed he was the one who was going to do the jig! He paused with a hesitant limp paw, then wiggled his pom-pom tail to rev up encouragement. Then he did a kind of Crufts weave in and out of the horses' legs. One by one they neighed and picked up their hooves to dodge him in mild irritation from being interrupted in munching. Opal gasped in horror and held in the air she'd gasped.

'Stop!'

But wait... she knew what he was doing. She could now see the underside of the horses' hooves. Each one of them as they flipped up to avoid the tiny mutt.

Opal could clearly see that the horseshoes were well worn, tarnished with grown-out nail holes. Certainly not freshly done. They had not had their manicures yet. *Aha! It must have been someone else on that grinding wheel this morning, not the stable boy.*

Napoleon came out of the stalls, smiling up at Opal, showing all his teeth and pink tongue. She picked him up in case he put himself in danger again.

'Well, Napoleon, we've eliminated the doubt. We just need to find out who truly *did* sharpen the skate. We have to leave for Edinburgh shortly, but I will bring the evidence to confer with Detective Inspector Sinclair.'

THIRTY-THREE
EDINBURGH BOUND

The sea lapped up against the sides of the vessel and was the only sound to be heard. Lady Viola Blair, the Laplumes, Mr Finlay Roberts, Countess Angelina, Cecil Turks-Leyton, Effie and Augusto were speechless on the ferry across to the mainland. It seemed inappropriate to make any trivial comment about the water or any mundane conversation, but then it was too excruciating and maudlin to bring up Clyde. Besides, the trip's purpose was to lay the recently deceased Sir Seamus to rest, so for Lady Blair's sake, it was pertinent to focus on that if anything.

The verbal void was even more deafening in their compartment on the train to Edinburgh. The only sound was a couple of coughs from Turkey, the page turns of a book from Countess Angelina and whimpers from Lady Blair. It made it easy for Opal to keep shtum about the malicious ice skate because there was never a moment she was not around people she suspected.

On arrival in the misty city of Edinburgh, the Laplumes and Augusto took a Rolls-Royce to the Northbridge Grand Hotel. Finally, Opal could spill the beans. They were completely incredulous that Clyde was deliberately harmed. Appalled to boot. Who on earth would want to hurt such a young man like that? Lord Laplume suggested that the skate blades were simply a modern design. New innovations had all kinds of defects nowadays and it was never a surprise when something ended up breaking or hurting someone. But when Opal pulled the metallic evidence out of her pocket and splayed it on her palm, screws and all, the unanimous decision was that the ice skate had indeed been tampered with.

Once in her room, despite being late at night, Opal called for Detective Inspector Sinclair. It was too important to wait. They sat in the sitting area of the suite, and she watched him smoke his pipe as they touched base.

'I have a veritable *hoard* of evidence for you, Detective Inspector Sinclair.'

On the table, she poured out the fruits of her sleuthing labour: Seraphina's medicine bottle with the diagrams proving she couldn't read, the testimonies proving Seraphina's illiteracy from the bank and chemist, the macramé cord and thread from the tower and the sharpened skate blade and screws.

She went on to explain to him the tragic events of this afternoon with Clyde and how she was certain it was foul play.

Sinclair picked up the ice-skate blade and examined it close to his eye. 'That is some fine workmanship,' he said, shaking his head gravely. 'I don't see why anyone would do this unless it was to make it dangerous for the person wearing them.'

Opal then showed him the mismatched brass screw.

'There was a jar of these exact screws in the blacksmith's workshop at Dunvaloch Castle, and mixed in with them, an original silver one. Whoever sharpened them did so there with the tools.'

'We can deduce that Clyde knew or witnessed something that he had to be silenced for?'

'Yes,' said Opal. 'And Countess Angelina whacked him on the head with a branch when attempting to save him with it.

Seems a little suspicious to me. If she is a friend of the Parisian textile company that the gentlemen fought with, then she would have a motive for both Sir Seamus and Mr Martindale to be killed.'

'We must both keep an eye on her. I'm sure, if she is guilty, she may slip up during funeral events,' said Detective Inspector Sinclair, like he had seen it a thousand times. 'These things tend to make murderers nervous. A funeral for the victim of a killer is like the play commencing for a playwright. Nerve-racking and emotive.'

THIRTY-FOUR

IN SEARCH OF SOMETHING TASTEFULLY BLACK

In the morning, Lady Viola Blair left to make the last-minute funeral arrangements with the undertaker to finalise the coffin, and with the officiating clergyman to discuss the service. The funeral was to be held at the University Chapel at Edinburgh University, and her husband would be buried in the Dean Cemetery. Lord Edmund Laplume assisted her. Cecil Turks-Leyton and his new pal, Mr Finlay Roberts, went to the Royal Scots Club.

'What a conundrum!' Lady Phyllis Laplume's voice flew around the hotel foyer like a trapped hawk. The concierge she was yelling at evidently found it far too shrill for eight o'clock in the morning, and his eyelids flapped backwards.

'What is it, Mother?' Opal said, clacking down the stairs leading to the foyer, although not too quickly, as she was used to her mother's dramatics. There was a fifty per cent chance it would be utterly trivial.

Napoleon scrabbled ahead and sat at Lady Laplume's feet, his pom-pom tail standing to attention like a black lollipop, ready to hear the outrageous news.

'The trunk with our Laplume funeral hats from London

hasn't arrived this morning. This is my lesson to *always* bring a black hat wherever I travel, you never know when someone will spontaneously *vamoose* from the party of life.'

'It's a little inconvenient about the hats, but we have far bigger things to be in a flap over... like worrying about who has been bumping everyone off!' Opal retorted.

'Opal Marion Laplume. I'm in the millinery business, and funerals are the marquee occasion for us. I can't have any other milliner beating me to the punch. There are rumours that royalty may be there, Princess Marina. I cannot miss the chance to get a princess interested in Laplume Millinery. I shall never forgive myself if this opportunity passes me by.'

'It's too late, Mother. We shall simply have to buy some hats this morning. You will have many other opportunities; Ascot 1935 is just around the corner.'

Lady Phyllis Laplume sank her face into her hands.

'Come along with me,' butted in Countess Angelina's irritatingly sweet voice. 'I, too, did not bring anything black, and I may need your assistance in understanding the Scottish shopkeepers. The accents here really are something. It's like aliens trying to understand each other, them and I.'

'I think that is our only option, Countess,' said Lady Laplume, happy to take the advice of a countess over her daughter's. 'Thank you, though we only have a few hours.'

'We will try Jenners Department Store, the Royal Mile and George Street boutiques, they must have something suitable. Come on, Augusto,' said Angelina.

Opal felt quite unsettled by the way Angelina spoke to Augusto with such familiarity. After all, he was her protection officer and Napoleon's trusted marshal. It ruffled her feathers to think Angelina was taking such a fancy to him.

. . .

The mourning-attire section in the department store gave off a hushed reverence, as if every hatstand had just received bad news. Each mannequin frozen in a solemn restraint. But, Opal had to admit, with *simply ripping* black outfits on. Waiting for her mother to choose her headwear, Opal couldn't help but smirk. Every so often, Napoleon would jump up and scrabble his pom-pom paws at the glass of the window from the outside. He was excited by the feather in Lady Laplume's cloche as she swished her head back and forth. But she was scrutinising every angle of it with flared nostrils of distaste.

'It's got such a wide brim,' complained Lady Laplume.

Opal tried to explain that this was à la mode and that the Laplume millinery shop in London should be following suit, but her mother wouldn't listen until Countess Angelina confirmed this.

'I'd only just got used to brims shrinking and all but disappearing, and now the brims are on their way back to a width only seen in the Belle Époque.'

'I would like to try this,' said Angelina to the assistant, pointing to a black lace, drop-waist dress with a black sable collar, covered buttons and cuffs.

Opal watched as the assistant hung Angelina's coat and bag on a hook and took her behind the velvet curtain. Opal then inched towards the bag, pretending to inspect the glove stand beside it. How could she go through the pockets without anyone noticing?

'Mother...' Opal said, pretending to squint out of the window. 'Is that Papa across the street having a verbal joust with a clergyman?' The little fib immediately had Lady Laplume darting to the window.

'What?' she said and plastered her face up at the glass. The other shop assistant and ladies followed suit. 'Where? What on earth is he playing at?'

Opal fished inside Angelina's bag and plucked out a couple of small books. One of them appeared to be a ledger.

'Mama, they were outside the tobacconists, hats removed and jabbing fingers,' Opal said as she thumbed through the financial notebook.

'I can't see, there's so many confounded people,' Lady Laplume said, bobbing up and down on tiptoes.

With Opal's rather decent French language skills, she could make out the gist of Angelina's latest tab on her investment portfolio.

27th December 1934 Astonishing development: **Société des Tissus Parisiens** declared an extraordinary dividend of 12%, up from 4.5% last quarter. Word is they've secured an exclusive supply contract for Scottish tweed fabrics with several government ministries. Immediate implications for the European textile market. Must consider acquiring additional shares before word spreads too far.

Aha! Proof that Angelina did hold shares with Société des Tissus Parisiens, the very same company that was trying to sue Sir Seamus over a tweed loom patent. Opal noted they have done astonishingly well since his death. Was Countess Angelina some sort of assassin for them? She stuffed the notebook back into the countess's bag and scurried over to her mother at the window, who was about to dash onto the street with the unpaid-for hat still upon her head.

'Oh no, sorry, it wasn't Papa. I must have been mistaken,' Opal said quickly.

'My dear girl, I thought you had binoculars for eyes. They seem to be malfunctioning.'

Countess Angelina came out in her black frock and looked just like an illustration from a Parisian magazine. Opal eyed her up and down as you would a traitor of the state. Countess

Angelina tweaked her cuffs in the full-length mirror, and Opal glanced outside into the street. Augusto was waiting out there, cigarillo dangling from his lips, holding Napoleon and smiling at Angelina in her dress.

This is unbearable. Opal gritted her teeth. *Not only is she possibly a murderess, but she is also a temptress who is taking my sweetheart away.* Opal glanced back into the stand-alone mirror over Countess Angelina's shoulder and examined her own dress choice in comparison. Was she dressing too young? She was coming up to twenty-three, and perhaps she should be giving a shade more Riviera and a dash less schoolgirl fête.

The ladies purchased their ensembles and headed down the arcade to source some respectful jewellery. Lady Laplume examined some strings of jet beads in Hamilton & Inches jewellers. Opal was trying to think how to bring up Clyde's drowning incident with the countess, who was eyeing up jewels from the outside window.

'I do hope we won't have to wear these jewels back in Dunvaloch for a funeral for Clyde,' said Opal. 'The poor darling, I must call the castle later to see if he is pulling through.'

'Yes,' said Countess Angelina. 'If only we'd got him out of the water sooner.'

'Well, you tried your best with that branch,' said Opal. 'Shame it knocked him under again.'

The countess's hands that were splayed on the window stiffened, and only her eyes turned to Opal. 'He was bobbing up and down under the surface anyway. I didn't cause any further harm. It was just very bad luck that he came up where I was bringing the branch down.'

'Indeed,' said Opal. 'Very bad luck.'

Angelina narrowed her eyes. 'I don't recall you trying to help him.'

Opal batted her lids in surprise. 'Papa and I were trying to acquire a strong branch. We were too late, but we were trying.'

'Indeed. You failed on the time front, and I failed on the strength of branch.' Angelina looked up at Augusto, seemingly for moral support.

'I think we all tried our best during a very fast and delicate situation,' said Augusto, trying to diffuse.

'A delicate *accident*,' said Countess Angelina, emphasising the last word. She then jabbed her finger at an onyx cluster brooch dotted with seed pearls. 'If you'll excuse me, I'm going inside to enquire.'

'But it wasn't an accident, Countess Angelina,' said Opal.

'What are you suggesting?' Angelina halted in the doorway of the jewellers and snapped her head back. 'I did not hit him with that stick on purpose!'

'It's not the branch I'm talking about,' Opal said. 'Somebody had sharpened Clyde's skating blades. They were cutting into the ice with their razor surface area, making him get stuck in the groove and kick, making the ice weaken further.'

'Who would want to kill little Clyde?' whispered Countess Angelina, stepping back outside to hear more.

'I don't know. Perhaps he saw or did something he shouldn't have.'

Countess Angelina looked around and continued to whisper.

'I am a little scared for my own life. I, too, have seen things I shouldn't have.'

THIRTY-FIVE

'What?' asked Opal, flabbergasted.

'The lady of the house,' Countess Angelina whispered, 'the lady of Dunvaloch Castle. She has a gentleman caller.'

'This is no secret. I've seen it too, and Sir Seamus publicly mocked her for it,' said Opal, disappointed that she didn't have anything juicier.

'But if Lady Viola Blair was behind the murders,' said Countess Angelina vehemently, 'she's now free to pursue whatever dreamboat she wants. Perhaps she had to be swift if Sir Seamus was to change his will or divorce her... hence why the lawyer had to die too. She got that sycophantic butler of hers to help her.'

'I thought McWatt was more sycophantic towards Sir Seamus than Lady Blair.'

'You're right. But perhaps Lady Blair's reward to him for involvement was more appealing than that inheritance of the paintings he was promised.' The countess shrugged.

'You think the lady and the butler are behind it all?' Opal said, raising both brows, and she felt her inner sleuthing compass start to twitch.

'Yes... and perhaps that young lapdog of hers. He'd be set to benefit, wouldn't he if he moved in and curled up on Sir Seamus's armchair.'

'Is this the gentleman you saw dancing with Lady Blair on Christmas Eve?' asked Opal, giving Augusto a quick side-eye. 'The one you two were laughing about, who'd *muddled the energy of his hips?*'

'It must be,' whispered the countess.

Opal folded her arms and flicked her up and down with her lashes. Of course she would try and palm it off on someone else... even Lady Blair, who'd been so kind as to have her stay for Christmas.

'McWatt seemed to think you benefitted from Sir Seamus and Mr Martindale's demise. That Parisian weaving company you invest in have been after Sir Seamus for a loom patent for years, haven't they?'

Countess Angelina, cheeks quivering, went a shade of purple and a vein pulsed in her forehead.

'I do not know what you are insinuating, my dear. But, yes, I do hold shares in a company that has benefitted from Sir Seamus's and Mr Martindale's death. But if you knew as much about my financial affairs as you claim, you know that I also hold shares in a company that has *fallen apart* due to Sir Seamus's death, and I am, in fact, financially *worse off.*'

Countess Angelina then stomped into the jewellers and enquired after the onyx cluster brooch.

'Opal, my dear, I've found some simple black pearl-drop earrings for you, with that hat you'll need them to lengthen your neck,' Lady Laplume called, beckoning from the back of the shop.

Opal was about to step inside when Augusto put his hand on her shoulder.

'Opal, please lay off Countess Angelina. She is innocent,' he said with sincere eyes.

'*Is she now?* How on earth would you know *that?*' said Opal. 'How many mysteries have you single-handedly solved this year? I think leave the sleuthing to me, and don't forget you are here for *one purpose*, and that is to be my protection officer. You may need to protect me from Countess Angelina de Brisecloque!'

THIRTY-SIX
THE DEAN CEMETERY

Opal's feet sank into the dewy turf of the Dean Cemetery. Her kid-gloved fingers were clutching a clump of earth in one hand and a damp handkerchief in the other. Sniffs and whimpers came from behind black veils and moustaches. Croaked, unsympathetic commentary came from crows sitting atop stone angels. The coffin made its stately descent while the straps creaked and the minister began his committal. 'Earth to earth, ashes to ashes, dust to dust...'

Opal tossed her soil down onto the shiny oak. Tiny pebbles clinking on the surface like light rain. Maisie, the hawk, was loosed from the gauntlet of a tweedy handler, and she circled above as if carrying Sir Seamus's spirit. It brought a sting to Opal's eyes, which seemed to be contagious. The vast congregation that had shown up all seemed to hold a fond place for the eccentric lecturer and inventor in their hearts.

She stepped back into the earth-scattering queue and followed it round to the back of the crowd. There she found herself standing behind Augusto and Countess Angelina. She wanted to be embraced by him, but would have to wait until they were alone later. She felt so terribly sad about squabbling with him earlier.

His chiselled chin turned to Angelina, and he whispered something inaudible in her ear. Opal's stomach performed a slow undulation like the darkest deep sea. Then, to her horror, Countess Angelina whispered back into Augusto's ear, and Opal could hear it as loud as if it was an organ.

'I've always loved you, my Augusto,' Countess Angelina said, placing a hand on Augusto's arm.

He turned his head and smiled at her in a way that proved he'd known her for a long time.

Opal pressed her handkerchief to her mouth in what she hoped would look like a funereal, grief-stricken sort of way. She quietly tiptoed behind a tall gravestone where she could have a silent sob. It was not only a funeral for Sir Seamus, but a funeral of her heart. She was not the only girl in Augusto's life. How could she ever compete with such a dream of a woman as Countess Angelina de Brisecloque, who was clearly as enamoured by him as she was?

When she was able to open her eyes again, she noticed a pair of boots poking out from behind a tomb a good ten yards away. Hobnail trench boots. The very same that had made the boot prints on the isle of St Kessog's.

Oh, my goodness. It couldn't be... she slowly raised her eyeline above the tombstone and she saw him. A leathery tan face and a yellow eye, the other was covered by an eyepatch. The bristle brush of moustache sprouted orange and black hairs. The auburn curls on his head were crushed down by... the ivy cap of *Lord Sterling Peregrine.* He was scowling at the grave scene, emanating the sinister air of someone who cares nothing for death, and who poaches exotic and endangered birds for sport.

What did the confounded man want now? He must have received Opal's little note spelling the endgame. No wicked moves left for him now. But, of course, Lord Sterling Peregrine was also a student of Sir Seamus's, along with her father. They were, once upon a time, chums at Edinburgh University. Back before Lord Peregrine lost his marbles!

Opal gasped as his shoulder turned slightly. Revealing two black eyes – the twin barrels of his shotgun. *Who brings a countryside persuader to a funeral?* Opal thought bizarrely, before realising she was actually in grave danger indeed. He seemed to sense her looking, and his pupils darted right at her. He smirked evilly, his moustache becoming a freakish crescent moon.

The air turned to ice in her lungs. She glanced down at Napoleon. He had not noticed him, thank God, as he was busy looking up at the hawk and fantasising about catching it. The last thing Opal wanted was for Napoleon to go for Lord Peregrine and get blown to smithereens.

She looked back up at the crooked lord, but he'd disappeared. *Oh God, where is he now? He wasn't going to shoot Papa, was he?* Opal quickstepped silently back to Augusto and tapped him on the shoulder.

'Lord Peregrine's here,' she whispered. 'He's hefting twin barrels of trouble.'

'Where?' he said, his right hand jutting up inside his jacket lapels.

'Are you carrying a pistol?' Opal asked.

'Of course I am. What kind of a protection officer doesn't offer any protection?' he said, his dark eyes darting about the mourners. 'Where is he?'

'I don't know now... he was hiding behind that tomb,' Opal whispered, pointing towards a concrete angel.

The sermon and sniffles continued – the procession unaware of what was going on – while Augusto slipped away into the sea of black overcoats and furs. Opal stood on tiptoes, anxiously trying to where Lord Peregrine had got to. Countess

Angelina, too, craned her neck and whipped her chin back and forth, anxious to see where Augusto had gone.

Opal then saw the shotgun barrel poke behind another tomb. Augusto had evidently noticed this too, as his trilby bobbed in that direction. Then it halted. The shotgun barrel zoomed off away to the south of the graveyard towards the chapel. Augusto's trilby followed fast as if carried by a swift wind.

They disappeared into the stone archway of the chapel and into blackness within, Augusto about ten paces after Lord Peregrine. Opal felt a sleeve brush past hers. It was Countess Angelina's. She was obviously worried about her beloved Augusto and had decided to chase after them. Opal tugged Napoleon's leash, and she followed on too, anxiously awaiting a gunshot. Napoleon's ears were pricked forward, not entirely sure what he was running towards.

Countess Angelina's cloak, flowing ahead, was blocking Opal's view. *I'm not going to let her get to Augusto first*, Opal thought. She quickened her pace, but the countess was pummelling across the ground. Opal wanted to overtake but at the same time felt terrified of the guns. She halted and grasped at a gravestone to regain her breath. *I hope to God Augusto isn't going to get shot by Lord Peregrine. And if Augusto is the first to shoot, then I sincerely hope he doesn't go to prison for it. Why oh why did I have to choose him to protect us? I've got him into trouble... what have I done!*

Angelina was now close to the chapel, and her cape swished to the side as she abruptly stopped.

Napoleon, at Opal's side, barked loudly, not able to hold it in any longer. The mourners started to titter and shuffle as they turned to see what was going on. Opal squinted her gaze at the chapel's entrance. There was a shadow in the doorway, a broad hulk emerging. *Oh God, which man is it?*

THIRTY-SEVEN

SHOOTING SEASON PSYCHOPATH

A black dot held aloft emerged first. Augusto's pistol barrel. He then emerged and looked at Angelina and shrugged.

'I think he escaped through the side door that leads west,' he said, pointing the pistol in the direction.

Opal completely emptied her lungs of air and almost collapsed over the front of the gravestone she was clinging to. Augusto was unharmed. *If God was safeguarding that chapel, I promise to attend Mass every Sunday for as long as I live,* Opal thought. She never wanted Augusto to confront Lord Peregrine again.

She looked west towards the thick wedge of overgrowth and woodland beyond. They rustled, a sinister indication of Lord Peregrine's exit. *Could she feel safe in Edinburgh now that she knew Lord Peregrine was in town?*

'What the devil?' hissed Lord Laplume, ambling around gravestones towards Opal. 'What is Augusto doing?'

Heads from the funeral were jutting back and forth, trying to respectfully listen to the sermon but desperate to know what the ruckus was over.

'Why is Augusto wielding a pistol on holy soil?' Lady Laplume said, rather too loudly, bobbing behind her husband.

'Because he is our protection officer,' said Opal in a seething whisper, 'and that shooting-season psychopath we hired him to protect us from was here with his shotgun.'

Lord Laplume went as white as his collar. He opened his arms and jostled his family behind a tomb, away from onlookers.

'Where... where is he now?' he asked, looking over at Augusto.

'He went into the woodland,' said Opal.

'He needs immediate confinement in a lunatic asylum,' said Lady Laplume. 'We must alert the constabulary.'

'He's two stops short of Piccadilly... mentally, but he is as clever as a fox,' said Lord Laplume, 'though, with his illustrious connections, one imagines constables may be a touch too... understanding.'

Augusto and Countess Angelina approached. Augusto slid his piece back inside his coat and walked with twitchy adrenaline. The countess tottered to keep up at his side, clutching her cloak close and looking at him with scared eyes... like she was his anxious wife. Opal immediately threw her arms around him. It wasn't because of Countess Angelina, but it was because refraining had become quite impossible, given the fright she'd just had. And, for once, she wasn't bothered that her parents could see.

'Augusto.'

He accepted her hug with warm and sturdy arms. His familiar scent, brilliantine and smoke, was a comfort and brought her back to the feeling she had in Paris under the Eiffel Tower, where he had taught her the tango. Where all her troubles and loneliness had melted away, and she had felt secure.

. . .

In the hotel foyer that afternoon, the Laplumes and Augusto had a meeting with the Edinburgh City Police over tea. They firmly assured the family that an officer would be dispatched to inquire into the situation, ensure the safety of the family and determine if any action needed to be taken to prevent any harm.

'It's the kind of response I was expecting,' said Lord Laplume as the police departed. 'Thank goodness we've taken steps to have help of our own.'

Countess Angelina, who had been listening in from the adjacent table, interjected, 'Is it really necessary to put Augusto in harm's way when the police have already said they are dealing with it?'

Lady Laplume almost spat out her Darjeeling. She clattered the cup and saucer back onto the table and smoothed her skirts. Opal could almost hear her mental gears grinding. Lady Laplume, a woman so devoted to the art of social protocol, was struggling to form a rebuke without offending someone of Angelina's rank.

Opal turned her shoulders squarely to Angelina. 'Do forgive me, Countess,' her tone a blend of sweetness and frost, 'but I must insist that it is my papa and I that Lord Peregrine is after. If he wanted to harm Augusto, it would, I daresay, have happened in the chapel this very afternoon. And, I might add, he is in attendance for this *very* purpose.'

Countess Angelina smiled, but her narrow eyes told a different story.

'With all due respect, Countess, do not patronise Augusto's profession,' Lady Laplume added, seeming to take confidence from her daughter's straightforwardness, seeing as the damage was already done. 'He isn't a glorified poodle walker.'

Countess Angelina looked at Augusto and giggled as if he'd been hired by buffoons. Napoleon barked at her three times as if to say that he, in fact, was the sole protector of Opal's honour, ankles and afternoon tea, pom-pom tail standing to attention.

Augusto exchanged looks with Lord Laplume and muttered something about the time being later than expected.

'Pardon me for interrupting,' said a hotel clerk, with one hand behind his back in a slight bow. 'There is a Mrs Keith on the line for The Honourable Opal Laplume, calling from Dunvaloch Castle.'

Opal thanked him and marched off, her heels castanets of indignation on the tiles all the way to the telephone booth.

'Miss Laplume. I'm calling to update you on the state of Clyde.'

'Mrs Keith. How very kind of you to keep me in the loop. How is he?'

'He has pneumonia and is speaking gibberish, but he just keeps saying something that we can only translate as a message to you.'

'To me?' said Opal, blinking rapidly and pressing the earpiece closer. 'What is it?'

'We can only translate it as something like this... tell Opal... Mmmmmm. Rub. Sig. Netting.'

'Come again?' Opal said after a brief pause.

'He said... tell Opal... then these four sounds: Mmmmm. Rub. Sig. Netting. Can you make any sense of it?'

'I wish I could... but wait a moment, I shall write it down.' She jotted the cryptic message on the booth's paper pad.

'He has been adamant. The doctor says he is delirious, but I think there's more to it. He's desperately trying to convey something to us... or to you,' she said with an emotional quaver in her voice.

'Thank you for making me aware. I shall wrack my brains. And please let him know he is in my prayers. I'll call back in a few days to see how he is doing.'

THIRTY-EIGHT

SIR SEAMUS'S WAKE

'I haven't been in this room since I was eighteen,' said Lord Laplume, looking up at the echoing ceiling of the George Street conference room of Edinburgh University.

'Who is that?' asked Lady Laplume, looking at a portrait of a cloaked gentleman with an enormous walrus moustache.

'Oh... some long-forgotten provost,' he replied, swirling his sherry and knocking it back.

'Look, Opal, these were Sir Seamus's binoculars,' said Turkey, pointing to a small memorial table that Lady Viola Blair had set up, scattered with little inventions and gadgets. 'One of the lenses is taped. I wonder if he fell out of a tree.'

'Oh, yes, his bins. How sweet,' said Opal, absent-mindedly flipping through Sir Seamus's field journal that was on display.

'Doesn't your papa call you *Bins* after binoculars and your talent for spotting things?' Cecil asked, making a silly binocular hand gesture in a desperate attempt to flirt.

'Yes,' Opal said flatly.

'I say, isn't it just the tiniest bit mortifying, now that you've blossomed into a rather striking young woman and not, say, a Boy Scout?'

'Turkey.' Opal sighed and shut the journal. 'You share your name with sandwich meat.'

Mr Finlay Roberts stifled a laugh into his sherry glass, but then, on seeing Turkey's astonished face, cleared his throat and began a fond anecdote about the late Sir Seamus.

Opal left the tiresome men and walked to the sash windows and stroked the brocade curtain. It was only four o'clock, but it was dark already. She looked into the navy-blue sky and tried desperately hard to think what Clyde's message could have been. And why he'd wanted to send it to her in particular. What had been her last conversation with him? The day before, outside the barber's, they had been chatting about his encounter with Seraphina Serle and how she had asked him to pull off the bagpipes hoax. That directly made him involved in the double murder. His murder attempt was surely an effort to silence him. But the words... rub and netting, those themes had never come up in their conversations, and they certainly didn't know anyone named Sig.

A string quartet struck up a Scottish lament. Retired colonels, all manner of academics and business affiliates chattered away as if it were more of an old boys' networking event rather than a wake. Opal covered her ears. She couldn't think. She must think! What could Clyde have been saying? She got out the scrap of paper on which she'd written the ramblings. *Mmmm. Rub. Sig. Netting.*

A hand touched her shoulder. It was Augusto, looking concerned at her distress, his eyes dark and caring. He had left Countess Angelina alone by the sherry decanters. The countess flipped her sable stole over her shoulder and whipped her head away when she saw Opal looking.

Opal pulled Augusto's lapels close. She explained in hushed tones about Mrs Keith's telephone message and asked if he had any inkling. He shook his head. How could one make sense of random mumblings like that?

Opal sipped her sherry and said the sounds over and over in her head, trying to combine them to make a word. Lady Blair moved across the room, swathed in a dramatic black opera coat that made her seem a bit like a black cloud floating around, raining sadness. Walking at her side... quite scandalously, was a young man she'd seen kiss Lady Blair's hand at the Christmas kirk service. Opal heard him introduce himself to someone as a 'friend of Lady Viola Blair' quite confidently, with no qualms about how it may look. Lady Blair's countenance was completely detached, and it seemed she couldn't have given a damn either way.

As Opal regarded this little scene, she noticed something through the window, directly behind Lady Blair. A flickering orange light danced in the corner of the dusty pane. Opal blinked to sharpen her vision. Then marched straight towards it.

She put her hands upon the glass and peered at it. There was a fire, about five buildings down the street from where they were, on the adjacent side. In front of the Victorian commercial premises in question, a couple of silhouetted men were waving their arms and dashing back and forth as if not knowing quite what to do. The flame was a great tongue of yellow lapping up from a ground-floor window and coughing out black clouds that swirled into the indigo sky. It roared as another tongue of fire burst through the window above.

'Oh heavens!' Opal's eyes stretched wide, and she yelled, 'There's a fire down the street!'

A heave of people behind Opal moved towards the windows to get a look. There was a ripple of gasps.

'It's the Edinburgh Printing Works building,' said a voice.

'Is anyone injured?' said another.

'I'm going to call for the fire brigade!' shouted a third.

Opal kept peering through the window at the growing inferno. She scanned the six-floor building in case anyone was trapped above. Indeed, they were. Hardly visible, the silhouette of someone was frantically pawing at the window frame on the second floor. You could barely see the poor soul due to the opaque smoke rolling up the building. The people below seemed much too concerned with the fire to notice.

'There's someone trapped!' Opal shouted, but her voice was lost in the cacophony of voices echoing off the barrelled ceiling.

Opal felt an arm scoop around her shoulders and pull her from the crush. It was Augusto. He had Napoleon by the leash in the other hand, thank God. Her mama and papa were close behind, holding each other.

'Is it a big fire?' Lady Laplume asked. 'We can't see for the crush of people.'

'It's becoming a substantial inferno and travelling up the floors,' said Opal, 'but there's someone trapped on the second floor! I don't think they can get the window open. I'm not sure the fire brigade will make it in time!'

'Well, we must help them or at least sound the alarm,' said Lord Laplume.

'Quite right!' said Lady Laplume.

Augusto had already slipped out of the conference room and was halfway down the stairs to the hall, Napoleon galloping beside him like the charge of the light brigade. The Laplumes tried their best to keep up, dashing out into the air that should have been cold, but was warm from the fury of the fire at the end of the street.

They got as close as they could while staying within a safe range and stopped by a delivery vehicle, piled high with enormous rolls of paper from the print house. Opal could just about make out the signs of the premises, EDINBURGH PRINTING WORKS, in white, and below on the ground floor, MARTINGALE SOLICITORS, the gold lettering peeling in the heat.

THIRTY-NINE

RIBBONS TO THE RESCUE

'Good grief!' said Lord Laplume. 'That's Mr Martindale's office!'

Opal shaded her eyes while pointing up at the window of the print house above, where she'd seen the trapped figure. She knew the correct window, but the figure was now invisible due to the smoke.

'I can't see them anymore, but that doesn't mean they're not still in there!' she shouted.

'I'll try to work out how we can rescue them,' said Augusto. 'The fire brigade might be too late! There's an alleyway down the side of the building that isn't touched by the fire.' He strode away into a pillow of smoke that engulfed him.

Opal held Napoleon back, who barked furiously at the fire as if it was an impertinent dragon. Lord and Lady Laplume clung to one another on the pavement beside the delivery vehicle and said they would keep a lookout and inform the fire brigade of the trapped person when they arrived.

By now, other members of the wake had come to witness the blaze. They stood in a horseshoe formation around the burning building. Oranges and yellows dancing in their frightened eyes and flickering on their metal coat buttons.

Opal's nostrils got hit by the fragrant tang of singed pulp. She looked sideways into the open-topped delivery vehicle. Several of the great rolls of printing paper had been set alight due to embers and were licking with orange flames like fat marshmallows left too long on the fire.

It happened so fast. Opal saw a familiar boot appear at the back of the paper-delivery vehicle, then the sound of a latch being unhooked at the van's rear flap. The result was instantaneous. The burning rolls tumbled forth with a rumble, gathering speed and flame as they descended. Lord and Lady Laplume were currently in their path. Lord Laplume turned just in time to emit a yell and push his wife out of harm's way, before disappearing beneath an avalanche of flaming paper.

'Papa!' Opal screamed.

'Edmund!' Lady Laplume cried, getting to her feet.

The crowd gasped, and the attention was shifted from the burning building to Lord Edmund Laplume's predicament.

Where is Augusto? Opal thought, her hands digging into her hair, utterly helpless. As if she'd summoned him with desperate telepathy, Augusto emerged through the smoky alley and vaulted the pavement, knocking aside a startled onlooker. He grasped and yanked a roll of paper right out of the stack, making others above it fall away. Lord Laplume's smoking foot poked out. Augusto removed his coat and battled the flames with one hand, while dragging Lord Laplume out by the ankle with the other. A few of the braver assortment in the crowd mucked in and took Lord Laplume's other ankle.

Napoleon, legs splayed in readiness, growled and chased after the offending boots that had caused the disaster. Opal followed. *Who had done this to her darling papa?* Her arms protecting her head from wafting paper cinders, she followed the boots that were trying to dash down the side alley. But thankfully, the person's coat had caught fire from a flying cinder.

Napoleon skidded to a halt and backed up. The person spun in a circle like a lacklustre firework, trying to pat themselves down. When they collapsed to the ground in a smoking heap, Opal could see the face... and the yellow eye and eyepatch of Lord Sterling Peregrine.

'You're nicked,' said a sudden voice.

Opal turned. It was a constable, a golden flame dancing on the metal badge of his helmet.

'I am Lord Sterling Peregrine,' seethed Lord Peregrine.

The constable cleared his throat. 'You're nicked... *m'lord.*'

'For *what?*' Lord Peregrine spat.

'For attempted murder,' said the constable, rolling the Scottish 'r'. 'I saw the entire calculated deed. You were eyeing up the gentleman in a suspicious manner. Then you took the opportune moment to undo the van latch to release those paper rolls, burying him in a bonfire. I wouldn't be surprised if you started the building inferno too.'

'I did *neither* of those deeds,' said Lord Sterling Peregrine, trying to sit up straight. 'I was merely on my way to Sir Seamus's wake at the conference rooms and came across the commotion. It's not my blasted fault I was at the wrong place at the wrong time!'

The constable tilted his head doubtfully down at the barbecued viscount. Napoleon promptly urinated on Peregrine's scorched shoe as if to show how much respect his little story deserved.

'Wretched, odious creature!' Lord Peregrine shouted, kicking his foot. 'And that goes for you as well, Opal Laplume.'

'Do write, if they let you have paper in jail. And give our regards to the warden,' Opal replied with a smile.

He was cuffed and dragged under the armpits by two other officers who had approached. Napoleon and his pom-pom paws did a little victory dance. Opal was relieved that at least it was one less thing to fret about. She scooped Napoleon up. She buried her face in his bouffant, then looked up over his fur. They were close to the backend of the building, and her gaze fixed on the second-floor window. She gasped. A soot-streaked figure waved frantically at her behind the thickening smoke. The poor person was still trapped!

'Hold on!' she yelled.

She dashed back into the street with Napoleon at her side. St Andrew's ambulance was the first to respond; a stretcher bearer was kneeling down at Lord Laplume's body, tending to him. Lady Laplume was standing over them, sobbing into her hands.

'Papa!' cried Opal. 'Are you alright?'

'Thank goodness for woollen coats being flame resistant, eh!' he said weakly.

Opal breathed a sigh of relief that her dear papa wasn't seriously hurt. And now that she knew he was safe, she would have to tend to him later. She must help the trapped stranger first.

'Señorita!' Augusto said, dashing over and embracing her, 'Are you alright?'

'Augusto, the trapped person is now at the rear window! Around the back!'

'Oh no,' he said. 'The fire brigade still aren't here. I'm going to have to rescue them myself.'

He rolled up his blackened sleeves and darted down the side alley.

'Wait!' Opal yelled, dodging a piece of flaming debris as she flew after him.

The back of the print house had not yet been engulfed by fire. The person in the window started banging on the glass when they saw Augusto and Opal. Was the window locked? Sealed? Perhaps it was a window that didn't open. Augusto began to scale the cast-iron drainpipe, but it came away from the wall with his weight. He caught himself by digging his fingers into the mortar lines and jumped back down. He then scurried around like a madman, building a tower with wooden crates and dustbins.

Opal's eyes flashed ingeniously. *I've got a better idea.*

There hung an old, wrought-iron shop sign bracket, still bolted to the brick just beneath the second-floor window in question. A heavy sign, embossed with EDINBURGH PRINTING WORKS swung off it from chains. If Opal could somehow reach the sign and swing it sideways, it would smash the window.

Opal rummaged in her handbag and withdrew a ball of strong ribbon that she'd been pleating to make hat embellishments. She tried to toss one end up onto the wrought-iron loops of the signage. It pathetically floated up and fluttered down. *Blast.* She then knotted it around a rock she scavenged from the ground. This time the rock flew through the loop. *Hooray.*

Napoleon leapt and caught the rock in his jaws. Knowing exactly what was required of him, he began to yank, a bit like a caterpillar walking backwards. Opal, still holding the other end of the ribbon, joined him, and they began to heave the sign together.

'Good boy!' Opal called. 'Now let go, and as it swings back, I'll tug it!'

With one last growl of exertion, Napoleon gave a mighty tug – and the sign swung up high, swooshed back and then smashed into the second-floor window, shattering the glass in a rain of sooty shards.

Augusto, who had only been paying attention to his tower, looked up, aghast.

The trapped figure stared in wide-eyed amazement as the fresh air gusted in.

'Climb out!' Opal shouted. 'Use the sign... I'll guide you down!'

The figure clambered through the broken frame, then carefully eased himself down onto the swaying sign, and was able to put his feet onto Augusto's leaning tower of dustbins. Then his feet landed on the floor, and Napoleon did a celebratory twirl.

Opal exhaled in exhaustion and relief and patted her hair back into some semblance of order.

'Well,' she said, brushing ash off her gloves, 'that was very nearly *too* exciting.'

'However can I...' the main stammered, 'repay you?' Suddenly, they heard the bells of the fire engine, and the hoses start to gush around the front of the building. The man slung an arm over Opal and Augusto's shoulders, and they led him out to the street tremulously, spluttering and coughing. The poor chap would have had a lot of smoke inhalation.

But something made Opal stop them for a moment. There was something... written on the ground. Amidst the scorched pieces of newspaper and smashed glass, shone four letters in white paint.

ELAN

'ELAN? Is that a word? Or an acronym?' Opal said.

'Who knows, let's get this man to the ambulance before he collapses,' said Augusto breathlessly.

As they ambled along, Opal remembered she'd seen the word before... just that morning at the hotel over breakfast. It had been in the newspaper. The Edinburgh Labour Alliance Network. That activist society, causing all sorts of rows about industries hiring new machinery and sacking workers. Was it written to claim ownership of the fire? Had the printers been buying new, innovative presses that took people's jobs away?

If this was the case, was it just a coincidence that Mr. Martindale's office was below? It kept all his important documents: land deeds, business contracts, family wills, divorce settlements, and other bits of paper that caused the upper classes to turn pale and whisper, 'Good God, burn it!'

Then there was the chance that Lord Sterling Peregrine started the fire. He denied it, but at the very least, he was an opportunist, seizing his moment to try to kill her dear papa.

'Did you see at all who started the fire?' Opal asked the man.

'No...didn't see a damn thing.' He spluttered in reply.

When they emerged from the alleyway like hobbling soldiers, Opal's dear friend Detective Inspector Sinclair turned to look at them. He was prodding the reservoir of his tobacco pipe with a stick, as if stoking at his own little fire, took a drag, then said, 'Opal, my dear, you've rescued someone. Are you a pioneering fire lady?'

'Looks like it,' she said, pulling off her cloche. 'Not the most appropriate uniform though, I've singed the ostrich feathers in my hat.'

'You must get checked over, then wrapped in a blanket, given the sweetest cup of tea the hotel can muster and off to bed. Meet me back here in the morning. We'll have sniffing to do.'

FORTY

ASHES TO AFFIDAVITS

Morning of 30th December

Steam was still rising from the shell of the building in the morning. You could almost hear the hiss as the hot mist was distinguished by delicate rain. The air was thick with the smell of damp charcoal with a chemical tinge of ink. How many thousands of typed letters of the law and signatures were devoured in a flick of Hades' wrist? What law-binding secrets had been lost? Had they lost all evidence of Mr Martindale and his dealings? Were some of them crooked?

Detective Inspector Sinclair stood stoutly on the opposite side of the street to the blackened office. His hands were in the pockets of his plus-fours. The green tweed was billowing outwards, making him look even wider than usual. He had donned a deerstalker hat, seeming to fancy himself a bit of a Sherlock that morning. His eyes twinkled with the anticipation of exploring inside the carnage.

Napoleon trotted up to him and sat to attention at his feet. He clearly respected this good-egg of a gumshoe. All the other detectives he'd ever met whiffed of stupidity. Opal followed suit and stood with her feet slightly turned out and fur muff hoisted under her bosom, awaiting Detective Inspector Sinclair's instruction.

'Ah, The Honourable Miss Opal Laplume,' he said and removed the deerstalker, 'Feeling better this morning?'

'Yes, thank you, Detective Inspector Sinclair,' she replied and glanced aside at the office. 'Seems the case got so hot, it decided to roast itself.'

'Indeed, the building's now toastier than a crumpet,' he replied. 'Are you going to come and have a poke about with me? The fire department confirmed it's safe to enter through the back.'

'Happy to oblige, Detective,' said Opal, pretending to be a female Doctor Watson, while fully cognisant of the fact that she was, in actuality, Sherlock.

'I need your sharp eyes to ferret out anything that might be lurking among the cinders,' he said as they trod through rubble. 'And while we're at it... find Sir Seamus's file.'

'If it's not toast,' said Opal.

Once they'd manoeuvred themselves through the alley and arrived at the back of the office, Opal pointed to the ground and said, 'Have you seen the letters painted here, Detective? ELAN?'

'Indeed, I have, my dear, but the Edinburgh Labour Alliance Network are denying they started the fire,' he said, making many chins wobble as he analysed the graffiti.

'You mean, you think it was someone *pretending* to be this activist group?' asked Opal.

'Indeed, I do.' He nodded. 'They wouldn't bother denying it as they usually own up to their antics. I did believe for a moment it was them because the printing factory above was slashing the workers' hours and buying new machines... but it seems not to be the case.'

'So, from what we can deduce, the target was not the printing factory above, but Mr Martindale's office below?'

'Yes,' he said, and the line between his brows deepened in confirmation.

Opal tapped her foot, and her lashes fluttered in thought. 'All of our suspects for the murder of Sir Seamus and Mr Martindale were at the wake with me at the time of the fire, so none of them could have started it.'

'Drats,' Detective Inspector Sinclair said emphatically. 'I was going to ask you about the attendance and see if anyone had done a Houdini.'

'Afraid not,' Opal said as she followed him through the back entrance. It was now just a cavern as the wooden doors were a pile of ash.

The sturdy stone foundations gave Opal the confidence that the ceiling wouldn't fall on top of them. It was like stepping inside a blackened oven, shelves lining the walls held manila folders that curled up, like burnt pastries. The once beautiful desk, carved probably from a beautiful Highland tree, now lay on its side, legs splayed like a fainting lady's. Papers, once bound with red tape, now lay in ashes, reduced to ghostly confetti. The chandelier above was like a melted insect in filthy jewels. There was a grey metal cabinet behind the desk that had warped, causing the door to be blown open, and the innards resembled not much more than a coal shed.

'I say!' was the only thing Opal could think of to utter.

'Ironically,' Detective Inspector Sinclair said, 'I was going to snoop around in here soon after Mr Martindale's funeral. I had to obtain a warrant first due to client privilege and all that. But now the fire's happened, I've been able to get inside, only to be presented with' – he reached inside the cabinet and pulled out a triangle of paper – 'crisps.'

'Tasty.' Opal giggled. 'Class action, salty flavour.'

Detective Inspector Sinclair, usually cheered by the

mention of food, remained very serious, holding the legal crisp in thumb and forefinger, clearly paralysed and not knowing where to start.

Napoleon, having been rescued from a coal sack as a pup, felt quite at home and even invigorated at all the ashy muck to roll in. He did several barrel rolls at once, tongue lolling out as he did so.

'Thank goodness you're not a white poodle,' said Opal, and picked up a piece of broken bottle from the floor. 'And careful of glass!'

His pom-pom tail brushed the shelves in excitement, better than a maid after three coffees. Opal noticed a gleaming metal plaque become visible. It read ESTATE TAXATION. Opal rubbed some fallen ash off her lashes and blinked at the plaque while crouching down.

'Everything is organised with metal plaques, thank goodness!' she said with a surge of excitement. 'If they were paper labels, they would have burned.'

'That's all well and good, my dear, but I don't think the literature is etched onto metal plates,' said Detective Inspector Sinclair with a sigh.

'Oh, don't be such a negative Nancy,' said Opal. 'Even the crisp you're holding has a few legible words on it. We just might find something interesting.'

'That's why I needed you,' said Detective Inspector Sinclair. 'Enthusiasm to the point of madness.'

They spent the next half hour using a hanky to clean the plaques and found a section on the top shelf that held BLAIR ELECTRICAL ENTERPRISES

'Aha!' said Detective Inspector Sinclair. 'If someone deliberately burnt this office to destroy any reason for them to kill both Sir Seamus and Mr Martindale, it might just be up here.'

The folders were half devoured, but the documents inside seemed to have the odd phrases legible on one edge. They took the bundle and wrapped it in Detective Inspector Sinclair's cardigan.

They clambered out onto the street and started off towards the hotel. They bumped into the fire department, who were having a cigarette break, with grey bags under their eyes.

'Do we know how the fire was started yet?' enquired Detective Inspector Sinclair to the chap with the most authoritative-looking fireman's hat.

'Incendiary device. Had a timer attached to a milk bottle. We found it in the office, someone had dropped it through the back window.'

'Interesting,' Opal commented as they carried on to the hotel. 'A timer would give the arsonist time to leave and not be seen when the fire started.'

'Could have been anyone at the wake, then.' Detective Inspector Sinclair nodded. 'The ELAN most certainly did *not* do it.'

They were tutted all the way up the stairs by the hotel maid. She glared at Napoleon's sooty footprints splodging up the white marble. Opal tried to scrub one of the marks with the hanky she'd used in the office, but made it worse, so hurriedly carried on upstairs with mumbled apologies. She simply couldn't wait to try to read the remnants of the contracts wrapped in Sinclair's cardigan.

Once in her room, Sinclair plodded over to the vanity and fished about the pots and bottles.

'Aha!' he said triumphantly and brandished something.

He then brought back a pot of loose powder and a brush.

Opal was transfixed as the detective sprinkled and dusted on one of the blackened papers.

'The powder will settle into creases or ink residue and possibly reveal where marks once were,' he whispered quietly as if any louder would disturb the delicate powder.

He managed to reveal a queer complaint letter about someone's singed moustache from using a shoddy electric trimmer. Detective Inspector Sinclair sighed with disappointment.

'I'm not sure Sir Seamus was murdered over a singed moustache,' muttered Opal. 'Crumbs. There's so much to get through. Hundreds of pages.'

She sifted her fingers over the pages until her eye stopped on something at the edge of one page.

'December 25th,' Opal mused. 'Sir Seamus died just before the turn of December 25th.'

Detective Inspector Sinclair didn't seem to notice her comments and kept blowing and shaking out papers. Opal shrugged and decided to dust it off anyway. Her heart began to beat faster and faster as she revealed more and more.

'Subject to provisions under the Official Secrets Act, 1911'
'In collaboration with the War Office Technical Division'
'...royalties... fifty per cent (50%)...'
'...exclusive rights...'
'...renew automatically and annually on... December 25th... voided only if renegotiated or should either party become deceased...'
'...revert to surviving party...'

At the bottom was 'Blair Electrical Enterprises' and Sir Seamus's signature and his metal seal with the stag. Next to it was 'Invention Contractor'. The signature was missing, but there was a seal with a cow on it and the letter 'K' inside it.

Opal gasped and dropped the brush. 'Detective Inspector Sinclair. We know that Sir Seamus's electrical inventions company worked for the War Office for classified inventions. It looks like he employed a contractor. And this contractor could get out of the contract by either re-negotiating terms or if one of them were to die. It is renewed on the 25th of December every year. Did this person bump Sir Seamus off to get out of this contract? Was Mr Martindale murdered because he also knew about this agreement?'

'Miss Laplume,' Detective Inspector Sinclair said very slowly and took the document.

It trembled in his hand as if it was carrying an electrical surge.

'I think... I think this is it,' he said, after a long pause. 'But why is the damn signature burnt out?'

'I know. Blithering fig!' said Opal. 'But at least we have the seal... a cow and a K.'

'Yes, how very helpful,' said Sinclair sarcastically. 'But, Opal, you must be very careful with whom you share any of this information. These are government secrets, they're not for civilian eyes. We don't know how far they are willing to go to keep it secret.'

Opal gulped. 'I know,' she said and wriggled on her pouffe uncomfortably, imagining little listening devices tucked under all the pieces of furniture in the room.

A sudden sharp trilling sound made Opal almost jump out of her skin.

'What in the deuce is that?'

'The telephone, my dear.'

'Oh yes, of course.'

They eyed each other, spooked.

'You better pick it up, Detective.'

'A gentleman in a young lady's room? I think not. You better get it. It'll be nothing sinister, we just have the jitters.'

'Quite.' Opal gulped.

She slowly picked up the receiver with shaking hands and pressed it to her ear.

FORTY-ONE

THE ROYAL PAISLEY CLUB

30th December

Opal slumped forward in relief as the sound of Turkey's pathetic voice warbled through the earpiece. Though, unfortunately, her comment about sandwich meat at the wake evidently hadn't thrown him off.

'Opal, my sweet,' he said. 'It's Cecil. You're right, Turkey is an absurd moniker, and I shall give it up. It is foolish that it is both mine and Papa's tags and we are always getting mixed up besides.'

'Oh, Turkey, I mean *Cecil*, you don't need to do that,' she said, exasperated.

'Well, I'm afraid, my sweet, I have to inform you that I will not be present for the New Year's Eve fireworks. How I would have loved to see the sparkles light up your pretty face.'

'Oh... how terribly disappointing,' Opal said, but inwardly perked up at the fact he'd be out of her hair soon.

'But not to worry. You can come and play a game of billiards with me tonight at the Royal Paisley Club. I'm off to Norfolk tomorrow, so it'll be our last chance to talk before God knows how long.'

Talk? Opal thought. What on earth was there to talk about with this grovelling yes-man? He was the last person she wanted to waste time with before cracking the case. But... she sat up straight as the idea came to her. She could do with speaking to someone close to Sir Seamus. Could Mr Finlay Roberts perhaps know of an inventor that Sir Seamus worked with? She'd have to bring Augusto, of course, to keep Cecil at bay.

'Why don't we play doubles, with Mr Finlay Roberts and Augusto?'

'Augusto?' Cecil said, sounding a little deflated. 'Yes, your chaperone... of course. A four o'clock sundowner?'

'Splendid.'

The billiard rooms at the Royal Paisley Club were self-contained chambers designed for private competitions and backroom wagers whispered over a dram. So, it was just the four of them in this room. Being the only lady, Opal broke the triangle with a confident thwack. The balls clonked the sides of the table and then each other with satisfying percussion. The table glowed a bright green under the brass pendant light suspended from the low ceiling. It illuminated the skin of the players in a slightly ghoulish green hue.

'You know, Opal, my sweet, that snooker is really all about *geometry*. Once you understand that, it clicks!'

'You don't say?' said Opal, in mock astonishment. 'Then surely you can remove your lucky cufflinks and rely on your, ah, mental faculties? Your turn.'

Cecil fiddled with his horseshoe-linked cuffs a little abashed and watched her saunter around the table to the back of the room. She leant her cue at the fireplace and picked up her dram off the mantle. The whisky she sipped was exceedingly oaky.

Cecil and Augusto discussed his next snooker move, and Opal took the opportunity to chat to Mr Finlay Roberts, perched in the fireside armchair. He was holding the cue in front of him like a staff, staring into the green rectangle of the billiard table.

'All this chat about geometry and snooker makes me wonder if Sir Seamus could have made a snooker-playing machine as a companion for lonely bachelors.'

'I wouldn't be at all surprised if that was on his list of conquests,' replied Mr Roberts distantly.

'Do you think he engineered all of his ideas by himself... or hired inventors to work for him silently? Ghost inventors, so to speak? I mean, he was an old boy, he couldn't have been completely up to date on the engineering side... and had so many ideas to get through.'

Mr Roberts's fingers drummed on the cue, and he glanced up sideways at her. 'I never thought about it. But I shouldn't imagine he'd ever let on if he did. He was very proud. Why?'

'Just curious. Somebody may come out of the woodwork and claim ownership of his patents. Doesn't seem like all this mess is over yet,' Opal said, trying to sound conversational. 'Did you know, he had a secret workshop on St Kessog's Isle?'

Mr Roberts sank his dram and clonked it on the mantle. 'He did spend a lot of time there, so I'm not surprised... Cecil, it's my shot. I wouldn't let you take that shot even if your cufflinks were blessed by the pope.'

Opal got the feeling Mr Roberts didn't want to talk about Sir Seamus. It was possibly too raw for the man who was practically Sir Seamus's son, too upsetting so soon after the funeral. She hugged herself with one arm and brought the whisky to her mouth with the other. As her hip leant on the fireplace, she felt a sharp prick.

'Ouch!' she couldn't help but yell. 'Something sharp is in my blasted pocket.'

She dug her hand inside her tweed skirt pocket and pulled out a piece of shattered glass. She frowned.

'Opal?' Augusto looked up from chalking his cue, concerned.

Opal turned the thing in her hand as the orange light from the fireplace shone through it, illuminating the words embossed 'Kerrybride Creamery'. It was from the piece of glass she'd picked off the floor when Napoleon was rolling around in the soot in Mr Martindale's office.

Augusto came over. 'Are you alright? What is it?'

'Oh, it's nothing... and I'm fine,' said Opal, frowning at the glass triangle. Something about it was intriguing.

'Let me dispose of it.' He plucked it out of her palm and went to leave the room.

'No wait, Augusto,' Opal said, suddenly coming to the realisation of what it might be. 'It might be a piece of the broken milk bottle. It says *creamery* on it.' She tugged Augusto's arm.

'So, what if it *is* a piece of milk bottle?' asked Augusto, gently handing it back to her.

'I'll need to give it to Detective Inspector Sinclair. I found it on the floor of Mr Martindale's office. It may be from the milk bottle used as the incendiary device,' Opal said, then trailed off as she realised she may not want everyone to know she was investigating.

Cecil leant across the table and peered into Opal's palm. 'Indeed it is. Kerrybride Creamery... isn't that the dairy farm you're from, Finlay, old chap?'

Mr Roberts was currently aiming his cue with his hands splayed in the snooker bridge. His sinews looked like a puma that was about to pounce. He was moving the pole back and forth to make a precise shot. He'd paused when he'd heard the word 'Kerrybride'.

The air went static. Opal noticed something twinkle on his splayed pinky finger. A golden sheen passed over the signet ring, and it was the emblem of a... cow.

Opal blinked a singular, strong blink to make sure what she was seeing was correct. Yes, yes, it was. And what's more, inside the engraving of a cow, there was something else...

Her heart forgot to beat for a moment. She looked up from the ring into Mr Roberts's face. He was looking back at her, dead in the eye. A brief glimpse of acknowledgement that she had been ogling his ring. He then resumed his gaze on the ball.

'Yes, Cecil, Kerrybride is my family farm,' he said casually and made a shot. It skimmed the red and was a bad shot. He clearly wasn't focused.

He then straightened up and leaned on the black marble mantlepiece. It was Opal's turn. She wrapped the piece of glass in a hanky and stuffed it back inside her skirt. Then stared at the snooker balls, feeling faintly nauseous. Her thoughts were on a sinister Ferris wheel. *Mr Finlay Roberts was from Kerrybride... a dairy farm. Clyde was trying to send her a message beginning 'Mmmm Rub'. Did he mean Mr Roberts? Only managing a few syllables?*

'I would help you, Opal, my sweet, but you are the opposition,' smirked Turkey.

Opal blinked out of her daze and grasped her cue.

Mr Roberts sniffed loudly twice and screwed up his nose. 'Is...' *Sniff.* 'Is that gas I can smell?'

Opal and the others sniffed the air; there was indeed the faint scent of gas.

'Oh, for God's sake,' said Cecil. 'Is that old gas fireplace playing up? We can't have another inferno!'

'Augusto, can you check the club's boiler or speak to staff?' asked Mr Roberts, slinging the ash bucket over the little fire in the hearth to be on the safe side. 'Cecil, grab a poker from another room, would you? We need to inspect if it's coming from here.'

Before Opal could protest and ask Augusto to stay close, the men slipped out and left Mr Roberts and Opal alone.

'It *is* coming from here, isn't it, Opal?' Mr Roberts pointed to a little valve behind the mantle and beckoned her to come and sniff.

Opal hesitated, though she wasn't sure whether that was because of the danger of gas or Mr Finlay Roberts's ambiguous smile.

'The fire is out, there's no risk of explosion,' he said calmly and began to pick at the valve with his finger. 'I don't have small enough fingers to get it and shut it off. This really is a terrible design.'

Despite the dread pooling in her stomach, Opal decided she'd better help in case something went wrong. There had been enough calamities already. She exhaled and walked to the fireplace. Her feet, tentative clonks on the boards. She reached behind the mantle and easily twisted the valve closed.

'Jolly good,' said Mr Finlay Roberts and shoved the lacquered wall panel behind her hard.

Opal gasped. The wall opened into a chilly blackness. *A hidden door?* Mr Roberts clamped one hand hard over her mouth and brought his snooker cue across as a barrier. Opal yelled behind his hand, which became barely audible as he pushed her inside the dark abyss beyond. The door thudded heavily shut behind them, engulfing her in darkness.

FORTY-TWO
CUE THE DARKNESS

Mr Finlay Roberts pressed Opal up against the adjacent wall of whatever passage they were in, barring her against the cold, damp bricks with the snooker cue. It was terribly hard on her chest and pinned her mid-arms, so she couldn't attack back. He then took his hand off Opal's mouth to grip the pole with his other hand. Opal could now yell for help.

'HELLLPP!!!! AUGUSTO,' Opal screamed.

'Nobody will be able to hear you, silly girl, we're in a vault of Mary King's Close...'

'What do you want?' Opal panted, when her lungs could scream no more.

'For you to shut up!' said Mr Roberts.

His snooker cue rose above her body, heading for her throat.

'No... don't hurt me, please!' she begged.

'You should have thought of that before meddling in my business,' said Mr Roberts. 'But, before I kill you, I can indulge your smug little brain in the knowledge that you are *right*. I was not simply Blair's falconer. I was his inventing apprentice. From the age of twelve, I was groomed as a lab assistant. He took me off the farm, he needed someone he could teach to do things his way and *silently*. Little could he have envisaged how talented I would become at the job. We didn't just make commercial gadgets, we worked on military briefs, and I became an anonymous inventor. When I was old enough to be paid, he presented me with a contract as a gift on Christmas Day. When Lord Turks-Leyton offered me a decent sum on a tea-making machine I'd worked on – many, many times more than what I would have made in the contract with Sir Seamus – I knew I had to get out of it... and that very night.' Mr Roberts's face turned into a freakish rubber mask. 'Shame nobody will know how clever you were, Miss Laplume.'

Opal began to hyperventilate in fear. A faint light from a grate above shone down onto Mr Roberts's hands. The gold signet ring shone silver, its cow rising higher and higher, and now Opal could see closely the K printed inside the cow... just like on the contract.

Now, with the billiard cue at her throat, all Opal could think of was Clyde's message, 'Mmmmm. Rub. Sig. Netting.' She now understood he was trying to say 'Mr Roberts's Signet Ring.' He must have seen it when he'd dressed up as Seraphina Serle and asked him to play the bagpipes. And he would have seen it again when Mr Finlay Roberts held him underwater, pretending to rescue him from the ice.

Opal almost gave in to the strangulation, just to get the pain of her throat to stop. She didn't know if she'd blacked out or if it was the darkness of the vault. But she could now see nothing. She couldn't make a sound; all she heard was her own gurgling as she desperately tried to suck air into her lungs. Her head filled with a thumping blood pressure.

His weight was right up against her, his elbows pinning her upper arms back so all she could do was claw and scratch his suit fabric. His knees were pressing into her legs, so she was unable to kick. She could do one thing though... stamp her foot.

It was a far-fetched pursuit... if nobody could hear her when she screamed earlier, they could probably not hear this, but the Morse code for SOS was the only thing she could do. She stamped three times, then a longer pause between the next three, and a final three, before it all became too much...

Opal awoke coughing, her face pressed against the stone floor. She gasped for air and her ribcage spasmed in desperation to catch up on oxygen. Her Adam's apple felt bruised and throbbing. She scrambled onto her knees, her back curved in a catlike position as she tried to regain a steady breath.

She then froze. She could hear footsteps running away from her down the long vault, echoing... two pairs of feet. Who could it be? Mr Finlay Roberts, and the person who'd stopped him from strangling her to death?

She heard a grunt at the other end of the tunnel. Augusto? She scrambled to her feet. She could barely see anything. Only the hazy outlines of alcoves and the odd grate, high above, letting slivers of the night sky in.

If she called out... it would signal that she was alive... and that would not be what Mr Roberts would want. But she could creep closer to the sounds. Mr Roberts had to be caught. How many more lives would fall in his domino game of murder? There were scuffling noises... wrestling?

Her foot knocked something that clattered. She crouched down and grasped at it in the dark. A broken-in-half snooker cue. She armed herself with it. Better than nothing.

The wrestling bodies moved under a patch of light, limbs jostling and twisting at all angles. She could decipher the orange hair of Mr Finlay Roberts. The other man's shoulders were broad and could have been Augusto's, but Opal couldn't be certain. They seemed to be fighting over an object grasped in all four hands. As the hands rose under the light, Opal could see it was a pistol... the same pistol Augusto carried.

Mr Roberts grunted and yanked his arms sideways... making Augusto slip and splash in a shallow puddle. Augusto let go of the gun as he tried to get his balance. Opal covered her mouth. The gun shone under the light as it was brought down and aimed at Augusto. Mr Roberts's signet ring glinted in arrogance as he prepared the shot.

BANG!

The vault was illuminated with the shot. A yellow freeze frame of horror. Then blackness again. Movement. Please God, let Augusto be alright. Splashes and stumbling and running feet towards her. Two pairs of feet. YES! Mr Roberts had missed.

But surely he would try again? She had to do something. She ducked into an alcove and held the snooker cue at the ready. After the first pair of feet came past, she thrust the cue out at ankle level. The second pair of feet clipped the pole and Mr Finlay Roberts yelled as he clattered to the ground. Opal dropped the cue and crawled back into the darkness of the alcove.

'Opal? Opal where are you?' Augusto shouted, he'd obviously realised she wasn't lying where he'd rescued her earlier.

Mr Finlay Roberts scrambled to his feet.

Opal could just make out his silhouette, the sheen on the pistol barrel aiming right down the alcove at her. 'Tough one to get rid of, aren't you?'

Her heart raced like a tiny bird as she scrambled back further. Dread washed over her as her back touched cold, hard brick. It was a dead end, in more ways than one. The sound of Mr Finlay Roberts cocking the hammer came. Opal curled into a tiny ball, her head tucked down into her arms. She screwed her eyes shut. *This is it.*

The sound of a chain being yanked sounded, and something ahead of her rumbled and crashed. A deafening shot rang out, and the sound of a bullet hitting metal.

'BLAST YOU!' shouted Mr Finlay Roberts.

Opal opened her eyes. She could see the dark latticework of a portcullis gate ahead. Augusto must have lowered the gate to protect her. She saw his shadow leap at Mr Roberts like a puma, and they resumed wrestling for the gun. Mr Roberts could come back any minute to stick his gun through the holes in the gate... or worse, kill Augusto. *She had to get out!*

She frantically patted the walls surrounding her, and to her left, she found a gap, some sort of drainage vessel, big enough to crawl under. Like a desperate snake, she wriggled through. Several shots were fired, making the tunnel flash in shocking bursts. But the bullets were simply hitting bricks as the men tumbled and fought.

Opal watched, shielding herself behind a boulder. She realised Mr Roberts was lying in a vulnerable position as he tussled for possession of the firearm. His midriff was below another portcullis. If Opal was to pull the chain, it would fall onto him. She'd better hurry.

It was so damned dark she could only just make out a chain.

'Opal, stay back!' shouted Augusto, as Mr Roberts's arm yanked the gun in her direction.

She ignored him, of course, ducked the gun blast, and pulled the chain down with the weight of her entire body.

A shower of brick dust fell onto her as the heavy gate fell right down onto Mr Roberts's chest. Fortunately for him, the gate was not a spiked base, it merely pinned him to the floor with its great weight. There was no wriggling out of this one.

His arms and legs flailed like a tortoise turned over, and Augusto plucked the gun out of his hand.

'*Muchas gracias,*' Augusto panted and wiped the sweat from his forehead with the back of the hand that was holding the gun.

He then pulled Opal into his arms and kissed her upon the head. They embraced, completely ignoring the expletive demands coming out of Mr Finlay Roberts's mouth.

'Where is your hat?' he said, blinking at the crown of her head. 'I am not used to kissing your hair.'

'For once, I don't give a damn,' said Opal, her throat stinging as she spoke. 'How on earth did you find me down here?'

'I heard you stamping SOS with your foot, my dear girl.' Augusto smiled, and his moustache curved upwards.

'How?' said Opal croakily. 'I only did it out of sheer desperation. I was certain I was a goner.'

'I was in the vault below... looking at the gas boiler for the club. Your stomping came through above. I ran back up to the billiard room. I could not see you, but the back panel next to the fireplace looked disturbed. I got him off you, but I wasn't sure if I had been too late...'

She nestled her face against his lapel and tears pricked her eyes. To think she may not be here if it wasn't for this man. She coughed.

'Come on. We will need to call the police and get you to the hospital... your poor throat.'

'If I survive this,' Mr Finlay Roberts seethed, practically foaming at the mouth, 'I swear on Queen Victoria's ghost, I'll sue you both. This is entrapment of the highest order!'

'Would you like a pillow, Mr Roberts, or are you still pretending to have dignity?' Opal giggled, but stopped when her throat ached.

'Shall we leave him there? Give the next intruder something to *trip over?*' Augusto said, leading Opal away.

Opal leant back into her pillows and held a cold compress on her throat. Napoleon wasn't allowed on the ward, and she missed him dreadfully. All the aspirin in the world couldn't be more healing than being able to cuddle him. She stared at the mint-green wall opposite, where a lithograph of Edinburgh Castle hung annoyingly askew, and listened to the radiator tickle and hiss. She might as well distract herself with her sketchbook until they let her out of this blasted place.

A nurse entered Opal's hospital room with a tray. The sister's uniform was an exceedingly flamboyant white cap, shaped like a sideways canoe. Opal quickly did a line drawing of her and her delightful matching apron.

'Thank you, Sister,' said Opal, as the nurse exchanged the cold compress on her throat with a new one and placed a cup of sugary tea and a couple of aspirin on her bedside table.

'Doctor said you should be alright to leave in the morning,' the sister said. 'We should keep you in just in case, mind. Oh,' – she stopped on her way out – 'and you have a guest here to see you… a Detective Inspector Morven Sinclair.'

The detective, holding his deerstalker cap gravely to his chest, entered the room as the nurse exited.

'I am so terribly sorry, Opal,' he said, his eyes filling with water.

'What for?'

'Not catching Mr Finlay Roberts sooner,' he replied, wiping his eyes on a cuff. 'How is your throat feeling?'

'It's a lot better since using these cold compresses. And it's not your fault, Detective. He had us all bamboozled. But I was always right about one thing... Seraphina Serle's innocence,' Opal said with a smirk.

'You were indeed.' He sighed and perched on the edge of her bed. 'But, please, do enlighten me on how he managed to execute all these dreadful things? And what's more... *why?*'

Opal turned a page in her sketchbook and started to draw Detective Inspector Sinclair. 'Put your hat back on a moment, Detective. I'm going to draw you as I explain.'

He obeyed and then looked at her as wide-eyed as an owl, desperate to know.

'Mr Finlay Roberts wasn't simply Sir Seamus's falcon handler. He'd been his apprentice growing up, groomed as his anonymous engineer, while Sir Seamus took all the credit. One Christmas Day, as a present, Sir Seamus offered Mr Finlay Roberts a business collaboration contract. Blair Electrical Enterprises would fund the talented Mr Finlay Roberts's research as long as Blair Electrical Enterprises would own the rights to sell these inventions, paying Mr Finlay Roberts half the profits. They would work on commercial enterprises *and* secret military apparatus. Hence why Mr Finlay Roberts had to be a silent inventor.'

'Oh dear,' said Detective Inspector Sinclair. 'The contract we found would renew every three years on the 25th of December. The only way out of it was either by negotiation or if either party were to die.'

'Exactly,' said Opal. 'A little short-sighted of Sir Seamus and his lawyer, Mr Martindale, to put that clause in.'

'But why didn't Mr Finlay Roberts simply negotiate his way out of it, if he had wanted out?' Detective Inspector Sinclair said. 'No need to *electrocute* Sir Seamus to death at his party!'

'Unfortunately, there was no time for negotiations as he only wanted out a day before the cut-off date, 25th December. This was the festive period and Sir Seamus would not likely allow it at this late stage and then Mr Finlay Roberts would be tied in for another three years.'

'Yes, yes, of course. *Why* did he want out though?'

'He'd received a huge offer for a tea-making machine he'd quietly been inventing without Sir Seamus's knowledge, and Lord Cecil Turks-Leyton, the meddling fool, offered him far more cash for it than he would ever have made being tied into Blair Electrical Enterprises.'

'So, he acted extremely fast and conducted a frenzied plan that very evening,' mused Detective Inspector Sinclair, making a triple chin.

'He would have to kill both Sir Seamus and his lawyer, Mr Martindale, as he was the only other person who knew about the contract clauses. Mr Martindale would be the only one to deduce Sir Seamus's death and the sudden monetary windfall, and put two and two together. They both had to go. But Sir Seamus, before midnight. Mr Martindale's demise he could plan a little longer.'

Opal paused in her speech to sketch a deep furrow in Sinclair's brow, then continued.

'Mr Finlay Roberts's method would have to depend upon who he could frame. It had to be someone easy and vulnerable to pin the murders on. He knew Seraphina, a poor clairvoyant, was the sister of Euphemia, the seer that Sir Seamus had put in prison for spying. Very conveniently, Mr Martindale had been involved in Euphemia's demise also, all the newspaper clippings were there in the scrapbook. It was the perfect revenge motive that Mr Finlay Roberts could bestow on Seraphina.'

'What an evil cad.' Detective Inspector Sinclair shook his head.

'On Christmas Eve, before the guests arrived and everyone was dressing in their chambers, Mr Roberts tampered with the Christmas tree switch, remembering that Lady Blair had previously told us all the exciting plans of Sir Seamus turning on the lights at ten o clock after his speech. He had placed a gramophone inside the tree and tampered with the switch and cords so that when Sir Seamus turned on the lights, it would turn on the gramophone as well. Mr Roberts chose "The Twa Corbies", due to its eerie, ghostly themes.'

'That tune gives me the willies,' said Detective Inspector Sinclair, shivering.

'He planted the metal shavings under Seraphina's wardrobe and the manual and screwdriver behind her radiator,' said Opal, speeding up. 'He also pinched some of her hair out of her brush and a few beads in case he needed them later.'

'What about the part when crows appeared in the tea-leaf reading with Seraphina and Mr Martindale? Was this a coincidence? How could Mr Roberts make the crows appear?' asked Sinclair.

'No coincidence. He was trying to get a ghoulish crow narrative going. Mr Roberts himself was the first one to point out in a very loud voice that he *saw crows*, to put that idea in Seraphina's head. But crows are a very easy thing to see in tea leaves. They can fall in a wingspan shape, a mere "M" shape in the sky, the twist of a beak or the curve of a body pecking in the ground. The black colour of the tea leaves and crows. People see what you tell them to see. A kind of placebo effect.'

'I see!'

'Once gathering in the ballroom, Mr Roberts got scared when the children were playing around the tree, in case they turned on the switch and got electrocuted. He distracted them with a game of I Spy. Something Lady Blair noted was very out of character as he detested children.'

'He would have been a dreadful parent,' said Sinclair.

'Then the electrocution happened, and the creepy sound of the gramophone played. He knew Seraphina would be hysterical about the link between the crow song and the crow tea leaves, making it look like she was trying to create a ghostly cover-up. The police were called and, of course, everyone had to retire to bed.'

'And poor Seraphina was arrested and locked in a room while Mr Roberts planned Mr Martindale's death.' Sinclair sighed.

'Sadly, yes. Mr Roberts had thrown on a cloak and went to visit Clyde at the dock in the night, where he knew he'd be the lone watch-boy. Everyone knew Clyde's talents for playing the pipes. He put on a wench's voice and told him his name was Seraphina Serle and instructed him to play "The Twa Corbies" tune on the cliff in front of the rock, but behind the tree. He said to start that night at 3.30 a.m. on the dot and to stop once Clyde had seen a person pass the last window before the top of the tower. To keep the boy quiet, Mr Roberts told him there would be more lucrative jobs in the future, but only if he kept his mouth shut. The problem was that Mr Finlay Roberts forgot about his signet ring. When he handed Clyde the money, he noticed the Kerrybride Creamery crest.'

'What a very silly oversight,' said Sinclair.

'On the night of Mr Martindale's death, Mr Roberts started by placing the bagpipes from one of the knights in shining armour on the tower floor. He planned on being the first up the steps so he could yank the flag's cord off and drop it out of the window. I noticed the cord on the ground the next day, and Countess Angelina noticed the flag was tight around the tower earlier that evening.'

'But how could Mr Finlay Roberts have been in the tower when the bagpipes played? Because that was the time Mr Martindale's murder happened!' asked Sinclair.

'Ah, but that is the point. The bagpipes and Mr Martindale's murder did not happen at the same time; it was simply Mr Roberts's alibi. He smothered the lawyer silently in his sleep, before the bagpipes, and made the murder scene look noisy, so that everyone assumed it was done whilst the bagpipes were playing.'

'What an absolute monster!' said Sinclair. 'He did this all for money? After Sir Seamus had supported him all these years?'

'Yes. And poor Clyde was to be his next casualty,' said Opal. 'He recognised Mr Finlay Roberts's signet ring outside the barber's shop and asked him if he had any more jobs for him. Mr Roberts couldn't possibly have anyone knowing it was *he* who set up the phantom bagpipes scheme, so he must rid himself of Clyde. Mr Roberts asked him to come and help collect foliage for Sir Seamus's funeral, and before we went on the ice, he sharpened Clyde's ice skates using the stable machinery, causing him to fall through the ice. Luckily, Clyde survived the ordeal,' said Opal. 'When poor Clyde was drowning, Roberts held him under instead of pulling him out, pretending the current was too strong. Though he was struggling to speak, he managed to get a message to me. But mmmmm, rub, sig, netting meant, *Mr Roberts's signet ring*. He was trying to help me connect the dots.'

'The very last thing he had to do was to destroy that damning contract in Mr Martindale's office,' Sinclair said with a nod.

'Indeed. Shortly before the evening wake, he went down the back alleyway behind the office and dropped an incendiary device through the air vent. But he foolishly used a milk bottle embossed with Kerrybride Creamery, which Mr Finlay Roberts's ancestors owned and was the seal on his signet ring.'

'That cryptic cow and K...' Sinclair rolled his eyes and then peered at Opal's drawing. 'I daresay if I looked like that, the criminals would turn themselves in out of sheer admiration! You've even given me lipstick!'

'I daubed it in parts of your face that have a reddish hue and for shading.' Opal laughed.

'The Honourable Miss Opal Marion Laplume, for the flattering portrait and for cracking the case, you have earned a bag of Berwick cockles, the finest sweeties in Scotland.' He pulled a brown paper bag of the things out of his jacket and patted them on the bed.

He then got up with the great creak of springs.

'Where are you going now?' asked Opal.

'I'm collecting the discharge order for Seraphina Serle.'

'Can you get mine too, please?'

'That is up to the matron!' Sinclair said and tipped his hat before squeaking down the hospital corridor.

FORTY-FOUR
GUNPOWDER AND CLAPTRAP

The Laplumes had arrived at The Black Kelpie pub in pursuit of hot toddies and general cheer, before braving the chill on Princes Street for the midnight fireworks. Shortly thereafter, Augusto swept in to complete the merry little cohort.

Although the murders had been solved, there was one mystery Opal hadn't quite cracked yet. Augusto's affection towards Countess Angelina had left her decidedly uncomfortable, and daresay, a little defeated. She feared that this Hogmanay outing might be the last she'd see of him. She could feel a painful little crack in her heart at the prospect.

As they passed by the barrier window looking into the public section of the pub, Opal noticed a blur of black feathers sprouting from a tall turban. Opal had a feeling that it could quite possibly be Seraphina. She grasped the door handle, but her mother gripped her shoulder firmly.

'Opal, my dear, that is the *public* bar,' said Lady Laplume, pulling a ghastly face. 'Ladies must stay in the saloon.'

'I've seen someone we know,' said Opal and pushed open the door.

Lady Laplume gasped at her daughter's defiance.

A group of builders looked up and saluted their foaming pints at the ladies. Opal smiled back, clutching her purse to her chest. Lady Laplume played with an earring and sidestepped out of view. The dark turban looked up with a scowl... it was indeed Seraphina Serle. She pleasantly bared her one front tooth when she recognised Opal. Her sister Malvina was next to her, also smiling with her crooked gnashers.

'Seraphina! What a delight to see you,' Opal said, and Napoleon dashed in and climbed at her calf.

'Detective Inspector Sinclair came and let me out of Saughton Prison,' Seraphina said breezily and ruffled Napoleon's head. 'We're going to watch the fireworks and then my sister is going to bring me home to our cottage in Dunvaloch hamlet tomorrow.'

'I daresay your cat Morag will have missed you. She will be waiting for you,' Opal said, beaming.

'I know. Thank you, Opal. You've always believed in my innocence, and I knew from the moment I saw you, you were an oracle. Look at those eyes, shining opals of truth.'

'Thank you,' said Opal, cupping her bob. 'But I daresay Mr Finlay Roberts was a real engineer of mystery.'

'Oh, don't give Mr Roberts the credit,' said Seraphina darkly. 'My sister Euphemia's spirit used him as her puppet. She was out for revenge against those two men. The twa corbies.'

Opal sensed a dark quaver in the atmosphere like something was cackling evilly in another world, and she shivered. Napoleon stepped down from Seraphina's calf and ducked behind his mistress's feet, pom-pom tail between his legs.

'Right... err, we'd better acquire our hot toddies before they become cold toddies,' said Lord Laplume, who'd earwigged from the doorway and was obviously feeling the jitters too. 'Wonderful to see justice done and all that.'

'One last thing,' said Malvina. 'There's been wonderful

news in Dunvaloch hamlet. Our wee Clyde is making progress and getting his speech back.'

'That is just the most joyous news!' Opal clasped her hands together.

The Laplumes nabbed a booth in the lounge bar and cupped their warm toddies in pewter tankards, glancing at the clock every few moments. They should venture outside at eleven forty-five to be ready for the fireworks display.

'I think we can safely say you are discharged as our protection officer, Mr Sevilla,' said Lord Laplume to Augusto, smacking his lips after a swig. 'Now that that blister Peregrine is shut away, he won't be bothering us anymore.'

'It is sad,' said Augusto. 'The only thing I liked about Lord Peregrine was that he brought me on this adventure with you all. Your daughter, The Honourable Opal Laplume, is my favourite person.'

Napoleon whined under the table.

'Yes, and you, little scamp,' said Augusto, ruffling the dog's bouffant.

What a Casanova, thought Opal. *Why is he pretending to be so fond of me when there is clearly someone else?*

'Don't forget Countess Angelina,' Opal said, thudding her tankard down a little too hard. 'You seem to have made a very good friend in her.'

Lord Laplume raised his eyebrows, evidently detecting Opal's shakiness.

'Exquisite woman,' said Lady Laplume and slurped some sherry with her pinky out, totally oblivious to Opal's sensitivity. 'Ruddy nuisance she's married to a count, isn't it, Mr Sevilla?'

'So where will you go now, Augusto?' said Lord Laplume, attempting to rescue the subsiding conversation.

'Paris, possibly,' Augusto replied. Opal held her breath. She couldn't bear it. It's where Countess Angelina would be travelling back to.

He looked at Opal and continued. 'But this is not yet to be determined.'

Opal turned her head away and looked at the blue tiled wall. She couldn't bear this pain.

'What will you do in London, Opal?' Augusto said.

'Ascot will come around before we know it, so I'll be busy with Laplume Millinery, I expect,' she said with a sigh. She didn't look at him but looked down into her mug. She tried her best to just smile and make their farewell positive and genial. After all, they had been through a lot together. But the corners of her mouth seemed so heavy, there was no chance of lifting them.

'And what will you be doing in Paris, Mr Sevilla?' asked Lady Laplume. 'Protecting more damsels from beasts?'

'I have many connections in Paris. I'll sort something out. Countess Angelina may have a position for me,' he replied and straightened his cravat, unaware that he had in fact dropped a bomb.

'Is that not a little... inappropriate?' said Opal, looking right in his eyes.

'What?' Augusto said, spilling a little toddy.

'What about Comte de Brisecloque? You can't work for the family when you're sweet on Angelina!'

'Sweet on?' Augusto asked, tilting his head, perplexed. 'I don't understand.'

'Opal Marion Laplume,' interjected Lady Laplume. 'What on earth has got into you?'

Opal lowered her voice to a whisper. 'I heard you at the graveyard. Countess Angelina said she loved you.'

There was a pause where their eyes met like two planets in retrograde... circling each other with ancient confusion and the distinct sense something had gone awry.

'I have known Angelina for a long time and, you're right, I do love her,' Augusto whispered, his eyes round with truth.

Opal's lower eyelids filled with tears. She looked down at the bowl of pork scratchings and crunched one to busy herself in this excruciating moment. She wasn't even able to factor in the humiliating idea that her parents were present.

'But that's because... she is my sister,' said Augusto, producing the last word slowly and exactly.

Opal spat the scratching out onto the table. Lady Laplume shrieked, 'Opal!' Napoleon, on cue, as if to erase Opal's uncouth behaviour, clambered onto her lap, snatched the expunged snack and disappeared again.

'I beg your pardon?' asked Opal, dabbing her mouth with a napkin. 'Your... *sister?*'

Lord Laplume, sensing the probability that this conversation would include scandal, shook out an *Evening Dispatch* and glanced sheepishly over it so as not to be left out.

'I concur,' joined in Lady Laplume. 'Explain yourself, Mr Sevilla! How can Countess Angelina be your sister?' And looked him up and down as if asking a muddy wellie how it got on the cover of *Tatler*.

'I think, it is about time, I tell you who I really am, Opal.'

Opal scrunched up a napkin into a tight ball as hard as she could, her fist shaking, then looked up at him, bracing herself for the whole world to morph in an abysmal direction.

'Your suspicions that I am from Argentina are indeed correct,' he said, then dropped his volume. 'But my name is not Augusto Sevilla. It is Augusto Escalada, and Angelina's birth name is Escalada too.'

Lord Laplume lowered his paper a smidgen further to ogle Augusto properly. Lady Laplume wriggled in her seat as if getting ready for a good radio drama. Napoleon's nose and little peepers suddenly appeared above the table. Opal lowered her chin and implored him to go on by widening her eyes.

'It's not exactly the best place to be speaking out loud about this, but I don't know if Opal will allow me another chance. So here goes,' he said in a hushed tone after glancing around the pub. 'My father was Don Enrique Escalada. An oligarch who dominated Argentina's lucrative beef exports.'

There was a brief silence in which all you could hear was a customer in the background complaining to the barman that his beer was flat.

'Claptrap. You're pulling our legs,' Lord Laplume broke the silence and chuckled, but his laughter trailed off hesitantly.

'He's not, Papa. It makes complete sense,' Opal said, the only part of her body moving was her mouth, the rest frozen.

'You're an *Argentine oligarch?*' Lady Laplume said and looked at him like he was a very expensive Rolls-Royce, albeit with blood on the bonnet.

'Why did you change your name?' asked Opal, not blinking.

'When the coup toppled the president a few years ago, the Escalada family's ties to the old regime became a liability. My father's refusal to bow to the new military junta made us enemies of the state, and he was assassinated in a staged robbery. Leaving me to manage what was left of our crumbling empire.'

Opal automatically wafted a hand over and rested it on Augusto's forearm. He glanced at it gratefully and continued. 'The regime moved to seize the Escalada assets, and Angelina and I fled to Paris with barely anything to our names. We adopted new last names and a Spanish background to avoid being traced. I worked as a protection officer, the only thing I could do. Angelina used her charm and connections to preserve her wealth, albeit separately from the family fortune and married Comte de Brisecloque. My sister and I became estranged when she blamed me for Father's death. We didn't flee when she'd asked us to, you see.'

'How did she end up at the ball?' Lord Laplume asked without being able to help himself.

'I sought her out in desperation when I found out that the

Argentinian government had planned to auction off our cherished childhood estate in Argentina. With her marital buying power, I wanted her to buy it back, perhaps covertly through a lawyer. I could only ask her face to face. I sent her a letter saying I had vital information that could ruin us both unless she met me at the ball. She wrote to Lord Seamus Blair that guff about studying culture, and it charmed him, and she got the invite she was after.'

'Did she agree to buy your pile back?' asked Lady Laplume, eyes sparkling.

'Opal witnessed a few arguments we had over it. Angelina was torn... helping me, her brother, would risk exposing her as an Escalada and jeopardise her French status, but the estate was the only thing we had left of our identity... of Father. Eventually, at Sir Seamus's funeral, which reminded her of our padre, she agreed to help buy back the estate via proxy... perhaps using a lawyer. But on one condition.'

'And what is that?' asked Opal, now smiling at the fact he had finally come clean to her.

'That I abandon my plans for revenge or political entanglements once the estate was secured,' Augusto said and downed the last of his drink.

'Well, that, I daresay, is the first thing she has said that I agree with.' Opal smiled and pinched his arm. 'I knew, with your drawing skills, you would have gone to a fancy art school.'

'I might have.' Augusto smirked.

Napoleon jumped onto his lap and started licking his face happily to let him know that, oligarch or street urchin, he was still his comrade. There was a hubbub under the grandfather clock, people pointing at the hand edging teasingly close to midnight. Then a cloud of fur hats wafted towards the exits.

'Let's carry this on after the fireworks. We can't miss those, no matter how interesting the chatter,' said Lord Laplume, and he led the way out onto Princes Street.

The street was steaming with hot toddies and excited breath. Edinburgh Castle loomed above them like an ancient monarch, waiting for its illuminating jubilee. A distant chime began to dong a little sooner than Opal had expected. She whipped around and threw her arms around Augusto and began to shriek, 'Happy—'

'No, love, that's the North British Hotel clock,' said a stranger in a flat cap. 'It's set a few minutes early to help travellers not miss their trains. Ignore it.'

Opal went pink and hid her face in Augusto's scarf. 'Golly, Augusto, I'm so embarrassed. I can't believe I let my silly feelings overtake me. I was so desperately unhappy when I thought you'd gone off me.'

'I could never go off you,' he said smiling and pulling his scarf up around his chin. 'In fact...'

'What's that?' asked Opal, as Augusto pulled away from her.

Augusto got down on one knee and ruffled Napoleon's flank, then looked up at Opal. Nobody paid attention to what he said next, apart from Lady Laplume.

'The Honourable Opal Marion Laplume, I have never met a prettier, kinder, cleverer woman in all my life. And believe me, I have travelled all over. Would you do me the honour of calling me... your husband?'

Opal felt as if she had turned into stone. She couldn't close her mouth, she couldn't blink. The midnight bell began to chime, and the crowd yelled Happy New Year, but they were distant noises. A firework whistled and crackled overhead with fizzing pinks, oranges and whites, like pretty feather sprays. Augusto's face and his skin tone changed with the colours of the sky. She only noticed that her mother had fainted when her hat tumbled onto Opal's shoes.

EPILOGUE

A TOAST IN THE TROPICS

Papua, Three Months Later

An al fresco banquet had been set up with a breathtaking view of the green precipitous mountains across the lake. Behind the long dining table, a lush part of the forest crept forth. On one of the trees hung a wooden sign that read 'Clementina Paradise Birds' Sanctuary'.

The hearty fish course had been keenly devoured by the guests, and they were now fanning themselves and leaning back in their seats as if they were deckchairs. The hosts were, of course, the Laplumes and their guests were those completely disconnected from the London circuit: Dutch friends from Port Moresby, local missionaries, Augusto and Countess Angelina.

'Right! Before it gets dark. Next on the agenda is a bird spotting contest!' said Lord Laplume, standing proudly upright in his pith helmet. 'First one to spot a blue bird-of-paradise wins a bottle of champers! Golly... steady on or you'll frighten the poor blighters off!'

The party guests, who knew how hard champagne was to come by out there, charged past him and scattered like primates into the forest reserve, their feet tossing up leaves and cracking branches.

Opal, her beaded gown getting caught on the undergrowth, weaved in and out of the thicket, pulling Augusto's hand. She was determined to get them lost so that they could have a moment alone. She pulled him behind the thick trunk of a merbau tree and encircled her arms around his waist.

'I am most irrevocably, most devastatingly in love with you, Opalita,' said Augusto, straightening her tiara and then looking down deep into her eyes.

Opal pressed against his chest and caught her breath. 'Look where we are now compared to last year... engaged.'

'I will never forget Paris. The oyster tricycle, when you first dared to splodge lipstick on one of my sketches,' he replied.

'And later, that improbable moment I saw you from the rooftop of the Hollywood Palatial Pines, my heart didn't beat... it positively bolted,' Opal said, feeling those emotions all over again.

'I can't believe some of the things we have done. We navigated the desert in California and camped under the stars with the lizards.'

'How you taught me that my fashion illustrations could be something quite more substantial. Art!' Opal whispered. 'With you, I felt not only admired but understood. A feeling at once terrifying and utterly intoxicating. Something I have never felt before.'

'And still, you said nothing. Why?' Augusto asked.

'Because, dear heart, I had not the words, or the training, or the gumption,' Opal said.

Suddenly, she heard a rustling sound. She held her tiara on with one hand and looked up into the forest canopy above. *Oh, jolly marvellous!* She'd spotted a blue bird-of-paradise, for the first time!

The bird hung upside down from a branch, his flank plumes sprayed out in a glorious 'V' shape, the blue-flame colour tipped with licks of cinnamon-orange gave the resemblance of a hand-fan on fire. The oval of his chest was puffed out, black and eclipsed with a slit of scarlet, emphasising its prominence. His two thin black tail feathers shot upwards into arches like amorous antennae. His whole body was pulsing in a beautiful fan dance.

The brown female near it, the ironically less effeminate one, looked at the blue bird with her head cocked. She blinked as if to say she'd been chirpsed better down the pub, plucked a leaf with her beak and flew away.

'Oh dear. Better luck next time, little chap,' Opal whispered to her blue friend.

'Did I win your hand with my Tango skills?' said Augusto as he pulled her into a clearing.

He took Opal's left hand and put it to his mouth. He kissed the engagement ring. An opal stone, of course. Nestled in a platinum setting of crisp geometry, the gemstone at its centre glistened as if it had captured the bride-to-be's aura within it, blue one moment, green the next, with occasional flashes of a pink excitement.

Yap. Yap. Yappppp! Napoleon came bounding through the trees. His tail with the black bobble on the end, whipped up the leaves when he sat beside her. He continued to yap at the birds above, and they flew off.

'Napoleon!' Opal said and lifted him up into her arms. 'This is a sanctuary for the birds. They have been rescued from poaching territory. You, too, are a rescue, always remember that. I found you in a coal sack in Piccadilly. Now don't go around scaring them like a miniature marauder.'

The dog's barks seemed to have summoned everyone else, and they emerged from behind trees to gather around the betrothed couple.

'You just missed a blue bird-of-paradise,' Opal informed them.

'Botheration! I always miss them!' Lady Laplume cursed, looking up into the canopy.

'That's because you're so shrill and gauche, my dear.' Lord Laplume laughed.

'They're terribly conceited animals.' She sniffed, arms folded. 'They probably believe they are the dukes of the avian world, and we are mere underlings.'

'That they do.' Lord Laplume nodded. 'But well done, my Bins.'

'They are the bluest blue you can behold,' said Opal. 'Far better than any painting I've ever seen of one.'

'Only correct that the subjects of this engagement party win the champers,' said Lord Laplume as he cracked open the hamper and served everyone coupes of bubbles.

'My deepest thanks to you all for gathering here at my daughter's... shall we say, somewhat discreet engagement party,' Lord Laplume said, raising his glass. 'As trusted friends, you are, of course, aware that Augusto's background is of a rather delicate nature. Now then, may I propose a toast... to my darling daughter, and to the newly appointed gamekeeper of this sanctuary... Opal and Augusto. To their health.'

Glasses clinked. Lady Laplume and Effie wiped tears from the corners of their eyes. Countess Angelina struck up a guitar and started strumming a Tango tune. Napoleon circled Opal and Augusto, dancing on his hind legs as if they were under the Eiffel Tower again. Augusto swallowed his champagne in one gulp, took Opal's waist and twirled her.

Was this really happening? thought Opal. Her life was not destined to be an endless solo in silence, but a full-blown tango duet, full of twists, surprises and Augusto's hand firmly on her waist.

Thank you so much for taking the time to read my third book – *Murder at the Scottish Ball*. It was thrilling to write! I do hope you enjoyed it and that you felt part of the adventure with Opal and Napoleon. If want to stay updated on my latest releases, please do sign up using the link below. Your email address will never be shared and you can unsubscribe anytime.

www.bookouture.com/millicent-binks

The central inspiration for this novel was taken from the remarkable true story of Helen Duncan. She was a Scottish medium arrested in 1944 after allegedly revealing the sinking of HMS *Barham*, a fact that was classified at the time. Authorities feared she had obtained military secrets and might threaten wartime security. She was charged under the Witchcraft Act of 1735, accused of fraudulent spiritual practices. Her trial sparked a cause célèbre about freedom of speech, state control and belief in the esoteric. She was sentenced to nine months in prison, becoming the last person imprisoned under that law. It is now believed she heard about the sinking of the HMS *Barham* through word of mouth, as several families would have been told about the tragedy through condolence letters.

Though Helen was essentially a con artist, I found the crossover of the witchcraft and wartime secrets fascinating. Her subterfuge and publicity stunts were very audacious and, though scary at the time, are really quite humorous today, an example being her infamous use of cheesecloth as 'ectoplasm', a ghostly substance. One can't help but imagine her laughing at the spectacle she orchestrated.

Many poor women turned to making money from clairvoyance if there were no other jobs available to them other than prostitution. If you gained credibility, you could make a good business out of it, especially from customers who'd lost men in World War I and were desperate to see or speak to them again. While my Serle sisters are fictional, the treatment they receive – dismissal, mockery, then imprisonment – echoes the ways in which women have been vilified throughout history for this idea of witchcraft. It fascinates me that there isn't the same persecution for men. Though there are records of men being punished under the Witchcraft Act, the high proportion were women.

Opal Laplume is a feminist or 'progressive woman' in the language of her time, and I enjoyed making her serve as Seraphina Serle's advocate, while Detective Inspector Morven Sinclair's support provides an unexpected counterbalance. This novel is dedicated to the many women in history who have suffered under the weight of moral systemic misogyny – those condemned not for their crimes, but for daring to survive in a world stacked against them. While the language of condemnation has shifted, its essence lingers. Witch hunts rarely disappear. They simply change their disguise.

The second part of my letter is in memory of my beloved calico cat Queenie, who died during the writing of this book. She was the most loving cat, filling my home with joy for the sixteen years I was blessed with her. When I was twenty-one and living in Streatham, my neighbour said, 'I have a bathroom full of kittens!' An hour later, I'd adopted Tarquin (Queenie's brother). I then decided he was lonely and picked up his sister the week after. I named her Queenie after Queen Elizabeth II. She looked like a bumblebee and sometimes Gizmo from *Gremlins*. A timid and unsure girl at first, she came out of her shell in midlife, and it was a delight to love her little character. Queenie liked sitting next to Mummy – not on but next to! Sitting on everything else – including wire hangers (comfy choice). Watching melodrama on TV, particularly enamoured with water ballet when it came on during the Olympics, probably wondering why all the mummies were pretending to be fish. She enjoyed helping my mum with the NSPCC stair climb challenge, sporting a green bow! Licking condensation off windows (sophisticated lady). Wolfing tuna with zeal. Her little safe-space box. Squeaking as she snored. Surprising her brother behind a door. Looking down on you through bannisters. Squirming in the sunshine on the roof. Cuddling Mummy's elbow at night. I will hold you in my heart forever, Queenie. Mummy misses you, darling.

I would LOVE to hear from my readers – for any reason, ideas on new book themes or adventures that Opal could go on or even just to chat – you can find me if you search Millicent Binks on Facebook, Instagram, Tiktok and X. You can also contact me on my website.

Millicent Binks x

www.millicentbinks.co.uk

 instagram.com/millicentbinks

ACKNOWLEDGEMENTS

I am so very grateful to the many people who have supported me on my writing journey. Creatively, emotionally and practically.

Firstly, thanks to Nina Winters, my wonderful commissioning editor, who gave me this opportunity. I could never have dreamed of getting a three-book deal, and the experience has just been amazing. Thanks also to the whole Bookouture team, all thirty or so of you who've worked on my books with such attention to detail and who have pushed for my success.

To my parents, the most loving I could wish for. My mother, Mary Hunt, for reading drafts and offering help with her French expertise and my father for admin help.

My brother William, sister-in-law Ali and Willow and Ethan for your support and wonderful costumes at my launch.

Leigh Russell, crime writer, who took me under her wing at the early stages and with whom I had a wonderful time on her Greek writing retreat.

Morwenna Loughman, my agent, who never gave up on getting me a book deal.

A pat to my remaining darling cats, Tarquin and Madame de Pompadot, for the stress-busting cuddles and laughter. My third cat, Queenie, died during the writing of Murder in Scotland, which was devastating... I miss you and will hold you in my heart always, my little bumblebee Gizmo.

My darling friend, Robert Noble, for being the first to read

A Most Parisian Murder years before I got a deal and for your thoughtful feedback.

To Gentry de Paris, for inspiring the setting of *A Most Parisian Murder*.

Thanks to Adnams of Southwold and the University Women's Club for their support with my book launch.

To Louise Hulland and BBC Radio Suffolk for the opportunity to speak on air and connect with new readers.

To Patrick Süskind and the ghost of Dashiell Hammett, my favourite writers, for their breathtaking creativity.

To the London College of Fashion Library for letting me scan countless fashion images.

To Claridge's hotel for letting me bash away on my laptop behind a pillar in the foyer while you topped up endless pots of Darjeeling.

Jasmine Gardner, who in 2011 gave me a column in the *London Evening Standard*.

Eleanor Mills. who championed my crazy ideas and published my cover story for *The Sunday Times Magazine*.

To Dr Justine Ashford and Miss Branson, my English teachers from St Felix, whose lessons echo in my head as I read and edit.

To everyone who came to my *Opal Laplume series* launch – your presence meant more than you know.

And finally, to everyone who reads or listens to my novels: thank you. You're the reason I do it. I hope my stories offer you a moment of joyful escape.

PUBLISHING TEAM

Turning a manuscript into a book requires the efforts of many people. The publishing team at Bookouture would like to acknowledge everyone who contributed to this publication.

Audio
Alba Proko
Melissa Tran
Sinead O'Connor

Commercial
Lauren Morrissette
Hannah Richmond
Imogen Allport

Contracts
Peta Nightingale

Cover design
Tash Webber

Data and analysis
Mark Alder
Mohamed Bussuri

Editorial
Harriet Wade
Sinead O'Connor

Copyeditor
Jane Eastgate

Proofreader
Lynne Walker

Marketing
Alex Crow
Melanie Price
Occy Carr
Cíara Rosney
Martyna Młynarska

Operations and distribution
Marina Valles
Stephanie Straub
Joe Morris

Production
Hannah Snetsinger
Mandy Kullar
Charlotte Hegley
Nadia Michael

Publicity
Kim Nash
Noelle Holten
Jess Readett
Sarah Hardy